91.01. .9

TORRENT

The Alt Apocalypse Survival Series

Tom Abrahams

A PITON PRESS BOOK

TORRENT

The Alt Apocalypse Survival Series
© 2018 by Tom Abrahams
All Rights Reserved

Cover Design by Hristo Kovatliev
Edited by Felicia A. Sullivan
Proofread by Pauline Nolet
Proofread by Patricia Wilson
Interior design by Stef McDaid at WriteIntoPrint.com

tomabrahamsbooks.com

FREE PREFERRED READERS CLUB: Sign up
for information on discounts, events, and release dates:

eepurl.com/bWCRQ5

PITON PRESS

For Courtney, Sam, & Luke

You've helped me weather every storm

"Water is the driving force of all nature."

—Leonardo da Vinci

AUTHOR'S NOTE

I once told my editor, "People love reading about the apocalypse."

She corrected me. "People love reading about *surviving* the apocalypse."

She was right.

This series of books, THE ALT APOCALYPSE, is about that premise. It explores survival under the most extreme circumstances. It is, however, a new twist on the post-apocalyptic /dystopian/survival genres.

This series, which can be read in any order, features the same core characters in each complete story. But every book dunks them into a new, alternate apocalypse: a nuclear holocaust, an earthquake, a flood, a wildfire, a hurricane, a plague, and even zombies. Different heroes will emerge in each novel. Different characters will survive and perish. Your favorite character dies in one book? He or she will be back in the next.

The idea is to explore how people with different skills survive, or not, in alternate disasters. I hope you enjoy the fiction that treads close to reality (except the zombies) and choose to ride shotgun with me for what promises to be an exceptional set of adventures.

CHAPTER 1

April 5, 2026
New Orleans, Louisiana

Keri Monk didn't want to drown in her childhood bedroom. But as she pushed herself from the popcorn ceiling using her fingertips, and dove underneath the cold, briny, putrid water that rose inconceivably fast, she understood it was a real possibility.

It was inky black beneath the roiling surface as she held her breath in her cheeks and searched for the door that led into the hallway. She was disoriented despite having grown up in this room, a haven from the outside world replete with plush bears and dolls, trophies, posters of teen idols, and certificates of achievement tacked to a handmade fabric bulletin board.

Her lungs burned as she pushed through the water, bumping into floating furniture and other things she couldn't identify. She found the doorway, gripped its molding with one hand, and propelled herself out into the hallway. She kicked toward the ceiling and found a few inches of air, which she gulped down while frantically pedaling her legs in a modified scissors kick to keep herself afloat.

She was alone as far as she knew. Her parents were staying at her older sister's house on the southern, central edge of the city, near the Mississippi River, so she and her friends could avoid the cost of a hotel during their weekend visit from the West Coast. The house was technically located in an area called City Center, part of the garden district, but it wasn't as nice as most of the homes around it. The owner had let it go a bit and rented it out instead of pouring in the kind of cash that so many of the neighbors had done.

Her boyfriend had gone to a nearby convenience store to pick up their friend earlier in the evening. He'd gotten trapped by floodwaters and had called to tell her he was backtracking, trying to find a way home.

While waiting for him, she'd fallen asleep. She'd woken up when the flood forced her brass-framed bed from the floor and she'd rolled into the water. It was rising so fast, as if the Gulf or Lake Pontchartrain were emptying into her house. Her phone was gone, the power was out. And now, as she struggled to survive, the water was pushing her away from the front of the house, where she'd planned on swimming. The strength of the moving water, its incredible force, was too much.

Rather than fight it and exhaust her energy, she let it carry her back, past her door then toward the rear of the house. The current slammed her against the end of the hallway, her back hitting the corner of a gilded frame that held a family portrait taken years earlier. It featured her father, mother, two sisters, and herself in matching blue denim jeans and white pocket T-shirts. They stood barefoot on the beach, the sun in their faces, the glow of summer on their skin. All of them were much younger in the photograph, but they'd never taken another professional family portrait since. It had hung there until the flood and a collision with Keri knocked it free, sending it spinning into the rising water.

She grabbed reflexively at the spot on her back where the frame had jabbed her, wincing and stretching her neck to suck down another gulp of humid air. Her nose scraped the ceiling.

She tried getting her wits about her, understanding where exactly she was and where she had to go. She took one sip of air and dunked herself under the water again, this time swimming into the room at the end of the hall. It was her parents' room, the only other bedroom in the house.

On the far side of the room, on the wall opposite their accordion-door closet, there was a pair of windows that framed the back left corner of the house. If she could swim diagonally across the room and get to those windows, she might have a chance.

Keri extended her arms in front of her, her hands cupped, scooping the water to propel herself forward. She moved quickly in the black water, despite the weight of her light hoodie and stylishly torn denim jeans. She narrowly avoided a large antique dresser that had floated from the floor. The current that had pushed her back toward the end of the hallway was as strong here and headed in the same direction. She managed to fight it enough to reach the windows in the corner.

Feeling the glass with her fingers, she fumbled for a latch. Her chest burned now, her vision blurred as the last remnants of air stored in her lungs leaked out in bubbles through her nose. The water didn't feel as cold anymore.

Shaking her head while trying to fight off the intensifying sensation that she was about to black out, she struggled to thumb a latch and slide the window open so she could swim free of the house.

She found one latch and flipped it open, but before she could reach the second, something hit her on the back of the head, dizzying her. Without air in her lungs, she was sinking toward the floor, closer to blacking out. She let herself drop, but when she reached the floor, she found her footing and launched herself upward toward the ceiling. There, she found maybe two inches of air. She floated at the ceiling, her head pounding now, and sucked at the air as if through a straw, trying to avoid drinking as much of the oily, salty water as possible.

Keri took one last breath and pushed herself below the surface again. She could sense the cold tightening her muscles. Her joints stiffened. But she managed, somehow, to find the other latch on the corner window and flip it. She reached down and yanked on the bottom of the frame, gliding the window up on its hinges enough for her body to slip through.

Reaching through the opening, Keri grabbed both sides of the window frame on the outside of the house. Holding tightly with what little strength she had left, she pulled, launching herself through the gap and out into her flooded backyard. Her pants leg caught on the window ledge and tugged her backward as she lunged against the current toward the surface. She couldn't reach it. It was so close. Somehow, despite the power outage in the house, the dim yellow light of a streetlamp danced above her and undulated above her flooding home. She reached back, the current catching her weakened, oxygen-starved body, trying to work at the stuck fabric.

Unable to loosen the denim, she struggled to find the looped button at her navel. She squeezed her eyes closed and unbuttoned her pants, unzipped them, and tried to kick free; however, the wet cotton was too heavy and she couldn't free herself. The buzz in her head grew loud, and she could sense she was losing consciousness. There was no air left in her lungs as she worked to keep her mouth closed, to resist the urge to breathe.

From nowhere, a dark figure appeared next to her and pulled her pants free. Then strong hands grabbed her under her arms, propelling her up toward the surface. Together they broke into the night air, pulled by the current away from the house as they moved toward a large wooden fence struggling to maintain its hold in the ground. Only parts of the fence stood tall, at the posts cemented deep into the loamy Louisiana soil.

Keri gulped her first breath of air, catching a mouthful of rank-tasting brackish water that forced her to spit and cough. The man holding her was behind her now, having wrapped his forearm across her chest. He held her on his hip, helping her stay above the raging flood.

She couldn't see him, yet as she blew the last of the water from her mouth and caught her breath, she recognized the firm grip that held her afloat.

"Dub?" she gasped, her voice breathless. "Dub? Is that you?"

"Yeah," came a blurb muted by the water. "It's me."

She could tell by the bob of their bodies that he was diving his head underwater, digging with his free hand to move them somewhere safe. She heard him sputter as their bodies lifted. She kicked her legs as much as she could, trying to help propel them in whatever direction he was taking them.

The dim yellow streetlight glowed from above the water's surface. As she stared at it, she wondered how the light could still have power despite the ubiquitous water. She wondered too how Dub had found her. How had he seen her and plucked her from the depths?

Dub swung her around to his side when they reached a section of fence flapping to one side like a stuck rudder. He helped her grab the top of the post, a pointed finial of smooth pine replete with countless layers of chipping paint and stain.

She grabbed it with both hands while holding herself there, her legs pressed against the handful of board connected to it. Dub had one hand on her as he moved to the other side of the finial. His grip now on her bicep, he treaded water in the relative calm of the waters dammed behind the section of secured fencing and her body.

From that position, he could face her. His face was drawn tight, his eyes wide with fear-fueled adrenaline, yet somehow sagged with exhaustion. His blond hair was dark and matted against his head. He had a cut along one of his cheeks. It was superficial, as well as the scratches Keri could now see on his neck and his forehead. Blood mixed with floodwater trickled from the corner of his mouth. The sides of his face and neck were red and swollen.

"You're hurt," she said, her voice airy. Her pulse felt thick against her neck and chest. "Are you okay?"

"Let's talk about this when we get out of the water." He motioned over his shoulder. "The house right behind me is two stories. As fast as the water is rising, I think we can navigate our way there; then we won't have to climb much, not much more than a push from a second-story windowsill. Or something."

She looked past him, beyond the reach of the light, and saw the gray outline of her neighbor's two-story colonial. While the water was up to the roof that extended over the front porch, it hadn't yet reached the quintet of second-story, shutter-framed windows that ran the length of facade.

"You think—" she exhaled "—we can make it?"

Dub nodded. The water was above the final now. Their hands were underwater.

"Okay," she said at the moment the remaining fence gave way to the rushing water. She lost her grip on the finial, and Dub struggled to hold her arm tight. He squeezed hard. She winced but didn't complain. They floated for a moment, stunned by the sudden snap of the fence.

Keri kicked her legs and tried paddling to pull herself into Dub's body. She managed to find his shirt and grab handfuls of it as the gnarled branches of an ancient live oak raked across them, tangling them in a swirling water threatening to pull them under. They navigated it, letting the current carry them closer to the colonial.

The rain, which had stopped briefly, was beginning again. Cold, heavy drops pelted them and slapped the angry surface of the rising water. Their legs brushed against metal under the surface, what Keri thought might be the top vertical bar of a neighbor's cheap swing set.

Dub yelled something to her and tightened his grip, though between the rush of water and the din of the rain, Keri couldn't make out what he was saying. His words vibrated against her, but they weren't much more than that. She decided that as long as she held onto him or went where his arms guided her, she'd be okay.

The closer they got to the house, the darker it became. The dense curtain of rain and the barely visible sliver of the new moon that dipped in and out of the fast-moving black clouds high above made it harder for Keri to see where exactly they were.

She swallowed a gulp of the foul water and coughed again. Then she gagged and retched, suppressing the urge to vomit. She dipped beneath the surface, a rush of water rolling over her head, and held her breath. Water seeped into her nose and stung her sinuses. She shook her head like a wet dog as she resurfaced, disoriented and not at all sure where they were. Keri grappled for a better hold on Dub's shirt, loosening and then reaffirming her grip. A wave of exhaustion washed across her body, and the backs of her legs cramped. Then the arches in her feet tightened as her toes curled painfully. She cried out in pain, a gargled shriek that drew Dub's attention. He said something she could feel against her body, but she didn't understand him. She did know, however, the intensity of his hold on her had tightened. His body betrayed his own fear. His movements weren't smooth and controlled anymore. They were random and desperate.

The speed and power of the current was too powerful. She could sense that Dub wasn't able to navigate it, and they were going to miss the house. They would slip into the wider, open water she imagined had swelled behind her neighborhood beyond the levy.

The cold beats of rain on her head and face were painful now, as if the device of some sadistic torturer fixated on her agony. The countless pellets stung when they struck her, each colder than the one before it.

It was the dark, though, that was the most terrifying. Unable to see now where they moved involuntarily, she was certain that some unseen obstacle under the water would catch them, that a tree would ensnare them, that a power line might entangle them, or that the water itself would swallow them whole. That, combined with the white noise of rain and rapids, made for sensory overload.

At the very moment her knotted, shivering body was about to give up, there was something solid under her feet. It was rough, and as Dub struggled to keep her relatively in place, it scratched across the tops of her feet and roughly across her bare knees. Then her shoulder slammed into something solid. The water pushed her against it, trapping her there. It was the house.

They were on the roof of the colonial's porch. Somehow—she neither knew nor cared how—but somehow Dub had gotten them there. He was next to her now, his body pushed against the siding and held there by the racing, rising water.

He took her hands with one of his and pulled them from his shirt, guiding them to a gutter downspout between them; then he led her to grab hold there, which she did.

Her vision hadn't adjusted to the darkness, but here on the roof and under the protective soffit of an overhanging eave, the blur of rain was diminished. The dark figure of Dub's body rose from the water and stood. He wavered against the rush at his calves but managed to pull himself up onto a window ledge and then climb onto the roof above, some three or four feet above the water.

He reached down, extending his arm to her. His fingers were wide and he called to her. She couldn't move. She tightened her hold on the downspout, threatening to pull it free of its anchors. There was no way she could let go and risk being sucked into the abyss. No. Freaking. Way.

"Keri!" Dub called with more force, more urgency. "Keri!" He shook his open hand, imploring her to take hold.

Water splashed against her face, freeing her from her paralysis. She let go of the downspout with one hand and reached skyward, toward Dub's hand. It wasn't enough. She couldn't grasp it from that distance.

She tried repeatedly to reach his hand without letting go of the downspout. She couldn't. It was inches out of her reach. Slowly, apprehensively, she pulled herself up onto her feet and stepped around the other side of the downspout. The composite tiles on the porch's roof were coming loose and she slipped twice, but managed to maintain her footing long enough to reach Dub. She grabbed hold of his arm above his elbow and planted one foot on the windowsill he'd used to launch himself onto the roof above.

Her stomach scraped along the edge of the gutters as Dub lifted her up. She collapsed into his lap, and the two of them lay in the rain, free of the floodwaters.

After what felt like a quarter hour, but might have been only a few seconds, she inched her face closer to his. She rolled onto him and kissed his lips, holding the sides of his wounded face in her wrinkled, dehydrated hands.

Out of breath, she said, "I love you," then rolled off him and onto her back next to him. The rain was steady and hard on her face and body. Her torn shirt and underwear were all that kept her from lying nude in the elements. The cramps in her feet and toes were gone, but the soreness remained, and she could sense the muscles might seize again.

But she was alive. Dub was alive. They'd made it. That thought was comforting for a moment, only a moment.

"We can't stay here long," Dub said amidst heavy, chest-heaving breaths. "The water is still rising. The rain isn't letting up. If somebody doesn't rescue us, we're screwed."

Her stomach tightened and, despite her complete exhaustion, she leaned up on her elbows, the rough composite digging into her skin. Oblivious to the pinch, she gazed into the darkness. In the near distance she could see the sheet of rain in the dim yellow streetlight, as well as that same light absorbed into the water that had drowned her childhood home, the place where her parents lived.

Dub was right. The water was moving higher. The danger was real.

CHAPTER 2

April 3, 2026
30,000 feet above Fort Meyers, Florida

Ellen Chang had always, half-jokingly, said that if she could choose her own death, it would be in an airplane crash. When challenged, she'd argued that the adrenaline spike for those final moments would be exhilarating. She might enjoy knowing the end was close.

"What a rush," she would say. "So frightening yet exhilarating," she would suggest. "Epically violent and final," she would defend. Such was the contention of a woman shamelessly bored with her existence. If any of her friends, who looked upon her with contempt, could step into her existence for a month, or even a day, they'd understand the attraction of death by plane crash.

Yet as the passenger jet aboard which she flew dropped altitude faster than she could down a bottle of Prosecco, Ellen Chang reconsidered her position. Her final moments were not in any way exhilarating or epic.

She gripped the armrests of her first-class seat, digging her freshly manicured nails into the leather, and clenched her jaw. Her stomach lurched with the shuddering pitches of the aircraft as its pilots fought to maintain control. A wave of nausea coursed through her Pilates-thin body, and bile crept up her throat into her mouth. She fought the urge to vomit, especially when she heard the man behind her retch.

This unplanned descent wasn't as she'd imagined. Instead, it was ear-piercing. The engines whined, the fuselage rattled, and passengers prayed or cursed the heavens. Grown men howled with fear. Women screamed and cried.

Ellen had the oxygen mask around her face. The yellow cup dug into her cheeks and chin. She'd pulled the band too tight above her ears, but she wasn't about to let go of the armrests to adjust it. She closed her eyes and tried to block out her senses.

In the early minutes of the flight, as the plane climbed to its cruising altitude at the Florida peninsula's western edge, the captain had warned of turbulence. He'd suggested a growing storm over the Gulf of Mexico might slow their trip from West Palm Beach to Los Angeles.

That hadn't bothered Ellen. She wasn't in any hurry to get home, and extra time in first class meant extra pours into the glass flute she kept at arm's length. She was on her third glass, rubbing the stem unconsciously with her thumb, and had been warned by the flight attendant it was her last for a while when the captain had corrected himself.

"Hello again," he'd said in the familiar tone and cadence of an airline pilot. The mic was too close to his mouth as he spoke, and his overmodulated words were drawn out between long pauses. *"We're going to have to adjust our altitude pretty significantly to avoid this storm ahead of us,"* he'd said. *"That's going to mean keeping your seatbelt on for now. I ask that you remain in your seats. No moving about the cabin for the time being. I'm also asking our flight attendants to move to their seats and buckle up as well. If you could, please avoid punching the call button for a bit. Could be bumpy until we find smooth air. Bear with us. I'll be back to let you know once it's okay to get up and stretch your legs."*

That announcement never came.

The plane shifted to one side and then tilted sharply, as if they were banking hard to one side. Ellen's seatbelt strained against her hip and she used her core to keep herself centered in her seat.

The plane dropped suddenly as it banked, and behind her she heard a loud thump, an air-filled grunt, and a woman's cry. That's when the masks had dropped. Above the high-pitched whine of the engines, someone announced a passenger was unconscious and bleeding. Multiple voices called for help.

The inertia of her body, fighting the turn of the plane, prevented her from turning around to see what had happened. Then the plane surged skyward, forcing her back against her seat. The aircraft pitched up and then abruptly leveled and dove. Ellen's body rose from her seat, lifted weightlessly, and the belt strained against her hips.

The urge to vomit surged and waned. She closed her eyes, cursing herself. Her doctor husband had long told her to be careful of getting the many things for which she'd wished. Of course, she'd always gotten what she'd wanted and scoffed at his witticism, much as she'd scoffed at much of what he'd said.

She had the house perfect for entertaining and praise in *Los Angeles Magazine*. The most recent accolades had proclaimed the Brentwood midcentury modern revival a *"loving ode to Herman Miller and George Nelson."* She'd smirked at the praise but framed the article nonetheless and hung the piece above the toilet in one of the two powder rooms on the main floor.

Ellen always drove the newest imported sedans, save the one time she'd deigned to buy a Cadillac, and never sat behind the wheel of one older than twenty-four months or with more than twenty-thousand miles on its engine. At that point, she'd explained to her husband, she might as well drive a Honda.

She attended gallery openings and donated charitably to causes. That is, she gave to charitable causes so as to attend the associated "see/be seen" galas. The giving was as much charitable as it was a way to appear engaged and concerned.

The carousel of galas and openings required the requisite attire. Ellen was a regular at many of the high-end boutiques peppering the western enclaves of Los Angeles. She had a collection of bunion-producing heels and designer handbags. Balenciaga was among her favorites, and she had lunched with the head designer, Demna Gvasalia, at the Getty more than once.

These were the things that preoccupied her frightened mind as the plane's movements deteriorated into spasmodic jerks and rattles. The sour acid climbed her throat once again while she swallowed hard against it. She knew definitively that none of that had brought her happiness; none of it filled the holes that existed deep within her.

Her son, whom she'd cajoled and guilted into attending UCLA despite scholarships on the East Coast, was spending an extra semester overseas and hadn't come home for Christmas, opting instead to stay longer to strengthen his relationship both with the Spanish language and with his Catalonian girlfriend. Ellen resented him for that.

She resented her husband for the long hours he worked and the time he didn't spend with her. On the rare occasions he was available, she chose to be otherwise occupied. They'd long since stopped communicating beyond the mundane, the logistical workings of their daily lives.

Ellen Chang chose not to think of those things, focusing her final moments on the newest collection opening at the Hammer Museum. It was the next Tuesday. She had tickets to the VIP cocktail reception. Rather, she had *a* ticket. Her husband had a surgery scheduled for that afternoon and would likely have missed it had she bought him one.

She thought about the landscape architect with whom she had a scheduled consultation on Wednesday morning. They were interested in xeriscaping the front yard. Many of the neighbors had converted to the low-water landscaping as the drought had worsened. Although Ellen wasn't much for the look of it, it far exceeded the side eyes of judgmental party guests who commented on what they imagined was a hefty water bill as they ate canapés and sipped fruit-infused cocktails.

If she died here and now, she'd miss out on the exhibit. She worried other guests would talk about her for not attending or, worse yet, not even notice her absence. She bit her lip underneath the oxygen mask at the thought of mourners at her wake traipsing up the long path that cut through the center of her thirsty yard, thinking as much about her environmental neglect as about her death. How many mourners would there be? Would anyone attend?

The plane rattled so hard Ellen bit the inside of her cheek and drew blood. Alarms sounded, the cabin lights flickered, and the warm metallic taste filled her mouth. She turned to look out the window at her row and saw slaps of rain against it. A red light strobed from somewhere farther back on the plane. Then there was a deafening bang, followed instantly by a blinding explosion of light outside the window and the sound of grinding metal. The cabin shuddered violently. Her ears popped painfully.

Ellen was certain the plane was coming apart. A rush of cold air filled the cabin. She trembled from the drop in temperature. People behind her were screaming in terror. Men and women made noises that sounded painfully inhuman, their voices indistinguishable from one another. Babies cried.

She couldn't see what was happening behind her, but from the sucking sound, the amplified volume of the whining engines, and the bitter cold that caused her teeth to chatter, she knew the cabin had been breached.

Her ears popped again. A thick ache in her throat crept behind her jaw. Ellen was crying now too. Tears welled in her eyes and traced the outer edges of the oxygen cup on her face.

As the plane violently shook and threatened to break apart, she couldn't tell whether they were pitching up and down or shaking from side to side. Her head pounded from the disorientation and the loss of air pressure. Her pulse thumped against her temples and her neck. Her heart was beating thickly against her chest, her breathing labored now, each intake more ragged than the one before. Ellen was on the verge of hyperventilating.

And then she wasn't.

The violent storm, an upper-level low, which had widened unexpectedly and trailed from west to east across Florida's Gulf Coast, had captured the plane. It struck it with force, its winds and lightning lashing out and pummeling the craft. Those threats and the captain's misplaced confidence in his ability to circumnavigate the widening threat had doomed them.

The plane's nose pitched downward steeply, and the wounded bird dove toward the angry Gulf, accelerating toward its terminal velocity with a gaping hole in its port side. It began to spin out of control and, at that moment, most all of its two hundred and ten passengers and crew were unconscious. It slammed into the inky black water, exploding into countless pieces large and small, among them Ellen Chang.

The woman whose life was about rising above the tide of wannabes and has-beens that littered the Southland sank deep beneath the surface of the bubbling ocean. She was part of the deep now, part of the storm that had killed her and everyone aboard that plane.

CHAPTER 3

April 4, 2026
New Orleans, Louisiana

Dub glanced up at the scoreboard. There were three minutes and forty-eight seconds left in the game. UCLA trailed North Carolina State by seven. He calculated in his head the combination of possessions that could give his Bruins the lead over the pesky Wolfpack.

Keri elbowed his side and tugged on his sleeve. "Hey, why are there so many time-outs?"

"TV time-outs," Dub replied. "There's one every four minutes, or the closest dead ball to every four minutes."

"This game is taking forever."

Dub turned his body toward hers but referenced the court with big sweeping moves of his hands. "You're not loving this? It's the Final Four."

"Meh," Keri said. "We're in the end zone. We've been standing all game. We haven't slept much. I—"

"I thought you loved basketball."

"I love watching *you* play basketball," she said, pinching the back of his arm.

He leaned over and kissed her on the side of the Bruins' baseball cap she wore on her head backwards. Then he looked past her to his friend and roommate Barker, who stood on the other side of Keri. Barker was rolling his eyes.

"What?" asked Dub. He checked his wristwatch, a gift from Keri he wore every day.

"Nothing," said Barker, waving his hands. "You two, though."

The buzzer sounded before Dub could respond. The two teams worked their way back onto the court to thickly syncopated music laced with heavy, chest-pulsing bass.

On the opposite end of the court, the NCSU pep band was playing a brass-heavy fight song. Their fans, which primarily occupied one decidedly red corner of the arena, were chanting something Dub couldn't understand.

Three rows in front of him at the court's baseline were half of UCLA's cheerleaders. They were chanting into megaphones, eliciting an 8-clap cheer from the assembled Bruins in the student section.

"Fight, fight, fight!" they chanted, moving their hands in the prescribed movements of the cheer.

One of the referees motioned for the cheerleaders to move, which they did, and he handed the ball to the Bruin's star player, Mark Helms. He was a freshman who everybody believed would enter the NBA draft after the season ended. He inbounded the ball to the point guard and then trotted up court.

The guard moved the ball into the front court and passed it to the tallest of the Bruins, a six-foot-eleven junior named Kevin Boxell, who blocked shots more than he made them. Boxell was standing at the top of the key, near the free throw line. He faked to his left and then, without looking, bounced the ball behind him to his right as Helms bolted toward the basket, caught the pass, and elevated toward the basket. He slammed the ball through the basket, a thunderous dunk, which shook the backboard. The Bruins were down five.

No sooner had NC State inbounded the ball than Helms stole it.

He took two steps back and launched a long three-point shot, which sailed through the net without touching the rim.

The Bruins were down two. There were more than three minutes on the clock. The Wolfpack took a time-out.

Keri planted her hands atop her cap, lacing her fingers, and drooped her shoulders. She sighed audibly. "Another one?" she asked rhetorically. "You have got to be kidding me."

Dub's phone buzzed inside his front pocket. He plucked it out and tapped the screen. There was a link to a weather alert at the center of the display. Dub, surprised he had any cell signal at all, tapped the alert. The phone cycled, trying to load the new page, and he looked up. Many of the attendees in the arena were all looking at their phones. Barker was too. He held up his phone in front of Keri, apologizing, and showed it to Barker.

"You get the alert too, Barker?"

"Yeah," said Barker, nodding. "It's taking a while to load though."

Dub nudged Keri. "You didn't get it?"

Keri shook her head. "My phone's deader than a doornail. No service. Haven't had any since tip-off. Too many people trying to Snap and livestream."

Dub looked at the court. The players were huddled at their respective benches, listening to their coaches. The referees stood at the scorers' table talking amongst themselves.

NC State's cheerleading squad was on the floor, performing some spirited routine that Dub could swear they'd repeated twice already. Their mascot, a comically angry wolf, was prowling along the sideline opposite the benches.

"Hey," said Barker, drawing his attention. "Mine loaded."

Dub checked his display. His had loaded too. He read the warning on the screen. Then he read it again. He showed it to Keri.

EMERGENCY ALERT
FLASH FLOOD WATCH UNTIL
11:00 PM SATURDAY, 4/6/2025

STRONG STORMS EXPECTED
ACROSS SOUTHERN LOUISIANA

ROAD CLOSURES EXPECTED IN LOW-LYING AREAS

Keri shook her head and shrugged. "Okay," she said, apparently not concerned. "Not unusual. We get those all the time when it rains."

Being from Houston, Texas, Dub was no stranger to flash flooding. He had been in elementary school when Hurricane Harvey put his hometown underwater for days. There were countless storms and extended rains subsequent to Harvey that threatened to do the same.

It had gotten to the point that any time it rained, a subconscious uneasiness crept outward from his gut. A lack of rainfall had weighed heavily in his decision to move to southern California for college. Among all the things there were to love about Los Angeles, the dry weather was at the top of the list.

He didn't share Keri's *"laissez les bon temp rouler"* attitude toward the weather. Nonetheless, she had experience in New Orleans that he didn't. This was her hometown. She should know better than he about which watches or warnings meant something and which didn't.

"Seriously, Dub," she said. "Nothing to worry about. It's not even a warning."

"Yet," said Barker.

The buzzer sounded and the players returned to the court. The crowd, which had lulled into a low chatter, roared as NC State inbounded the ball. A series of passes took the shot clock down to five seconds and then the Pack missed a short jumper.

Boxell rebounded the ball for the Bruins. The student section at the baseline erupted, and Boxell fired a rocket downcourt to Helms. Helms stopped at the three-point line, checked his feet, and drilled another basket. The Bruins were up by one with two and a half minutes to play.

Dub was jumping up and down. His throat was sore now from the loud cheering and chanting he'd employed throughout the course of the game.

A lifelong basketball fan, who'd been a good high school player, he'd never been to a Final Four. It was a dream and, when his Bruins had earned a spot in his girlfriend's hometown, he made it his mission to go.

Now he was here, sitting near the court, his team winning its semifinal game with time running out. He was, as his west Texas grandfather would have said, happy as a pig in slop.

Dub pumped his fists as NC State missed its next shot badly and Boxell grabbed another rebound. He ran the court and passed it to the point guard, who in turn lobbed it back to Boxell, and he slammed it home. NC State took its final time-out with two minutes left.

The student section and the yellow and blue clad corner of the Superdome were thunderously loud. The team was up three and had all of the momentum.

"No complaints about the time-out?" Dub said to Keri, cupping his hand around his mouth so she could hear him.

She winked and adjusted her cap on her head. "Not now that we're winning. This is fun."

Music blared over the loudspeakers, and the oversized display over center court replayed the last several Bruin highlights, further inciting the raucous crowd there to see their team advance to the final.

They weren't supposed to get this far. Despite their talent, they hadn't played up to expectations. Throughout the tournament they'd been underdogs. They'd defied the odds. Round by round they'd survived and advanced.

That was what tournament basketball was about, Dub had explained to Keri during the long flight from LAX to MSY: survive and advance. He explained that UCLA didn't have to be the best team in the country to win the tournament. They just had to be the better team on the court each time they played.

Keri was sandwiched between Dub and Barker on the plane. Though Dub had offered her his aisle seat, she'd declined. He was six feet three. Sitting in the middle wouldn't be fair for him. But given the conversation during the length of the four-and-a-half-hour flight, which centered on tournament history, she'd confided in Dub that she should have taken the aisle.

"Survival," Barker had echoed amidst chomps of mini pretzels, "is all that matters. As long as you're alive, you have a chance."

"Sounds easy enough," Keri had said.

"Survival is never easy," Dub had replied. "It's the little things, the unexpected obstacles that are the most threatening. When you least expect it, things turn, the clock hits zero, and it's over."

Now Dub watched the seconds tick down in the semifinal and the slumping body language of the NC State players. He saw the dejection on the faces of the lip-biting fans. It was in sharp contrast to the elation of the Bruins and the energy of the players on the court. It was the difference between survival and its antithesis. It was a fine line.

The final buzzer sounded and UCLA won. For several minutes the students chanted and cheered. They high-fived the players as they moved toward the locker room. And then ushers came to escort the students out.

Their tickets were only good for UCLA's game. They'd have to watch the second semifinal, the University of Houston versus the University of Florida, on television. They shuffled toward the exits.

Dub followed Keri, his hands gently on her shoulders as she

guided them up the steps and out of the arena. Barker was close behind them.

When they reached the concourse and the thinning crowds, the smells of overpriced fried food and spilled beer filling the air, Barker lamented the absence of their friend Michael.

"I wish he'd been here," he said. "He loves basketball every bit as much as we do."

"He wouldn't have liked the noise or the crowds," said Dub as they inched their way to the large glass doors that opened to the outside.

"True," said Barker. "But remind me to get him a T-shirt."

Michael, Dub, and Barker were roommates. Michael was on the spectrum. He was high-functioning and did well in small groups with familiar people. He didn't, however, warm to strangers quickly or remain calm in crowded, loud places.

"I bet he was watching," said Keri.

Dub's phone buzzed in his pocket and he pulled it out. He had three new text messages, all of them from Michael. He held up his device and shook it.

"He was," said Dub. "He's hyped. And he asked for a T-shirt."

Keri and Barker laughed.

When they reached the door, it was then they saw it was raining outside. It was a heavy curtain of rain that made it difficult to see much beyond the immediate plaza outside the arena doors.

"Nothing to worry about, huh?" said Dub, pushing the door open and holding it for Keri.

She stepped out into the thickly humid evening, rain splashing off the concrete. Tucking her hair up underneath her hat, she tugged it lower on her head. Then she zipped up her white and yellow track suit jacket and motioned for Dub and Barker to join her.

"It's just a little rain," she offered. "You won't melt."

Dub flipped his hoodie over his head and tugged on the drawstrings. It was a useless exercise. The cotton would be soaked within seconds.

"It's not melting I'm worried about," he said and stepped into the pelting rain.

CHAPTER 4

April 4, 2026
New Orleans, Louisiana

Lane Turner adjusted his custom-molded earpiece and straightened his tie. Then he raised his phone, turned on the camera function so that the display showed a reflection of himself, and gauged his appearance.

He straightened a couple of hairs, checked his tie, then slipped the device into the breast pocket of his suit jacket. His mic was already clipped to the lapel.

"We have an umbrella lead?" he asked his newscast producer, who was in the production booth back in Los Angeles. He was referring to leading the newscast with two stories and not the downpour beating upon New Orleans. "We tease the plane crash latest and then get to the game here?"

The primary news anchor at LA's number two television station stood under a cheap pop-up tent that kept him dry, for the most part. He was outside the Superdome, waiting for his newscast to begin. Turner was there with his own field producer and a photojournalist, along with the station's sports director, Tank Melton, who was getting postgame reaction from the players and coaches. He also had a photographer with him and would join Turner on camera later in the newscast.

"Yes," the newscast producer answered. *"You're off the top with video of the search for survivors. Then we wipe to highlights from the game, and then you're on camera for the hello. We have your package ready to roll. We'll hit a quick weather with an outlook for Monday, you'll throw to our reporter in Florida for the latest on the plane, and then you'll toss it back to the studio and Courtney Leigh for the rest of the day's news."*

Turner acknowledged her and asked his field producer if she'd added the last couple of sound bites he'd gotten with UCLA fans before the game.

"I did," she replied.

He smiled and adjusted his jacket.

"The crowd's starting to file out pretty good now," said the photojournalist, who was manning the tripod-mounted digital camera aimed at Turner's mug. "If they get rowdy, I'll zoom in and frame you tight. That'll keep them out of the shot."

Over his shoulder, Turner saw the growing throngs of fans weathering the rain, figuring they wouldn't be a problem. They'd be more concerned with getting out of the downpour and into an Uber to make their way to Bourbon Street or elsewhere in the French Quarter. That was where he'd be heading as soon as he had a chance. He'd started his day with beignets and chicory-enhanced coffee at Café Du Monde. Might as well end it with a hurricane and ogling at Pat O'Briens.

The producer spoke in his ear. *"Thirty seconds."*

Turner repeated the countdown to his photographer. The field producer was on the phone, listening to the control room. She gave a thumbs-up to Lane and then motioned for him to adjust his tie knot. He obliged and she gave him another thumbs-up.

"Open is rolling," said the producer. *"Stand by."*

"Stand by," repeated Turner. The timpani-heavy theme music crescendoed. He cleared his throat and the field producer pointed at him.

"Terror in the sky turns into the search for survivors in the sea. We'll have the latest information on the Los Angeles-bound Pacific East Flight 2929 that crashed into the Gulf," said Turner. He was looking at an iPad slowly rolling his script from bottom to top, a portable teleprompter that helped him stay on track. "Also tonight, we're live from New Orleans, where the UCLA men's basketball team has taken another step closer to a national championship."

He could hear the audio from the game in his ear as he glanced at the prompter one last time and then eyed the camera lens with his trademark "concerned and credible, yet approachable and affable" gaze.

"And that is where we begin our newscast on this Saturday evening. Hello, Southland, I'm Lane Turner, reporting tonight from the Big Easy, New Orleans, Louisiana, where the semifinal matchup for the UCLA Bruins was anything but easy. They went down to the wire against the heavily favored North Carolina State Wolfpack."

Turner shot a quick glance at the advancing teleprompter, pausing for a breath. He then mentioned the many fans that had traveled east for the big game then introduced a taped piece, called a package, he'd spent much of the day putting together with the help of his photographer and producer. When the piece ended, a minute and fifteen seconds later, he was again on camera.

"For many of those fans, they are leaving happy but drenched. As you can see behind me right now, the skies have opened and we are under a flash flood watch here. Let's check in now with meteorologist Monica Muldrow for how the weather might impact travel here and Monday night's championship game."

Turner stared into the camera, and Monica Muldrow began her forecast. *"It doesn't look good,"* she said. *"That flash flood watch is likely to become a warning, Lane. Of course, here in Los Angeles, the weather is sunny and a temperate seventy-four degrees with no chance of precipitation. But as we move the map and zero in on Texas and Louisiana, we can see this upper level low-pressure system is intensifying. This is the same low that created the violent storm that brought down Flight 2929. And what we have here is a system that isn't moving. It's just regenerating line after line of intense storms with heavy rainfall. They are moving east to west, as all systems do this time of year."*

Lane half-listened to the forecast while he checked the paper scripts he held in his hands. His field producer had paused the iPad at the beginning of the next story. He pressed his earpiece more snugly into his ear as Muldrow finished her forecast.

"Be careful out there, Lane, and stay dry," she concluded.

"Thanks, Monica," said Lane with a smile that quickly evaporated as he transitioned to a more serious story. "You heard Monica mention the rain falling in New Orleans is part of the same low-pressure system that took a Pacific East crew by surprise late yesterday. The aircraft, carrying two hundred and ten people aboard, lost communication and then altitude before crashing into the Gulf some seventy-five miles off the Florida coast. Joining us now from Miami is Southland reporter Damion Smith. Damion, we understand federal investigators are there, as are some family members of those on board the plane."

There was a brief pause and then Smith began the live portion of his report. Turner could hear it in his earpiece.

"It's too early to know an exact cause of the crash," said Smith, *"but we do know that what was an active search and rescue mission has, within the last few minutes, become a recovery mission. That means authorities believe all two hundred ten passengers and crew aboard Flight 2929 are dead."*

There was another brief pause. Then the taped portion of Smith's report began. In his ear, Turner heard a woman's wail. It sent shivers along his spine. *"It is unmistakable,"* said Smith, *"the sound of a mother learning her child is gone, killed in a senseless plane crash for which there are no answers. At least not yet."*

Next came the voice of the spokesperson for Pacific East Air. *"We extend our deepest condolences to the families and loved ones of those aboard Flight 2929,"* he said, clearly reading from a prepared statement. *"We too have lost people close to us, and we grieve with you."*

"The plane, a Boeing 737-300, was en route to Los Angeles International Airport from Miami," came the reporter's voice again. *"The twenty-three-hundred-mile journey began normally, we're told. There was no cause for alarm as it reached its cruising altitude."*

A spokesperson for the National Transportation Safety Board was next. She was answering a question from a news conference held earlier in the day.

"At some point," she said, *"we know the pilots communicated an issue with weather. They were instructed to alter their flight plan to accommodate the sudden change in conditions off Florida's southwestern Gulf Coast. Shortly after those initial adjustments, air traffic control noted significant anomalies with respect to the aircraft's altitude and speed."*

Smith again. *"Investigators have not clarified what those anomalies were, and they have not yet released an official manifest containing the names of the ill-fated passengers and crew. Families here are awaiting those answers, as are we. Reporting live from Miami, Florida, I'm Damion Smith. Lane?"*

"Thanks for that troubling update, Damion," said Turner. "We'll return here to New Orleans with game highlights and the latest postgame reaction from the Bruins' players and coaches later in the newscast when Tank Melton joins me with sports. For now, let's head back to the Southland and my colleague Courtney Leigh. Courtney?"

"Thank you, Lane," said Courtney. *"Tensions are mounting—"*

Turner pulled out his earpiece and disconnected the thin cable that attached to his cell phone. He hung up the phone, which had provided the audio of the newscast, stuffing it into his jacket pocket. Then he pinched the small alligator clip at his lapel and handed the lavalier microphone to his producer. He turned around to face the arena and the falling rain.

"Whew," he said, exhaling, "that's some rain there. Not sure how we're going to get out of here without getting wet."

"Uh, Lane," the producer said, the lilt of a question in her inflection, "we have another segment. It's…" She asked the newscast producer how long they had until the next segment. "It's fourteen minutes from now. You might want to keep your mic on and be listening to the newscast."

He waved her off and checked his watch. "I'm good. Plenty of time. I want to soak in the environment. I don't often get this chance, you know, being cooped up inside the station."

The producer, a woman whose name escaped Turner, crinkled her nose and narrowed her eyes. "Okay," she said, drawing out the second half of the word. "I guess that's fine. But control may need to talk with you and—"

Turner turned his whole body toward her, flashing her his billboard smile. "That's why you're here. You can talk with the control room and let me know what they need. Good?"

She pressed her lips into a flat smile, blinking back her frustration. "Sure."

Turner could taste the chicory on his own breath. He hadn't had anything to eat since his breakfast overlooking Jackson Square from his undersized chair and table at the edge of Decatur Street. He tugged on his belt, pulling up his suit pants to his navel.

"What are you thinking for dinner?" he asked. "Po'boys? Jambalaya? Crawfish?"

"You're just listing every stereotypical New Orleans dish you can think of, aren't you?" asked the photographer.

"Rice and red beans?" Turner added without answering the question. "I'm thinking Brennan's for breakfast tomorrow. A little bananas Foster? I hear they do it tableside."

The producer sighed. "I hadn't given it much thought. I'm kinda focused on the newscast right now. Maybe you should be doing that too, Lane?"

"Maybe." He shrugged. "But I did a lot of research on the food scene here. Spent a fair amount of time on Google looking up where to eat. There are many good options."

"I was just going to eat at the hotel," said the photographer. "I'm exhausted. We were up at seven this morning. That's five o'clock on the West Coast."

"I'll probably grab something at the hotel too," said the producer. "They've got twenty-four-hour room service."

Turner raised his hands, waving them off. "Suit yourself. I'm getting something that sticks to my ribs. Then maybe I'll hit Bourbon Street. I've never had a Hurricane."

"We've got seven minutes," said the producer. "Tank is on his way out right now. Apparently the second game is getting ready to tip off."

Turner sighed and dialed the most recent number on his cell phone. He plugged in the cord that connected to his earpiece and slid the molded plastic back into his ear. Then he motioned for the mic, which the producer took from the photographer and handed to him.

The newscast was in the middle of the main weather segment. Weather in southern California was a joke. Unless they were in wildfire season or mudslide season, there was virtually no difference in the forecast from one week to the next. Lane Turner was convinced he could be the chief forecaster if they'd let him. He was convinced a five-year-old could be the chief forecaster if they'd let one try.

Monica Muldrow was explaining how the high temperature on Sunday would be the same as the high temperature on Monday but slightly lower than Tuesday. The lows would be consistently in the sixties. The highs would never reach above eighty degrees. Turner chuckled to himself.

From behind him he heard the heavy panting of a man running, out of breath. It was Tank Melton. He was already dialed into the newscast with an earpiece in place.

"Hey, Lane," he said breathlessly. "Good game, right?"

"Sure thing, Tank," said Lane. "Fantastic."

Lane and Tank had worked together for the better part of a decade. They were cordial to each other, though neither ever spent time with the other off the set. Lane took a second lavalier mic from the producer, whose name he still couldn't recall, and handed it to Tank.

"Thanks," said the sports director, gathering himself for their imminent live report.

"Sure thing," Turner repeated. "Hey, you interested in grabbing some dinner tonight? I've got a list of places the Internet insists we try."

Tank smiled and shook his head. "Thanks, Lane, I appreciate it. I'm probably going to take a rain check, so to speak. I've got a lot to do tonight and I'm pretty tired. I'll grab something from room service."

"Suit yourself," said Lane, listening to Monica wrap up the weather and Courtney Leigh read a tease for their upcoming report.

The producer gave them an updated time. "Three minutes," she said. "Right after the next commercial break."

Turner adjusted his tie. The temperature was dropping. The rain, which was steady, was blowing at an angle now. He cursed the weather, hoping it wouldn't force him to resort to room service like the others.

CHAPTER 5

April 4, 2026
Los Angeles, California

Perspiration stung Danny Correa's eyes. He tasted it. It was in his ears, dripping down his back, lathering his chest. Even the palms of his hands were sweaty.

His thighs burned from the pressure of having partially squatted on them for more than a minute now.

"*Ich,*" he said, throwing a punch forward.

"*Ni,*" said the instructor, moving his arm into a blocking position.

Danny mirrored the movement with the rest of the class. "*Ni,*" he said and blew a drop of sweat from his face.

"*San,*" said the instructor, throwing another punch, this one with his left hand.

"*San,*" said the class collectively and threw punches with their right hands.

Danny eyed the clock above the mirrored wall in front of him. Class was nearly over, and he was exhausted. Though the dojo's sensei had insisted the air-conditioning remain off to induce muscle flexibility and strengthen endurance, Danny was convinced it was a cost-saving measure. Electricity costs in California had skyrocketed as an unusually warm spring had strained the grid.

Another bead of briny sweat dripped into the corner of one eye, blinding him momentarily as he continued through the progression of prescribed moves from memory. He pulled his fisted hands to his sides and kicked his right leg into the air, then planted that foot firmly on the dojo's spring-loaded, padded floor before pivoting on the balls of his feet ninety degrees.

He'd been coming to the dojo for a month after having taken a decade-long hiatus from the martial arts. There was something in his gut that told him he'd need the skills that had rusted in his muscle memory. It was an overwhelming sense that he'd have to defend himself against a coming attack.

It wasn't anything concrete and he didn't tell anyone about it. It was merely something that nagged at his psyche and had him looking over his shoulder whenever he left his modest apartment. He had recently installed three slide-bar locks on its front door and a metal bar that prevented the back slider from opening.

"Hachi," said the instructor.

Danny imitated the eighth move back toward the mirrored wall. The nape of his neck was soaked. Only two more moves and class would mercifully end. He wasn't in the shape most of the other students had attained. He was the newbie and there were no exceptions for him.

"Juu," said the instructor.

Ten.

Danny completed the final move, held his position, bowed to the instructor, and bent over at his waist, the cool streams of sweat trickling along the sides of his face, and he held himself upright, his hands on his knees.

He stayed there for several moments, the droplets of sweat splashing onto the floor, painting an abstract picture of the effort he'd put forth for the past hour. A strong, viselike hand touched his shoulder, gripping the stiff cotton fabric of his *gi*, the white karate uniform all of the students and instructors wore inside the dojo.

Danny lifted his head to see his instructor standing in front of him.

"You did well today, Mr. Danny," he said. "You are improving."

Danny stood up and planted his hands on his hips. *"Arigato."*

A polite smile spread across the instructor's chiseled face, revealing his dimples. He nodded. *"Ieie,"* he said. "Not at all. You need not thank me for noticing your effort."

Danny wiped his brow with the back of his arm. He sucked in a deep breath and exhaled. Then he stepped back deferentially. "As soon as I change, I'll be back to clean."

"Of course," said the instructor. "We don't doubt you'll earn your lessons both through labor of many kinds."

Danny thanked him again, this time in English, and backed away. He moved toward the far wall, the one opposite the mirrored one, and found his belongings: a black duffel bag so worn it appeared almost pink, a pair of scuffed athletic shoes, keys to a high-mileage Volkswagen, and his cell phone. He was out of data and hadn't made it a point to reload his prepaid plan.

He slung the duffel, heavier than it was before class, onto one arm, tossed the keys into the shoes and picked them up, palming his phone. There were message notifications on the screen: one missed call, one voicemail, and several text messages, all from the same number.

What little energy Danny had left in his body left him as if osmosis had sucked into him, taking his energy away from him and sliding into the ether. The call and messages were from Derek.

Derek.

Danny gritted his teeth while moving toward the locker room. He shouldered open the door with force, pretending it was Derek, and wound his way to an empty spot on a varnished wooden bench surrounded by lockers.

He dropped his belongings onto the bench, not paying attention to the conversations playing out around him, while leaning against a locker to read the texts. His blood pressure was rising, the tension in his shoulders hardening, and the acid in his gut was beginning to leak its way up into his throat.

Derek.

He held the phone up to his face to unlock it, then thumbed the screen to reveal the string of text messages. He wanted to puke. There were four messages, each of them sent only minutes apart.

DANNY, I NEED 2 TALK WITH U. CALL ME PLZ.

DANNY, LEFT A MSG 4 U. IMPORTANT.

DUDE, R U IGORING ME? SRIUSLY.

PLZ CALL ME. ASAP. URGENT.

He was reading the last of the messages when the phone buzzed and the screen changed to reveal an incoming call.

Derek.

Danny's thumb hovered over the icon that would allow him to ignore the call, but he answered it instead. *Might as well get it over with,* he thought to himself. He hadn't even said hello when Derek started his staccato soliloquy.

"Danny," he said breathlessly. *"Sheesh. I've been trying to get ahold of you for an hour. You haven't answered. Are you ignoring me? Never mind. It doesn't matter. I've got you on the phone now, so it's all good. You're there, right? You can hear me? Danny?"*

Danny puffed his cheeks and sighed, exhaling all of the air stored in his lungs. "I'm here," he said with all of the excitement of a man about to undergo a digital exam.

"Okay," said Derek. *"Great. I mean not great. But we need to talk. It's critically important."*

Danny remained silent, waiting for Derek to keep talking.

"You there? Danny?"

"We're talking," said Danny. "What do you want, Derek? You're not supposed to call me unless it's an absolute emer—"

"It is an emergency, Danny. Are you somewhere private?"

"I'm in a locker room."

"By yourself?"

Danny surveyed the others in the room. They were in various states of undress and topics of conversation. "Yes."

"You know I work in tech," Derek said, *"and I dabble in VC. So I—"*

"VC?"

"Venture capital," Derek said, speaking as if he were on the clock and running out of time. *"I invest some of the money I've made into other start-ups, other companies that I think show promise. Some win, some lose. But that's beside the point. The point is, there is this one company I've been spending a lot of time advising the team. They've got some incredibly unique and forward-thinking applications that transcend anything else that's happening in Silicon Valley right now."*

"Uh-huh," Danny said, resisting the urge to scream at Derek for ruining his life, for sending him into a spiral that had him out of data on his phone and trading Shotokan karate classes for janitorial duties.

"The company is called Interllayar," said Derek. *"They've hit upon some things that haven't done quite what we expected. That is to say, the underlying application is solid. The execution needs work."*

"Interlayer?" asked Danny.

"Yes. But it's spelled i-n-t-e-r-l-l-a-y-a-r."

"So what does this have to do with me?" asked Danny. He lowered the phone without awaiting the answer and shrugged his shoulder onto his sweaty ear to dry it.

"—of it," Derek was saying when he put the phone back to his ear. *"Really, I just need to ask you some questions. But they're critical."*

"Derek, I'm not interested," he said. "And let's be honest. I don't owe you anything. Good luck with your venture capitalizing, or whatever it is you do."

Danny disconnected the call and then turned off the phone. Of all the people on the face of the planet, Derek was one of two he'd gladly watch die a painful death.

That wasn't entirely true. As much as he'd like to think of himself as heartlessly vengeful, Danny wasn't the kind of person to let anyone else suffer.

As he aggressively showered and then angrily dressed himself, he couldn't shake Derek from his head. The jerk had ruined what had been, up until his desperate plea for help, a decent day. Danny didn't have a lot of those. The wounds were raw. His sleep was sporadic, his bank account was near empty, and his ex had had the audacity to give his cell phone number to Derek.

Unpleasant, X-rated memories flashed like a taunting slideshow as he forcefully tugged on clean socks. Derek. In his bed. With *his* woman.

His stomach lurched and he swallowed the urge to vomit. He squeezed his eyes closed as he sat on the varnished bench, alone now, merely trying to push the images from his mind. Those images were burned there on the backs of his eyelids.

The more he thought about Derek's phone call, the more his jaw tightened. He stuffed his soiled *gi* into his duffel bag, zipped it up, and stomped from the locker room, entering the dojo. His instructor was standing in the center of the room, performing a gracefully effortless *kata*.

Danny stood and watched him, admiring the sweeping movements that glided from one to the next. It calmed him. His pulse slowed. His shoulders slacked.

When the instructor was finished, Danny moved toward the far end of the large space with a storage closet. Inside it, he found his mop and bucket. He dropped his belongings to the floor and picked up then carried the empty bucket to a wall-mounted tub.

He cranked on the hot water and began filling the bucket, which he'd placed inside the tub and filled with a thin layer of liquid soap. Danny didn't hear the instructor until the man rapped his thick knuckles on the open door.

Danny swung around, knocking over the mop he'd rested against the corner of the tub. His face flushed. He bowed his head. "Sensei," he said, "I'm sorry. I didn't see you there."

"No apology needed," answered the blocky instructor. As fluid as his movements were, his physique was made of stone. He stepped into the closet and reached down to pick up the mop by its handle.

"I won't be long," said Danny. "I'm happy to lock up if you need to leave. I got delayed in the locker room."

The instructor handed him the mop. "Phone call?"

Danny bowed his head, eyeing his feet. He nodded. "You heard me?"

"No," said the instructor. "I did see the expression on your face when you checked your phone after class. Is everything okay? I know you don't have much money. Is it—?"

"No," said Danny, shaking his head vigorously. "It's not that. You're right. My cash flow is poor, and that's on a good day. But no, the phone call wasn't about money."

"Still," said the instructor, "I sense trouble."

Danny turned off the running water. The suds bloomed and popped, crackling in the silence between him and his instructor.

The instructor took a step into the closet. "May I offer some advice?"

Danny nodded. "Of course."

"Whatever it is," said the instructor. "Whatever the source of your trouble, you should confront it. Don't avoid it, Danny. I assure you that the source loses no sleep while you lie awake restless."

"Thank you," said Danny, considering what amounted to a Ruism. The instructor was right. He was positive that his ex and Derek lost absolutely no sleep over what they'd done to him. Though he did wonder if, because of the urgency and desperation in Derek's voice, the bane of his existence was struggling in some way.

The instructor left Danny to his work, crossing the dojo to an office and reception area at the front of the building. The dojo held a corner spot in a strip mall off South Hewitt. It was in an area of the city called Little Tokyo, northeast of downtown. He could have spent as much time cleaning the outside of the building as its interior, but thankfully the chores were limited to mopping and disinfecting the dojo floor and the locker rooms. That alone took him more than an hour and a half. But it was worth it for the free lessons.

At least he kept telling himself that.

***

Danny stepped onto the Gold Line Metro Bus and slid his card through the payment kiosk next to the driver. The driver didn't look up from her phone, sliding her fingers across the data-rich device, trolling a social media site he didn't recognize. It might have been a dating app; she was swiping past a parade of smiling faces. She must have sensed Danny watching her while he awaited the green light from the payment kiosk.

"You need something?" she asked with one eyebrow arched higher than the other.

Danny shook his head, spotted the green light, and shuffled toward a window seat at the back of the bus. He had a ten-minute ride to Union Station, where he'd switch to the Purple Line then take that to Santa Monica. His job there was a two-minute walk from the bus stop.

Despite having the Volkswagen, Danny rarely used it. He might take it to the beach to play with his dog, Maggie, or a road trip up the coast. Otherwise he took the bus. It saved on the extravagance of gasoline and prevented him from having to pay for regular maintenance more frequently than he did.

He plopped into his seat and leaned his head against the window. The exhaustion hit him instantly. He wanted to close his eyes and sleep, but he had a six-hour shift he'd picked up as an extra at the diner, so he'd muddle through. What else did he have to do anyhow? He had nowhere else to be.

The bus rumbled while pulling into traffic. He reached into his pocket and pulled out his phone, turned it on, and waited while the display cycled to the home screen. He had another series of messages, a combination of voicemails and texts. Again, they were all from Derek.

Whatever the source of your trouble, confront it.

Danny ignored the messages but returned Derek's call. It rang once before Derek answered.

"You hung up on me," he said. *"Why would you—"*

"Look, Derek," Danny interrupted, keeping his voice low so as not to include the half-dozen other bus riders in his conversation, "I'm not interested in anything you have to tell me. You stole my wife. You pretty much ruined my life. So you could tell me a huge asteroid is about to slam into the Earth and I'm not sure I'd care, given that you're the one telling me."

Danny felt at once invigorated and nervous as he spoke. He was short of breath, his pulse beating faster and faster. He was light-headed. But it was good.

"I really want you to stop calling me," he said. "I don't care what you're doing. I don't care what she's doing. Have a great life, but leave me out of it."

"I get that," said Derek quickly, as if he'd been waiting for his moment to counter, his sentences running together as if his speech were rolling downhill and gathering momentum. *"I'm not proud of it. She's not proud of it. It is what it is. I can't go back. Not where that's concerned. I can't fix that. And trust me, it's not as though I'm particularly interested in relying on you, of all people, for help."*

"Of all people?"

"I didn't mean it that way," said Derek. *"You know what I meant."*

The bus lurched to a stop with a squeal and a hiss of its brakes. A couple of people got up from their seats and exited; a few more climbed aboard. One of the arrivals, a heavyset man wearing a bright yellow Lakers jersey and denim jeans, sat in the aisle seat next to Danny despite the countless other empty seats on the bus.

Danny leaned into the window as the bus accelerated from the curb, merging into slow-moving traffic. "What *did* you mean?" he asked, lowering his voice.

"I meant," said Derek, pacing himself now, seeming to consider his words before they accumulated speed, *"I know how you feel about me. If I could avoid coming to you with this, I would. This isn't any more pleasant for me than it is for you."*

Danny sighed. "So what is it, then?"

"Have you been paying attention to the news today?"

"No. I've been...working."

"There was a plane crash off the coast of Florida," said Derek. *"It was an LA-bound flight."*

Danny squeezed himself into the corner between the window and his narrow seat, trying to avoid contact with the Lakers fan taking up more than his share of space. "I know about that," he said. "It was yesterday."

"Yes. And did you know there's a storm circulating in the Gulf? It's one wave of intense rain after another? There are flash flood warnings from east Texas to the Florida panhandle."

"Okay," said Danny. He didn't know about that. It was obvious in the way the word trailed into a partial question.

"What if I told you the two are related?"

"They are," said Danny. "I saw on the news last night that they think the weather was a factor in the—"

"No," said Derek sharply. *"That's not what I mean."*

The bus slowed again. It was Danny's stop. He gathered himself into as compact a package as he could and motioned for Kobe to get up from his seat. The man complied, barely, and Danny headed to the exit. He stepped onto the curb, managing to keep the phone cradled between his ear and shoulder. There were a few minutes to kill before he'd need to board the Purple Line bus to Santa Monica.

"What do you mean, then?"

"So here's the thing," said Derek. *"I can't talk about this on the phone. Can we talk in person?"*

Danny adjusted the duffel on his arm. A waft of sweaty funk filtered from the bag. He wrinkled his nose and looked for the signage that would lead him to Route 805. "What does any of this have to do with me?"

"I don't know yet if it does," said Derek. Then he huffed. *"Look, I've said enough already. I'm in LA. Can we meet?"*

"I'm on my way to work."

"I thought you've been at work."

"I have," said Danny. "I picked up an extra shift."

"I can meet you there."

Danny found the sign and started toward his bus. "I'll be working," he protested.

"You get breaks, right?" Derek pressed. *"I can wait for you."*

Danny knew there was no winning this one. The more he tried to avoid Derek, the pushier he'd become. He was certain of it.

Whatever the source of your trouble, confront it.

"Okay," said Danny. "Meet me in three hours. I'll get a fifteen-minute break. You can talk to me then. Fifteen minutes."

"What's the address?"

"I'll text it to you."

"Will you? Or will I have to keep calling you?"

"I'll send it as soon as we hang up."

True to his word, and truer than his ex, Danny sent the address to Derek. He really didn't want to talk to the guy. He especially didn't want the tech gazillionaire seeing he worked in a diner as a fry cook. But what did it matter? If he were honest with himself, in the grand scheme of things, not much.

He boarded the empty bus and swiped his card again. The driver was talking on his phone and didn't pay him any attention. Danny found a seat against a window toward the back of the bus and settled in for the longer part of his commute.

Nestled in the corner of his seat against the glass, with cool, damp air blowing onto the side of his face, Danny closed his eyes and thought about the bizarre conversation. Why would the weather and a plane crash thousands of miles away have anything to do with him? And whatever the connection might be, however tenuous, how did it involve Derek?

Before he dozed off, considering the unanswerable questions, he set an alarm on his phone. He didn't want to sleep past his stop. That would be a disaster.

CHAPTER 6

April 4, 2026
New Orleans, Louisiana

Bob Monk pinched the bridge of his nose and leaked the grunt of a man who didn't have the energy for much more than a weak attempt at attention-seeking. He was sitting in a cheap leather chair that faced the wall-mounted flat-screen television on the living room wall of his eldest daughters' rented home. The father of three women—Kiki, Katie, and Keri—he'd adapted the use of hyperbole to be heard amongst his loving but dismissive flock.

"What is it, Bob?" asked his wife, Kristin, in a tone of voice that expressed to him she didn't really care but was playing along for the sake of civility. She was sitting opposite him on a comfortable chenille sofa, rubbing her palms on and across the soft fabric.

"I don't like the look of it," he said. "Too much rain, too fast."

"We'll be fine," said Kristin. "Nothing real to worry about, Bob. Some street flooding maybe."

He shook his head. "I don't like being away from the house. We're close to water. Keri is there alone. I don't like the look of it."

"Keri isn't alone," said his wife. She folded her arms across her chest and looked at him over a pair of cheap readers she'd bought at

44

Costco the week before. "She has Dub with her and another boy. Barker, I think."

"What kind of name is Dub?" asked Bob. "That's not a name, it's a verb. And I don't like that she'd be getting so serious with the boy."

"Is there anything you do like, Dad?" asked Kiki, emerging from the tightly quartered but functional kitchen. "You don't like the forecast. You don't like Dub." She handed him a drink, a whiskey and ginger ale.

"I like this," he said, taking the glass from his daughter and toasting it toward her. "Three cubes and two fingers of whiskey. Perfect, thank you."

He took a long sip of the drink, and Kiki slinked across the room to sit next to her mother. Rain was now falling with more intensity; it was slapping the roof and pelting the windows. Its rhythm might have been hypnotic had it not been for the concern about how much of it would fall over the next two days.

"Speaking of Keri," Kiki said to nobody in particular, "she still at the game?"

"She texted a few minutes ago," said Kristin. "The game's over, and they're on their way to get something to eat, and then they'll head back to the house."

"She'll text you when she gets there?" asked Kiki. "I know she's in college and all, but she's still little Keri. I worry about her."

Bob took a pull of his drink and smacked his lips. "I got her on a tracker. One of those apps. I know where she is all the time."

Kristin put her hand on her daughter's leg. "Your father is a worrywart. Always has been with all of you girls."

"Yeah," said Kiki, "but we never abandoned you and went to California."

The three of them chuckled.

"This storm is going to put New Orleans underwater," said Katie, Bob's middle daughter, bounding into the room from her bedroom on the opposite side of the one-story house. She'd been sequestered there for much of the afternoon, sulking over something unspoken, as she frequently did. She'd learned from somebody that hyperbole was effective.

"She joins the living," her mother announced. "To what do we owe the pleasure of your company?"

Though Katie was in her mid-twenties, she frequently behaved as a seven-year-old who hadn't comprehended the idea of how reason might sound. Everyone in the family blamed this on her being the baby for several years, until an unexpected third child slid her unceremoniously into the middle slot. Alfred Adler would have loved her. She proved his theories correct every time she feigned aggrievement for the sake of attention.

"I've been watching the news," she said, waving her hands dramatically. "I had plans tomorrow. Big plans. It's the last day off before a long work week. But this rain is going to kill everything."

Kiki rolled her eyes. "I forgot," she said, aiming her veiled sarcasm directly at her younger sister.

Katie crossed the room to the sofa. "Forgot what?"

"This is your world and we're all just living in it," Kiki cracked.

Katie plopped onto the sofa on the other side of their mother. "At least you remember now."

Had they been in their tweens or teens, Bob or Kristin might have felt compelled to play peacemaker, to gently chastise one or both of their children and caution them against their behavior. But the girls were adults now. They were free to be asses to each other, especially in their own house. Bob wondered sometimes how the two of them managed to coexist under the same roof without clawing each other's eyes out. Deep down though, he knew the two were thick as thieves, and if push came to shove, which sometimes it did, they'd have each other's backs.

He took another sip, savoring the electric buzz that coursed through his body as he swallowed, and tipped the glass toward the screen. He shook his head. "I don't like the look of this. These bands of rain, one after the other, are going to cause a problem bigger than you missing an outing tomorrow, Katie."

The four of them sat silently for a few minutes, watching the local news team talk about the weather. The anchor announced the city would be opening its emergency operations center, then introduced a press conference about to begin.

The mayor of New Orleans was at the lectern speaking. Her chief of police, fire chief, and director of the Office of Homeland Security and Emergency Preparedness stood at her side.

"...*real potential for serious flooding,*" said the mayor. "*We have initiated our emergency response plan. We're staging assets where we see the need, and we will be here around the clock until the threat has passed. We remain hopeful that our precautions are just that, precautions. Still, given the forecast from the National Weather Service and data from our own meteorologists, we are being proactive.*"

Bob looked at the couch to his right. All three of the women were paying close attention to the television now. Maybe his concern about the storm wasn't as hyperbolic as they'd thought. He emptied his glass and held it in his lap, relishing the last of the sweet drink.

"*We have also initiated our seventeen Evacuspots,*" said the mayor. "*These are typically reserved for use in advance of a category three hurricane. And we have historically begun the process some seventy-two hours prior to the storm hitting us. But we are so confident of the risks tonight and tomorrow, we are asking those who can leave their homes to go to one of the spots within the next thirty minutes. They are marked with identical fourteen-foot sculptures. From there, we can accommodate up to thirty thousand of our friends and neighbors. We will transport you from the city and return you to that same spot once the threat is over.*"

The director of the OHSEP stepped to the microphone, adjusted it to his height, and cleared his throat. His tie was already loosened at the collar, and the swells under his eyes betrayed his perpetual lack of sleep.

"*As many of you know,*" he began, his gravelly voice as much distracting as reassuring, *"we've been through this many times before. Unfortunately, our response has not always been adequate."*

Bob glanced at the women and chuckled derisively. "I'll say."

"We've worked hard for the last decade to implement effective measures to keep you safe. As the mayor suggested, we have already activated our real-time warning systems. These are computer-aided projections that help us deploy assets ahead of any problems. We have also initiated our early warning system. This will send alerts to motorists who may be approaching any of our eleven most frequently flooded underpasses."

The mayor put her hand on the director's arm, and he paused, then stepped aside. She adjusted the mic. *"This is not to say we want anyone on the road tonight. We highly suggest that, unless you have absolutely no choice, you stay home."*

She stepped back and motioned for the director to resume his comments. He offered a nod and weak smile and readjusted the mic. *"Our pumping system is functioning at full capacity. We've tested it as recently as three weeks ago, and despite past failures, we are confident in its ability to mitigate flooding in the most prone areas of the city."*

When he finished his remarks, both the fire and police chiefs gave short updates about their staffing and readiness. Bob thought it wasn't much more than a pep talk.

"What are they going to say?" he asked. "Of course they're going to tell us they're ready. They always tell us they're ready."

"Let's hope they are," said Kristin.

"Let's hope. But this evacuation plan? Ridiculous. You can't take a system designed to work over three days and cram it into thirty minutes. They're panicking. They don't want to be accused of doing nothing. And I think they're making things worse."

The mayor was back at the lectern. She was taking questions from the assembled media, who were not on camera.

"Yes," she said, *"I am aware of the concerns about the pumps. We know they've failed in the past. But as you know, when I ran for office, flooding was a top priority for me. We are a sinking city. We all know that. I've seen the studies.*

Some areas are two inches lower than they were a year ago. Upper and Lower Ninth Ward, Metairie, and Bonnet Carré Spillway are settling at more than an inch and a half every twelve months. I can't do anything about that. Mother Nature doesn't listen to me. But my team does, the Army Corps of Engineers does, and I am confident we are as prepared as we can be."

"I didn't vote for her," said Bob.

Kristin nodded. "We know."

"It didn't have anything to do with her being a woman," he said.

"I know."

"I just don't buy what she's selling. I liked that other woman who was running against her. What was her name?"

"Penny Rogers."

"Yeah," said Bob. "She's whip smart. A real firecracker. I would have rather seen her behind that microphone."

"She did just fine for herself," said Kristin.

"I guess," said Bob. "If you consider Congress 'fine'."

"That's the thing of it, Bob," said his wife. "If it weren't for Rogers, this mayor wouldn't have gotten anything done. All of that flooding mitigation was Rogers's doing. She's the one who greased the wheels and got the money from Washington. It wasn't the mayor."

"So you're agreeing with me," said Bob.

"I suppose."

Bob's wife didn't speak much. She preferred to observe. When she did speak, it carried weight. She lived by the idea that one who speaks can't be listening and therefore can't be learning. Bob knew this about her. He respected it. It was one of her many traits he adored, in fact. That didn't stop him from forgetting sometimes that she knew more than he did about subjects on which he considered himself an expert, or at least someone with a strongly held and correct opinion.

The hair on his neck tingled.

Lightning flashed again, strobing outside the window and casting a pale blue flicker across the room. A bone-shaking clap of thunder instantly followed.

Bob dropped his glass on the floor, spilling the ice onto the tile. The tumbler shattered.

"Cut him off," joked Kristin. "No more drinks for you, Mr. Monk."

"Sorry, girls," Bob said, pushing himself from his seat to pick up the shards of glass.

Katie sprang from the sofa and hurried toward the kitchen. "No, Dad, I'll get it. It's no big deal."

Bob picked up the larger pieces of glass and carefully laid them in his open palm. Katie emerged from the kitchen with a broom and pan and knelt on the floor beside him.

"I don't want you cutting yourself," he said. "I've got it. I'm sorry though. It was a nice glass. I don't know what happened. That thunder—"

Another flash of angry light filled the room at the same time a deafening crack of thunder shook the house. Bob fell back from his feet and onto his rear. His back hit the front of his easy chair or he might have toppled over completely.

Katie put down the pan and touched her dad's leg. "You okay?"

Bob steadied himself and nodded. "Yeah. I guess I'm on edge, that's all. I don't like this one bit. And I certainly don't like that Keri is out in it."

Katie offered her father a reassuring smile. "She's a big girl, Dad. She can take care of herself. Plus she's got Dub with her."

He picked up the shards of glass he'd dropped and noticed his hand was bleeding. He held it up with a smirk. "True. I'm the one everyone should worry about."

CHAPTER 7

April 4, 2026
New Orleans, Louisiana

The hotel bar reeked of desperation. It smelled like bottom-shelf liquor and flat soda. Steve Konkoly, who went by the nickname Doc more than his own, was as familiar with the odor as he was with that of death. Neither was more appealing than the other. He slugged the last piece of ice from his drink and crunched the cube between his teeth.

He was a well-known lecturer at medical conferences the world over and had spent more nights than he cared to count in bars exactly like the one in which he now found himself ordering another dirty vodka martini.

He leaned on his elbows, feeling the heft of his gut weigh on his lower back, and mentally reminded himself to work out in the morning. He glanced up over his reading glasses at the large flat-panel display hanging on the wall behind the bar. The game wasn't on anymore, which was fine with Doc. It was a blowout. The Gators were up by thirty with a few minutes left. Instead the screen was awash with a rainbow of colors on a map of the Gulf Coast.

"The rain's getting worse?" Doc asked the bartender as the man replaced his empty glass with a fresh one.

The bartender checked over his shoulder. "Yeah. Could be flooding. But don't worry about it. The French Quarter is high enough. It'll stay dry. City wouldn't dream of letting the cash cow drown."

"Thanks," Doc said, raising his glass to toast the bartender. "To cash cows."

"You here for the medical convention?" asked the bartender, taking a soiled rag to the mahogany as if it might clean it.

"I look like a doctor?" asked Doc.

The bartender smiled and motioned to his chest. "You have a lanyard around your neck. Says you're a speaker."

Doc took a swig and rolled the sweet drink around in his mouth. He swallowed. "That I am."

A waitress sidled up to the bar next to him and gave the bartender an order. She smiled at Doc and then drifted back into the sea of desperation behind him. Doc was acutely aware of a woman's throaty giggle.

The bartender moved to the tap and held a pilsner glass underneath for a pour. "What do you speak about?"

"End of the world…medicine," said Doc.

The bartender raised his eyebrows and stopped the pour, pushing back the handle on the tap. He slapped a napkin on the mahogany and the glass atop the napkin. Then he moved to fish ice from the cooler. "What kind of medicine is that?"

Doc took another sip of his drink, relishing the buzz. He had to remind himself he was in New Orleans. The week before he'd been in Florida, and the week before that it was Michigan.

"It's conceptual," said Doc. "I've written some papers about it. I'm essentially the only one who talks about it, so I get asked to lecture on the subject."

The bartender pulled a bottle of Beefeater from the top shelf. "Sounds fun."

"Sometimes. I get a lot of frequent-flier miles. That's a bonus.

And I have some free nights built up at a couple of hotel chains. So there's that."

The waitress returned. She put the IPA and the gin and tonic on her tray, gave the bartender another order, and slid back to the pit.

"What's conceptual medicine?" asked the bartender.

Doc didn't really want to talk about it. He doubted the man on the other side of the mahogany gave two flips about him or what he did. Doc was certain he was feigning interest in the interest of a larger tip. Doc had been down this road before. In fact, he imagined that as many bartenders as practicing physicians had heard his spiel over the years.

He finished his drink and ordered another. "Shirley Temple this time."

"Seriously?" asked the bartender. "I can do that. It's weird, but I can do it."

Doc shook his head, eyeing the bartender above his glasses. "No. Not Seriously. Another martini. Just like the last one."

"Got it," said the bartender. "Are you going to explain?"

"Sure," said Doc, vaguely aware of a man pulling up to the bar a couple of seats down. "It's the idea that your world as you know it will end. That is to say communities all face reckonings. Your family…your neighborhood, city, state, country…are all susceptible to catastrophes large and small."

The bartender nodded. "I get it. Maybe my house floods. Maybe the whole country gets nuked, or my neighborhood burns in a fire."

"Yes," said Doc. "Or some asteroid slams into the planet. Whatever the scale, preparedness is an individual need. You take care of you…I take care of me."

The bartender held up a finger, asking Doc to hold his thought. He walked over to the new arrival and took his order. Then he was back. "Go ahead. Sorry about that."

"No…problem," said Doc. "As I was saying, preparedness is an individual responsibility. The government might be there to help. It might not be. I view it like I view Social Security. You'd like to think you'll get your share, but are you really counting on it?"

The bartender shook his head. He uncorked a bottle of white wine and poured a healthy glass.

"Everyone seems to think that preparedness has to do with living off the grid, hoarding canned food and ammo, and having bug-out plans," said Doc. "That's not enough. A basic first aid kit isn't enough. You need a medical plan too."

"So you're a prepper?" asked the newcomer at the bar. "I've heard of people like you. We've done stories about it."

The bartender delivered the wine to the man, and Doc noticed there was something vaguely familiar about him. He didn't respond to the intrusion, however.

"The end is nigh and all that," said the man, effecting the voice of a prophet predicting the apocalypse. "They have groups like that all over California."

Doc searched the man's face, his features. He was so familiar. Even his voice reminded him of—then it hit him. But he didn't let on that he knew the man. Not yet.

"I'm from California," said Doc. "I wouldn't say I'm a prepper. I'm more of a preparedness advocate. I look at it from the perspective of the medical community and how it can help ready the populace."

"But you know what I'm talking about, right?" asked the man, his identity clearer with every word. "Preppers?"

"I am," said Doc. "But that's a pejorative term."

The man sipped his white wine and then licked his upper lip. He seemed to be considering Doc's appraisal of the term. He swirled the wine in his glass, took another sip, and swallowed. "Tomato," he said, then pronounced it alternatively, "Tomahto."

"You're from California?" asked Doc.

The man nodded. "LA."

"Me too. Are you here for the convention?"

The man laughed as if Doc's question were ridiculous. "No. I'm here for the basketball tournament. I work for a television station."

"Oh really? Are you on camera?" Doc asked, already knowing the answer.

The man's smug expression softened. "Yes," he said, extending his hand. "I'm Lane Turner."

Doc took Turner's hand and shook it vigorously. "Huh. I'm sorry. I don't know the name."

"That's okay," said Turner. "A lot of people don't watch the news anymore. They get it from apps or websites."

"Oh, I watch plenty of news on television. I've just never seen you before."

Doc wasn't one to be rude, at least not generally. But he had an arrogance about him, born of intellect and experience that, when jabbed, forced him to fight back. He couldn't help it.

"I'm Doc," he said to Turner. "I'm here for the conference. Though I saw the Bruins won. It was a close game?"

"It was," said Turner. "Not much of a sports guy myself. I like real news. But I couldn't turn down a free trip to the Big Easy. A little bit of work in exchange for a little bit of fun."

Doc nodded and then motioned to the screen with his glass. "Not much fun with the weather this way. Looks like the weekend could be a washout."

"That's why I'm here at the hotel bar," said Turner. "I had plans to hit Bourbon Street, but it's pouring out there. We haven't had as much rain in LA in the last five years as has fallen in the past couple of hours here."

Doc looked back at the bartender. His attention was on the screen now. The volume was off, but closed-captioning populated at the bottom of the display. At the top of the screen was text highlighted in red and flashing.

FLASH FLOOD WARNING

The bartender was engrossed, his arms folded across his chest.

The waitress arrived with a new order, and he seemed not to hear her until she called his name a third time.

He blinked away from the screen and took the order. He moved toward the liquor and pulled down a bottle of Don Julio Reposado tequila.

"You look concerned," said Doc.

"Yeah," said the bartender, measuring a shot.

"I thought we have nothing to worry about in the French Quarter," Doc said, his attention split between the barkeep and the increasingly bothersome scroll at the bottom of the television on the wall.

"I did too," he said, his distant tone markedly different from the affable interest he'd employed for much of their conversation. "But that warning is for the whole city, and it looks like some parts are already flooding. It's pretty bad."

It *was* pretty bad. The darker colors on the screen were expanding in size. Much of the Gulf Coast, stretching beyond the borders of Louisiana, was under imminent threat of flooding. To the northeast of New Orleans was a trio of wide, parallel bands of storms marching southeast. The radar loop repeated over and over again, showing the bands inching closer, retreating to their previous positions, and inching closer again.

Doc slugged back his drink. "All right then. I'm done for the night. Can I settle up?"

The bartender punched up the tab and slid Doc the bill. He signed his name and room number to the bill, added a generous tip, and thanked both men for their conversation. If this was going to be as bad as it now appeared, he needed sleep. Tomorrow might not provide the opportunity.

He maneuvered through the bar, using the occasional seat back to balance himself. Doc wasn't much of a drinker, but when he did imbibe, it was well past the edge of sobriety. He walked through the lobby and to the bank of elevators at the other end of a shiny, travertine-laden atrium, and punched the call button with his thumb.

While he waited, the weight of the alcohol now descending upon him, he tried to recount how many drinks he'd had. He listened to the elevator cars descend, trying to determine which one would make it to the lobby first. He told himself he was multitasking.

Was it three drinks? No. It was four. Four drinks. Definitely four. It was enough to take the edge off, hasten his ability to fall asleep, but not leave him with a nasty hangover in the morning. He couldn't handle a hangover. Not tomorrow. Not with the possibility of New Orleans slipping under water.

The elevator to his right chimed and the doors slid apart. Doc braced himself against the stainless frame of the opening and stepped into the car, pushed the button for his floor, and willed himself to the back of it so he could lean against the wall.

The elevator doors shut, but the car didn't move. Doc stood there for what might have been two minutes before he realized he hadn't ascended yet. He punched his floor button again before realizing he needed to insert his room key into a slot to activate his limited-access floor.

He fumbled through his pockets and fished out the key, poked at the slot until the key slid inside, then punched his floor. The elevator jerked upward, and Doc stepped back, falling against the wall.

The car zipped skyward, accelerating until it neared his floor. Then it slowed and lumbered to a stop. The doors whooshed ajar and Doc searched the hallway for the right direction to his room. By the minute, the fourth vodka martini was soaking into him more completely, but he managed to find his room. He inserted the key, which he thought so antiquated. So many of the hotels at which he now stayed used keyless entry. He could unlock his door with his phone. No such luck here in New Orleans. He ambled toward the closer of the two queen beds.

Doc liked having two beds in his room. One was for sleeping. The other served as a handy spot for his open suitcase. He'd forgotten he'd used the bed closer to the door for his baggage and collapsed onto the Samsonite, jabbing his hip into the hard plastic.

He cursed himself and struggled to the other bed, where he slid off his shoes and fell back onto the comforter. His head sank into the pillows and he lay there trying to abate the sensation of spinning.

The air-conditioning, which he hadn't noticed until now, shut off, and the sound of rain beating against the room's large floor-to-ceiling window proved an adequate lullaby. Doc fell asleep thinking of the end of the world, his planned speech the next day, and wallowed in the profound sense of loneliness that pervaded every aspect of his life.

CHAPTER 8

April 4, 2026
New Orleans, Louisiana

It was close to midnight by the time Dub and Keri dropped onto the couch in her parents' family room, having navigated the rain-soaked streets of her hometown. It had taken forever to fight their way through the traffic and the weather.

"What do you think Barker's doing?" asked Keri.

"You mean *who* is he doing?"

"Funny, Dub. You think he's okay?"

"I'm sure," said Dub. "Dude can take care of himself."

"I felt bad leaving him at the restaurant."

"I didn't. He was having fun. Plus he told us to go. He'll grab an Uber."

"He knows where I live, right?"

Dub nodded. "I think so."

Keri leaned her head on his shoulder and placed her hand on his chest. She wiggled as close to him as he thought she could get, and he adjusted himself to put his arm around her. Her hair smelled like the baby shampoo her mother kept in the guest bathroom.

"You as tired as I am?" asked Keri.

When they'd gotten home, they'd stripped off their wet clothes, Keri had tossed them into the washing machine, and they'd taken hot showers. Now they were dry, the clothes were on the spin cycle.

"Probably," Dub replied. "But I'm wound up from that drive back."

She spoke through a wide yawn. "It was intense," she said, and took his hand. She rubbed the face of his wristwatch with her thumb.

He kissed the top of her head. "That it was."

Dub closed his eyes and focused on her breathing. They sat there in the dark, the rain beating against the roof, the windows creaking from the wind. The occasional flash of lightning and the delayed, low grumble of thunder drew him into a trance.

He was awake but not lucid. His mind drifted to the game they'd enjoyed, to the classes he'd be missing on Monday, probably Tuesday, and maybe Wednesday, and back to Keri's breathing. It was deeper now, more contented. She was asleep.

Dub was nearly there too, his breathing matching the slow, full rhythm of hers when his phone buzzed on the coffee table in front of him, vibrating loudly against the glass top. He ignored it, choosing to let it go to voicemail. He ignored it a second time. It buzzed again seconds later. Reluctantly, cursing the phone and whoever was calling, Dub leaned forward and plucked his phone from the table. Keri didn't fully awaken, but she shifted her body away from his and snuggled herself into the opposite corner of the sofa.

Dub checked the caller on the display. It was Barker.

"Yeah," said Dub. "What's up?"

In the distance, he heard the beep of what sounded like a cash register and the low, familiar rhythm of reggae music. Barker's voice was higher pitched than normal. He spoke quickly. *"Hey, dude. Where have you been? I've been calling you."*

"I was asleep," said Dub, mostly telling the truth.

"Okay," said Barker, sounding as though he didn't hear Dub's response. *"I need your help."*

"What?"

"I'm stuck at a convenience store. I can't get an Uber to pick me up."

Dub pushed himself to sit up straight. "A convenience store?"

Barker was speaking to someone else, his hand was over the phone, and his voice was muffled.

"Dude," said Dub, "you there?"

Barker uncovered the phone. *"Yeah. Sorry. I'm just putting out a fire here. Anyway, my new friend and I need a ride."*

"New friend?" asked Dub. "You're bringing a stranger to Keri's parents' house?"

"Yeah," said Barker. *"It's cool. She's a Bruin. I met her at the restaurant. We clicked. Then we caught a ride to the store here. But when we were getting supplies, the Uber driver took off. I gave him one star."*

Dub sighed and an overwhelming sense of dread washed over him. He had absolutely no interest in wading back out onto the streets. The weather was horrible, and from the sound of the wind and rain battering the house, it was getting worse by the minute. Plus, he was immensely comfortable sitting on the plush couch with Keri. He had no choice though. He couldn't leave a man behind.

"All right," he said, intentionally dragging out the words to let Barker know he was being a pain in the ass. "Drop me a pin and I'm on my way."

"Thank you," said Barker. *"I owe you."*

"Yeah, you do," said Dub. He ended the call and awaited the pin notification. A few seconds later the message appeared, and Dub tapped it open. The red pin appeared on a map, and then the app traced the route from the pin to his location. The store was only three miles away.

Dub patted Keri on her hip and squeezed gently. He leaned over her and whispered her name, trying to rouse her gently from her nap.

"Hey," he said. "I've got to go get Barker. He's stuck at a convenience store a few miles from here."

Keri blinked and yawned, disoriented for an instant until her eyes met Dub's. She reached up and touched his face. "You're leaving?" she asked, a lilt in her voice. "Don't leave."

"I have to. Barker can't get an Uber in this weather. He needs a ride back here."

She rolled her eyes. "Barker," she said in the same frustrated tone she'd used countless times before. "Of course he needs a ride."

"He has a friend with him."

Her eyes widened and she sat up. "A friend? He's bringing a hookup back here?"

"She goes to UCLA," said Dub. "I guess he met her at the restaurant."

"I don't know about that, Dub. Some random chick…"

"I can't leave her there," said Dub. "Barker put me in an awkward position."

Keri was fully awake now. "He put *us* in an awkward position," she corrected. "What an ass. That guy is always thinking with his—"

"I know. We can deal with it later. But I've gotta go get them. Cool?"

Keri stretched, arching her back. "Not cool, but whatever. Just be careful and hurry back."

"Of course," said Dub.

"The roads are probably worse than when we came home," she said, putting her hand on his knee. "Don't do anything stupid. If you can't see the curb, don't drive through the water."

"Got it. You gonna hang here until I get back?"

Keri stood up, stretching again. She ran her fingers along the waistband of her sweatpants. Dub stood up and put his hands on her hips.

She kissed him on the cheek. "No. I'm going to my room. I don't want to see Barker until tomorrow morning. No telling what I'd say to him and his hookup if I saw them tonight."

Dub laughed. "Fair enough." He slipped his feet into a pair of sliders. "He'll probably appreciate that too."

They hugged, Keri traipsed toward her room, and Dub grabbed the keys to the rental car. He stood at the front door with his hand on the knob for several seconds, gathering the courage to step out into the cold rain and wind. Then he exhaled loudly and made the dash toward his midsized domestic. He swung open the door, slid into the driver's seat, and pulled the door shut in what felt like one fluid motion. He was soaked by the time he pushed the ignition and put the car in reverse.

He couldn't see through the rear window, so he used the backup camera to navigate from the narrow driveway then onto the street. It was blurry from condensation but was clear enough for him to see the driveway.

He fumbled for the windshield wipers and put them on high. It wasn't enough to clearly see his path as he put the car into drive and slowly accelerated. He sat as far forward as he could in the seat, his chest against the steering wheel. His fingers gripped the wheel as if he were a first-time driver's ed student unsure of himself on the road.

The radio was on. He turned it off. The rain was so loud against the roof of the car he couldn't hear the music anyhow, and he needed his full attention on the barely visible road ahead. Three miles seemed like nothing until he started driving in this mess. Now it felt like a blindfolded cross-country trek on bald tires.

The tension tightened in Dub's neck and shoulders. There were memories there, of another night where the water rose too high, he was trying to keep at bay. He pushed them aside and glanced at his phone. He noticed a turn ahead, but he couldn't tell from the obscured windshield where the intersecting street met his. He slowed, leaning toward the passenger's window to get an alternative view.

He reached the turn and made it slowly, deliberately. In the dim wash of the headlights, which he'd flipped to high beam, he saw the water pooling on the street, rushing along the gutters, and spilling into curbside drains. The dull streetlights that dotted the street showcased the sheets of incessant rain as he passed. A well of anger made Dub clench his jaw. He was not happy with Barker.

He kept the car in the middle of the road, the standing water not having covered the pavement there, until he reached the next intersection and saw the bright lights of an oncoming SUV or truck. He eased through the intersection and crept toward the deeper water near the curb. He could feel it rushing under the floorboard as he held steady on the gas pedal. The approaching vehicle, however, wasn't moving to its side of the road. It was maintaining its path along the center. And it was moving much faster than Dub had originally thought. The closer it got, the more Dub could make out its speed and shape. It was a truck with large tires that sprayed a thick wash of floodwater up and out from its treads.

Dub toggled the high beams, trying to get the driver's attention. If it maintained its course, it might swamp him or, even worse, force him off the road and into the flooded gutter.

He flicked his lights again and took his foot off the accelerator. The truck kept coming. Dub held his foot above his brake, but did not press it. If he stopped the car, he'd flood, and might not get it going again. The water was likely just deep enough to creep into the tailpipe. He kept moving forward, at a crawl above idle, and steered toward the right.

The truck wasn't slowing. In fact, it seemed to Dub it was speeding up. Dub braced for the wave sure to come, and the truck rumbled past him.

A large spray slapped the driver's side of his car as Dub swerved to try to avoid it. Then a large wake splashed against the car, and Dub felt water on his bare heels as it leaked through the bottom of the driver's side door, pooling in the well underneath the gas and brake pedals.

He managed to maintain control, weaving back toward the center of the road before slamming into the back of a car parked at the curb. The car was struggling. The engine protested as he carefully accelerated and straightened his course. It sounded like the motor was coughing as he advanced along the street. He was sweating now, perspiration blooming on the back of his neck and on his forehead. He cursed Barker again and leaned even closer to the wheel. His muscles ached as if he'd been holding them taut for hours.

The GPS on the phone showed him it was less than a mile from the convenience store where he was told by Barker to pick him up, along with the girl Barker had met. He had two more turns to make before reaching the convenience store. His concern, as he reflexively checked the rearview mirror and then each side mirror, wasn't getting to the store. Sure, he was worried. But the real stress came from thinking ahead to the drive back.

He picked up his phone and voice dialed Keri. She answered groggily.

"Hey," he said. "I'm having trouble. There's water everywhere. I may have to come back home. Not sure. I might or might not be able to get Barker. Just letting you know."

"*Okay,*" she said, the sleep thickening her response. "*Be careful.*"

"You too," he said. "I'll keep you posted. Love you."

Dub hung up, not waiting for her response. He tossed the phone onto the seat beside him. He had to concentrate. There were a thousand moves running through his mind, a million options, countless bad outcomes.

If the rain persisted, there was no way he'd be able to take the same route home that he'd taken on the way to the store. It was already treacherously close to impassable. Another ten minutes and it would be inundated, no doubt. A swell of anxiety quickened his pulse. He tightened his grip on the wheel, forcing himself to stay in the moment and not let himself drift into his suppressed past.

He made the first of the turns, the car spitting water from its exhaust. The accelerator was struggling when he pressed it coming out of the turn and straightened onto the next street. There were cars lining both sides of the road, making a center path the only possibility. As the wipers made quick passes on the windshield, he saw the water was halfway up the rims of most of the sedans parked on the street. The SUVs had a little more clearance, though not much. The center of the road, not visible underneath the rising water, didn't have quite the depth, as far as he could tell.

A flash of lightning strobed and illuminated Dub's surroundings for a brief instant. His pulse was already thumping thickly against his chest. The perspiration was building. The sight of the flooding street, the sheets of rain, and the homes with water already creeping up their driveways made him want to vomit.

Thunder crashed overhead. He felt it in the steering wheel. He loosened his sweaty grip and readjusted it, making sure he had control of the vehicle as he neared his final turn. The GPS told him it was only a few feet ahead and to the left. When he reached it and started to make the turn, his headlights revealed not a street, but a torrent of water rushing toward him. It pushed against the front tires and rocked the carriage, threatening to lift both from the asphalt.

Dub bore down on the wheel, narrowed his focus, and swung the front of the car around, sloshing through deeper water as he bounced up onto a curb and off again. He pushed the gas and somehow managed to keep the car moving back toward the street from which he'd just turned. He turned left and found the center of the road. He exhaled. His muscles relaxed infinitesimally. But it was too soon for relief. The engine coughed and the wheel stuttered under his grip. The car stalled. In that instant, without the motor to propel it forward, the water lifted the vehicle from the ground and carried it back into the flooded intersection from which the rapids were angrily crashing and roiling. The car's headlights dimmed and it tipped toward the driver's side. Water rushed in through the door, quickly pooling at Dub's ankles.

The wheel locked. Dub struggled fruitlessly to regain control. He unbuckled himself and climbed to the passenger seat. The car was spinning now, bobbing like an unevenly weighted canoe. Dub reached for the button to lower the passenger window and pushed it.

It didn't work. He cursed himself and then grabbed the door handle, pulling it, and with every bit of strength he had left, shouldered the door open against the water.

He scooted to the edge of the passenger seat, water splashing against him while threatening to slam shut the door on his torso. He swung his feet around and then, gauging the depth of the water from the undulating reflection of streetlights on its surface, launched himself from the car.

The instant he hit the water, gliding through it before the rush of it tumbled him feet over head, his body seized from the shock of it. He resisted the urge to suck in a deep breath and cry out from the cold, as he somehow found his bare feet surfing along soft, muddy ground.

The force of the water diminished the farther he slid from his car, and as he gathered himself, coughing out water, he realized he was in somebody's front yard a few feet from the porch.

He looked back, trying to find the car. It was gone. Either it had washed away or was wholly submerged now. He couldn't be sure which. It didn't matter though. He did try to remember if he'd purchased the accident insurance when he'd rented it the day before.

Kneeling in muddy grass, the water up to his chest, Dub pushed himself to his feet. The taste of grease and rubber coated his tongue. He spat into the water, trying to rid himself of it. It didn't help.

Standing there drenched and shivering, water bubbling and rising toward his waist now, he reached in his pocket for his phone. It was gone, lost in the missing car. The tension in his neck returned. In his panic, he'd forgotten to unplug it from its charger. Now it was a sunken, useless treasure somewhere out of reach.

With each heave of his chest and heavy breath outward, the foul-tasting water that coated his body and mixed with the icy rain sprayed from his lips. He spread his feet shoulder-width apart to steady himself against the water, which was now bringing the current he'd experienced a block or two upstream.

The heavy rain made it hard to see much more than ten or twenty yards in any direction. Some of the streetlights had flickered off. It was darker, colder. He was lost.

Wait. He wasn't lost. He'd been so focused on the GPS and the difficulty of the drive, he forgot he could find his way to the convenience store. He took a tenuous step forward, and then another, and another until he'd reached a street sign at the nearest intersection, which was only two houses from the one where he'd skidded to a stop.

Dub recognized the name of the streets, but he wasn't sure which way was north. He was disoriented. He tried looking up to the skies. The rain and clouds made it impossible to see any stars. He couldn't see the sliver of a new moon either. Then he remembered his wristwatch.

It was an analog watch, perpetual motion with a sweeping second hand, with its numbers that were luminescent. He unstrapped it from his wrist, holding it horizontally in his palm. He wiped the face of it with his thumb and checked the time. Before he recognized it was after midnight now, he cursed himself again. It was nighttime. He couldn't check the sun in reference to the time.

He spit rainwater from his lips and clenched his jaw. He wasn't altogether there. The combination of exhaustion and stress was making him loopy. He took two steps then leaned on a tree. His hand slipped from its slimy surface, but he caught himself before he stumbled forward into the water face-first.

He touched the tree again, lightly running his fingers across the slimy surface of the bark. He looked up at the towering and wide-reaching branches of a grand magnolia tree. The slime wasn't slime. It was moss. Dub slapped the tree and laughed.

"Moss," he said. "Freaking moss."

He shuffled beside the tree and faced in the same direction as the mossy, *northern* side of the tree. Now he knew where he needed to go.

Wary of open manholes or water-sucking gutters he couldn't see beneath the rising water, Dub carefully waded north as close to the flooded houses as he could get. He occasionally stepped on popped sprinkler heads or decorative lawn ornaments, but managed to stay above water. It was painstaking, and with each successive inch forward, he couldn't be sure what he'd find when he reached the convenience store. Worse, he couldn't know what was happening a couple of miles away at Keri's house.

Trudging the final stretch, he came across three separate families, all of them wading with varying degrees of difficulty toward higher ground. Dub helped one family, whose belongings had spilled into the water when a large plastic tub had tipped.

He imagined that what these people wore and what they carried encompassed the whole of their salvaged belongings. He tried not staring at what looked like refugees as they passed him or moved more quickly in the same direction.

But one family, a mother and father and teenage son a couple of years younger than Dub but taller, didn't leave his side. They trekked with him toward the store.

"We don't know where else to go," said the mother through chattering teeth. "We don't know where is safe."

"I don't either," admitted Dub. "I'm not from here. I'm visiting."

He thought of two men who long ago had saved him from a similar fate. He had to help. He had to pay it forward.

"Our house is gone," said the son. His eyes were swollen, and even in the dim light, Dub could tell he'd been crying.

"Everything," echoed the mother. "The water is halfway up the walls. It's over the tops of our beds."

The father was almost catatonic. He was slogging silently forward at a pace equal to his wife—a water-logged zombie of a man, balding on the top of his head and empty in his countenance. Twice, when Dub glanced at him, he thought the father was mumbling to himself.

"He's a veteran," the wife said when she noticed Dub looking. "He suffers from PTSD. This isn't good for him. I'm just glad he came with us. At first I thought it might be a struggle, but he came."

She smiled weakly and moved closer to her husband, looping her arm in his and holding it with both hands. He glanced at her for a moment, then turned back to the watery path ahead.

"I can take that," Dub said, taking the floating plastic bin from the son. "You worry about your dad."

The boy nodded and thanked Dub. The four of them fought against the rising water another several blocks before they reached the convenience store, where they found a half-dozen people and an aluminum jon boat with a running twenty-horsepower engine rumbling and spurting water and smoke from its stern. The water thinned here. It was at most ankle deep, and the convenience store still had power. From the looks of it, the interior hadn't yet flooded. There were more people standing inside, gathered around the service counter, appearing as though they were in no hurry to go anywhere.

A half-dozen cars were as close to the storefront as they could get, parked at odd angles to one another to avoid the water. None of them had flooded yet, though Dub imagined it was only a matter of time. They were on an island that was surely sinking. One of the people loitering by the boat emerged from the others and sloshed a couple of steps toward Dub and the family he'd accompanied during the last part of his journey.

"Dub?" asked Barker, narrowing his eyes and peering into the rain. "Dub? Is that you? Holy crap. Seriously? Dub?"

He splashed through the water like a kid in a baby pool and extended his arms toward Dub. When he reached him, he wrapped them around his friend and grunted.

"Man, it's good to see you. I got so worried. These guys here in this boat, they're so cool. They're giving us a ride. They were going to go look for you."

Dub pulled away. "Well, I'm here."

Barker eyed him up and down. "You look like hell, dude."

Dub wiped the newly replenished sheen of water from his face, shook the excess from his hands, and nodded. "I feel like it. The car's gone."

"I figured." Barker glanced over Dub's shoulder. "Who are these people?"

"A family whose home is underwater," he explained. "They needed some help."

"That's my Dub," said Barker. "You're a hero, dude."

"Hardly," Dub scoffed.

"Seriously," said Barker, with a level of excitement Dub imagined had to have been born from nerve-fueled adrenaline. Or alcohol. "You're the kind of dude who'd run into a burning building when everyone else is running out."

"I doubt that," said Dub. But as he pushed the floating tub toward the teenage boy, he knew in his gut that Barker was right. He couldn't help but be nice to others, even when it was at his own expense.

Barker motioned toward the boat with his head and lowered his voice. "Look, I think I can get these guys to take us back to Keri's house."

"Really?"

"Yeah. They're looking for people to help. Half of those people inside the convenience store came here in their boat."

"But we're three miles from her house," protested Dub. "What makes you think they'll go that far out of their way when there are other people much closer they can ferry over?"

"I gave them the twelve-pack I bought," said Barker. "Cheap stuff, but they were thrilled. It was payment to go find you. Now they don't have to find you, so they can take us to Keri's. If there are others on the way, there's room for four other people."

Dub started counting. "So two guys with the boat, you, me, and your new friend."

Barker nodded.

"Which one is she?"

"The cute one in the overalls," said Barker, shooting a glance toward the woman without obviously trying to be obvious.

Noticing Barker's attempt to be sly, the woman high-stepped through the water toward him. She wore her hair in a scrunchie-affixed ponytail, and her face had the wide-eyed look of a person who knew they were the subject of conversation.

"I'm Gem," she said, offering her wet hand to Dub. "You're the famous Dub?"

Dub's brow furrowed with confusion. "Famous?"

She squeezed the water from her ponytail and wiped her hands on her overalls. Her mascara had run, giving her the appearance of an overdone smoky-eye. Even in the rain, her scent carried. It was an oddly enticing mixture of essential oils and wood.

"Barker talks about you a lot," she said. She nudged Barker with an elbow. "I'm thinking you're his hero."

There was that word again. *Hero.* He didn't much care for it.

"Well," said Dub, "I'm sure that's overstated."

"Probably not," she said, talking to Dub as if they'd been longtime friends. "Dude has a man-crush. No doubt."

Dub clenched his jaw. He didn't know Gem from pyrite, but she rubbed him the wrong way. Barker was smiling at her, mouthing her words as she spoke. He was entranced and appeared oblivious to Dub's disinterest in small talk. He started to move toward the man at the back of the jon boat. He was smoking a cigarette in the rain, blowing the smoke upward into his own face, contented.

Gem edged into his path, eyeing him with arched, meticulously waxed eyebrows dewy with rain. "Your girlfriend, Keri is it? She's at her house?"

"Yes."

"We should totally go get her. Barker paid the boat dudes with beer. He was saying we could get them to take us to her." She lowered her voice and leaned into him. "It's the worst beer. Cheap. I wouldn't drink it. But it's beer, right?"

He exhaled, wiped the rain from his face with the back of his arm, and faked a smile. Whatever he might have found cute or exotically attractive about her had washed off of him as soon as it had stuck.

Fortunately, the mother of the family he'd escorted interrupted them.

"I'm sorry," she said, touching his arm. "I don't mean to interrupt. I wanted to thank you. The store clerk is going to let us rest here for a while. They think the National Guard is on its way with some big trucks."

She squeezed his arm and offered him a grateful smile peppered with sadness he imagined was tattooed onto her face. Dub placed his hand on hers, returned the momentary affection, and wished her well.

Gem began to speak again. Dub held up a finger and winked at her politely, suggesting she hold her thought, and he sloshed to the boat. He waved as he approached, drawing a suspicious blow of smoke from the man at the motor.

"My friend Barker said you might be willing to take us to my girlfriend's house," he said. "Would that be okay?"

The man, who at first seemed wary, softened. He smiled under the steeply curled brim of a purple and gold baseball cap. Then he nodded, took a final drag from the cigarette, sucking in his cheeks, and flicked the butt into the rising water.

"I'd be happy to help." He exhaled, his words swirling the smoke that seemed like mist in the rain. "Sure thang," he said with a Southern drawl as pronounced as any Dub had ever heard in Houston. "Your buddy paid us up with a case, so we're good. You hop in and we'll make a run. You just give me turn by turn on the way and we'll figure it out."

Dub stepped forward with his hand extended. "I'm Dub. Thanks so much."

"Not at all," said the man. "I'm Louis. This is Frank."

Frank, a wiry man with close-cropped hair, was sitting in the front of the boat and finishing a pull on a can of beer. He nodded, swallowed hard, and raised the can. "S'up."

"Hey," said Dub. He turned and called to Barker over his shoulder, "Let's go. It's only going to get worse."

Dub, Barker, and Gem climbed into the boat, each of them taking seats on the wide benches that braced the shallow-drawing aluminum craft. Frank stepped out and held onto the bow, turning the boat around and tugging it out away from the parking lot. When he was knee deep, he hoisted himself back into the boat. It was then Dub noticed both of their hosts were wearing hip waders.

Louis took the rudder stick on the motor and pulled it toward his body as the fourteen-foot boat jerked forward. They were under way.

"You tell me where to turn," said Louis, thumping Dub on the shoulder. "I ain't much for street names. Some I know; some I don't."

Dub had taken the seat closest to Louis. Dub was in front of him and to the left. Barker and Gem sat next to each other at the center of the boat. Frank was in the front on the right.

"You're going to go straight for a while," he said, trying to recall distances. He remembered street names, but in the dark he couldn't see them any more than he could see the street under the black water.

"Hey," said Louis, as if reading his mind, "take this. It'll help."

Dub took a flashlight from Louis's outstretched hand. It was cold from the air and wet from the rain. He ran his hand along it to strip away the beads of water clinging to its metal battery compartment. He punched the button on its handle and, without thinking about it, looked directly at the bezel. A bright collection of LED lights nearly blinded him.

Dub squeezed his eyes shut and shook his head from the blinding error.

Louis chuckled. "I've done that," he said affably. "Stings, don't it?"

Dub rubbed the afterimage from his eyes with his thumb and forefinger. He nodded and readjusted his eyes to the night.

The rain hadn't subsided or given any hints that it might be letting up. It was a steady shower emanating from some invisible faucet high above without anyone to shut off the tap. It had gotten to the point, despite the discomfort and cold, the rain wasn't annoying anymore. Dub was so soaked through that more rain wasn't even an issue. He aimed the light up and out, away from the boat. He scanned the night, the sheets of rain the only thing visible at times, searching for street signs.

Occasionally he'd lower the white beam toward the water. From his seat aboard the jon boat, he couldn't determine how much higher the flood had risen. As the beam skipped across the black roil and bounced off the rounded tops of mailboxes or the fogged windows of curb-parked cars, it was apparent the tub was filling and the drain was stopped.

The farther they traveled in the murk, slowly advancing along the streets-turned-canals, the oil-burning odor of the puttering motor became more overwhelming. It consumed Dub's senses: the mix of fuel and grease, cold rain and stress.

"Straight?" asked Louis as they approached an intersection.

Dub angled the beam up to find the sign. He didn't recognize either name. "Keep going, please."

Barker and Gem were sitting against each other now, hip to hip. She leaned into him, and he had his arm around her waist. They were talking to each other, their voices inaudible over the sputter and gurgle of the motor. Frank was on his knees with a flashlight, checking for any obstacles in the water ahead.

"Turn up here," Dub said, spotting the right street. "Left."

"Got it." Louis maneuvered the boat, cranking the rudder handle hard to the right.

The boat's bow slid to the left, and the intersecting street came into view, as much as it could have given the rain and the dark. Frank's light, aiming directly in front of the boat, cast a dim cone into the inky distance. Ahead of them, another boat came into view. It was more of an inflatable pontoon, its engine whirring and its bow pitched out of the water, carrying eight people on its cramped deck. The pilot nodded at them as they passed each other. None of the shivering passengers, no doubt waterlogged survivors leaving behind their homes, said a word. Although none even looked up, Dub could see the shock and horror in their blank faces. They were a half a mile from Keri's house.

"Surprised we ain't seen more like that," said Louis. "I figure—"

"Help!" The voice was distant but close enough that the call was clear. It sounded like a young woman. "Help!" she cried again, her voice warbling through the din of the rain.

"That's just ahead," Frank said. "I can see someone waving a light stick."

"You mind?" Louis asked Dub.

"Of course not," said Dub.

Frank held his light toward the glow stick he could apparently see. Louis directed the boat in the light's path. The closer they got, the higher Frank aimed the cone of light. The glow stick, which was waving back and forth, was elevated high above the ground.

"Help!" called the woman excitedly. "Do you see me? Can you? I'm up here. Up here!"

Dub narrowed his focus, following the beam of light until he saw the woman. The shape of a woman, that was, waving her arms above her head, the bright pink glow stick waving, became clearer. He thought at first she was on her roof, seeking a perch above the water that was now at the eaves of single-story homes in this part of the city. But as they drifted closer, the boat pitching up and down from the current, he saw she wasn't on the roof. She wasn't anywhere near a house. She was in a tree, straddling the wide, strong branch that extended perpendicular from the thickly aged trunk of a commanding oak.

"Hold on!" Frank called, one hand cupped at his mouth. "We see you. We're coming."

Barker glanced over his shoulder at Dub, his jaw slack. He was shivering, his teeth chattering, and he appeared as bewildered as Dub had ever seen him.

"I can't believe this," he said. "How deep the water is. You see we just passed overtop a car?"

Dub nodded. "We'll be okay," he told his friend, saying it to convince himself as much as anyone else on the boat. "We'll be okay."

Louis skillfully maneuvered the boat, working the tiller handle of the outboard, twisting the throttle as he tried to get the boat as close to the tree as possible. He was feet from it, so close Dub saw the wide-eyed fear in the face of the woman above him.

Frank was calling out to her, calming her, reassuring her. He directed her to keep hold of the branch, to wrap herself around it like she was riding a bull. "And don't let go until I tell you."

She nodded vigorously and whimpered while she adjusted her arms and tightened her elbows against the sides of the branch.

And then, if it were possible, the rain intensified. Without warning, the drops grew heavier and colder. The speed with which they fell from the milky-black sky accelerated. The sound of the barrage slapping the water became deafening, like the thunderous applause of a crowd too large for a small auditorium.

A gust of wind buffeted the port side of the skiff. Dub nearly lost hold of the flashlight as he tried to grip the bench with his free hand to keep himself from falling over. Another gust of wind blew past them.

The boat swung wildly to one side, and the stern slammed into the oak's unforgiving trunk. The crash vibrated violently through the boat, shaking Dub's body.

"Hold on!" Louis shouted as he tried to settle his course. But the water now was flowing differently, more angrily ferociously, like a dam was opened somewhere upstream.

The boat swung around again in a cyclonic pattern, slapping the side of the oak a second time. The woman above called out with an urgent voice. Dub couldn't understand her words. He was focused on staying inside the boat as the water overpowered its small motor.

He dropped the flashlight and grabbed both sides of the boat as if to steady its hull himself, looking up in time to see the woman dangling from the branch, her arms stretched as far as her weight would extend them. He shot a look at Frank, who was trying to wave her off. She didn't listen. She dropped what had to be eight feet to the boat. Her body caught the side of it and tipped it precariously to one side. Dub's grip wasn't enough to hold him, and the blast of momentum shot him from his seat, slamming him into the cold, black water. Somehow, he managed to steal a breath of air as he tumbled headfirst overboard, falling tumultuously into the black turbulence. The hull raked across his back as the jon boat somehow righted itself. He struggled underneath it, unable to surface. They were both carried together in the increasingly strong current.

His heart racing, Dub struggled not to suck in a deep breath. His chest burned. He was blind. And then the boat was gone.

Not again. Not again. Not again.

His memories surfaced and flooded his mind. Water everywhere, cold, relentless rain, the darkness of night.

He tumbled in the blackness, weightless, and powerless to find his bearings. He wasn't sure which direction was toward the surface. Something sharp scraped against his leg. He grabbed for it and groaned, feeling the bubbles slide against his chin. The bubbles. They told him he was upside down.

He flipped himself over in the dark water. He couldn't know whether it was three feet deep or ten. Still, he righted himself and extended his legs beneath him. They didn't touch ground, but he kicked with both feet, fluttering as hard as he could, grabbing for the surface, reaching up with one arm and then the other, pulling himself toward breathable air.

His head dizzied; his vision blurred. Then he realized he wasn't swimming upward after all. He couldn't be. The water wasn't that deep. He wasn't swimming downward either. He'd have hit the ground. And then he did. His hands slid against the familiar muddy grass that had sucked in his bare feet an hour earlier. His fingers stuck into the muck, and cold mud filled the spaces underneath his fingernails.

He was out of air. His muscles quivered. The sensation of losing consciousness began to take hold, but having oriented himself, Dub found his footing and pushed against the muck with both feet, propelling himself upward at an angle toward the surface. He kicked, pulled, and shook his head, trying to fend off the pain as the final remnant of bubbles escaped from his mouth.

At last he surfaced. He thrashed against the water and gasped, sucking in both air and water. He coughed and spat the foul water from his mouth. He treaded water, breathing in and out with effort, until he'd regained control and left the panic behind.

Then he spun around, kicking his legs. His vision was blurred, by the torment of oxygen deprivation or from the water in his eyes. His breathing slowed to something closer to normal. He drew a hand from the water and wiped his eyes. As soon as he began to take stock of where he was, he felt a pinch on the back of his neck. And then another. Before he could slap at it, there was one on his ear. And on the back of his head.

He slapped at his neck, trying to tread water with one hand, and felt the bite on his hand. Then another. And another. Now the bites were hot. They stung. And there were more of them. All over his neck, the back of his hand, his jaw. The pain was spreading, deepening.

Fire ants!

Dub sucked in a quick breath and dunked himself under the water. He ran his hands across his neck and head and face frantically, washing his hair free of the ants. The poison bites swelled into a range of bumps across his neck and ears. He winced at the burning sensation throbbing across his raw skin, blowing out the water he'd stored in his lungs.

He flattened himself underwater and then swam deeper a couple of strokes before he resurfaced away from the ants. He pulled himself back to the surface, emerged, and shook the water from his face. He touched the back of his neck. The swelling had spread to the sides of his neck and across the tops of his ears. He scanned the water around him. Several feet away, where he'd been, he saw a floating ant pile, undulating but keeping its shape in the rain as it cruised the floodwaters. The top of the pile was swarming with angry, confused ants. Dub leaned back in the water and kicked himself farther away from the threat.

He cursed the pain and tried to refocus on the task at hand.

"Barker?" he yelled. His voice sounded flat, as if the pouring rain sucked it into a vacuum. "Barker!"

There was no answer. He listened for the sound of the skiff's motor, praying for the familiar rumble of its twenty horsepower. He heard nothing.

He sighed, exasperated and exhausted, treading water. There was no use searching for Barker or the jon boat. He needed to get to Keri. If the water was this deep so close to her street, there was no telling the conditions at her home.

He swam slowly, bobbing in the water and occasionally spitting the rainwater from his face, until he found a street sign only a foot or two above his head. It was an intersection a block from Keri's street. He took a deep breath, his chest stinging, and resolved to move faster. He leaned forward and began kicking. He kept his head above the water, except for his chin, swimming with effort.

His arms churned like a lifeguard hurrying out to a rescue. He cupped his hands and pulled them through the water at his sides, propelling himself forward. He was getting closer. Every stroke, every kick, every throb of the pain on his neck and ears brought him closer to Keri.

Hero.

That word stuck in his mind as he churned through the flood, hoping he would find his girlfriend high and dry, though he knew the idea of anything being high or dry right now was unlikely.

CHAPTER 9

April 5, 2026
New Orleans, Louisiana

Lane Turner was sitting at the bar, watching the weather report and nursing his second drink, when his phone buzzed, rattling against the mahogany bar. He cursed when he saw the number on the screen and slapped back the remnants of melted ice and liquor.

"Lane Turner," he answered, knowing it was the executive producer of the eleven o'clock newscast.

"*Lane?*" asked the voice on the other end of the line. "*How's it going?*"

"Fine," said Lane, resenting the false pleasantry. He knew they wanted something from him. He glanced at the flashing bright colors on the weather map that filled the television on the wall behind the bar, awaiting confirmation.

"*Good. So here's the deal. We're going to need you to give us a live shot tonight. Nothing big, just a straight live.*"

"Standing out in the rain?"

"*Exactly,*" said the EP. "*This storm is looking bad. The network says there's flooding. People are being evacuated already.*"

"Uh-huh."

"We were thinking if you could give us a scene setter, tell us what's going on around you. It's raining where you are, right? Where are you? The hotel?"

"Yeah."

"Yeah, you're at the hotel, or yeah, it's raining?"

Lane sighed. "Both."

He was an anchor for a reason. He'd chosen that avocation on purpose. It allowed him to stay inside, read aloud into a microphone, smile, and work a relatively fixed schedule in exchange for a good paycheck. If he'd wanted to work for a living, he'd have been a reporter. He'd have chosen to be one of the poor schlubs standing knee-deep in floodwater, breathing in the ash of forest fires, or knocking on the doors of widows or criminal suspects.

The only time he wanted out of the building was to travel on high-profile assignments that offered hotel points, airline miles, and a generous per diem. That or the occasional appearance at community functions, where an adoring public fawned over him and thanked him for giving so generously of his time.

"You look so much taller in person," they would say. *"You're so handsome."*

He would thank them when they'd tell him they'd watched him all of the time and wondered how long it would be before he left Los Angeles for the network. He would shake hands, take selfies, and sign autographs.

This wasn't part of that. This was street reporting. This was being in the trenches.

"Lane?" the EP prompted. *"You with me?"*

He sighed audibly in an obvious attempt to be passive-aggressive. "I am."

"Great. I'm leading with a string of juggings in the Valley, going to Tank with the latest on the Bruins. He'll also hit some highlights from the Florida game and talk about Monday and whether or not the game will happen."

"Okay," said Lane.

"Then we'll do a quick weather hit, and then have Monica Muldrow toss to you standing out in the middle of it."

"How long you want me to go?"

"A minute? I'll send you the latest stuff from the network's breaking news DL. You can throw in some numbers. But really I just want you in the rain, telling us about what you're seeing."

"Got it. You told the crew yet?"

"Yes. They know."

"Okay."

"I need you to be active too," added the EP. *"Nothing static."*

"Active?"

"Show me things. Move. Have the camera off the shoulder. I need to feel like I'm there. It'll give the hit some urgency."

It was going from bad to worse. Lane knew better than to complain though. So he sucked it up and agreed to whatever the EP wanted. No point in fighting it. He'd have to do what was asked regardless, and arguing the point only served to chink his reputation among management. He was already aware of the perception that he was lazy, which he was, and that he was above real work, which he was. There was no need to bolster the reality any more than necessary. He resolved he could suck it up for an urgent minute out in the rain.

"That it?" he asked. "I need to get changed. We've got what, forty-five minutes until the hit?"

"About," said the EP, then, as an afterthought, added, *"Oh, one last thing. Could you head to somewhere where it's actually flooding? Is that possible? I mean, don't put yourself in danger, but if you have some floodwater behind you, that would be optimal. So would posting a couple of quick pics or videos to your social media accounts. We can link to that from our app."*

Lane stood up from his stool, motioning to the bartender for his check. He clenched his jaw, holding his breath for a moment before blurting out something sarcastic and unhelpful, choosing to draw in a deep breath through his nose and exhale. "Sure. No problem. Gotta go."

"Great," said the EP cheerfully. *"I'll drop you an email with the info. See you on TV."*

He placed the phone on the bar without saying anything or disconnecting the call. The bartender handed him the bill, and he signed for the two drinks he now wished had been four, thanked him, tipped him, then went to his room to get changed.

*** *

The rain was harder than it had been at the Superdome. It was colder too. Lane cinched the elastic drawstrings that tightened the hood on his waterproof jacket. He had the wrists Velcroed tight and the snaps buttoned all the way up to his chin. He was also wearing rain pants he'd brought just in case, and with a pair of fashionable duck shoes on his feet, he was set. Except, as he sloshed through the ankle-deep water, he wished he'd brought boots.

They walked a few blocks from the French Quarter and found the water pooling in the streets. It was closer than they'd expected. But the valet at the front door to the hotel had suggested they could find high water by walking and wouldn't need their car.

He'd said it with a tone that mixed surprise and worry. Water had never gotten that close, he'd admitted. Even Katrina hadn't threatened the touristy center of the city the way this unnamed storm was in the midst of doing.

Lane, his photographer, and his producer slogged the short distance without much trouble. But it was as though they were swimming upstream, fighting the wind and driving rain that pushed into their faces as they marched. Their trek was lonely. Being nearly one o'clock in the morning, the crowd of drunkards and thrill-seekers was sparse. The occasional couple stumbled from a bar or late-night eatery but clung to the protection of the architecture's decorative overhangs.

Lane's photographer was carrying the rain-protected camera on his shoulder and had his tripod in his other hand. The producer had the portable live transmission unit over her shoulder. She had it wrapped in a rainproof bag but was careful to protect it as much as she could by keeping it close to her body and tucked under her arm.

Lane carried his attitude.

"This is ridiculous," he said when they stopped at a spot the producer deemed worthy of meeting the EP's expectations. "What's the point of this?"

"It is a big story," said the producer through the small circular opening of her own cinched rain hood. "And we're here, Lane. It would be stupid not to be on the air."

Lane bristled at the word *stupid*. It was a button for him. He frowned at her and then pulled out his cell phone. He fumbled with it in its waterproof case, then managed to swipe the screen that opened the camera function. He aimed the camera at the producer, zoomed in on the hood opening, and snapped a picture.

He opened his Twitter app and typed: *Big story. Bundled up. Ready to go live. #Cameraready #SouthlandNewsLeader.* Then he tagged the producer so she'd be sure to see his tweet, then posted it to his seventy-five thousand followers.

Almost instantly, her phone chimed. She was busy helping the photographer set up the shot. Lane chuckled to himself and flipped the camera around and tapped video. He began recording live, careful to show what he could behind him in the dim light.

"Hey, Southland," he said. "It's a few minutes before airtime and I'm here in New Orleans. The rain is coming down. It's torrential. Flooding is beginning to inundate this cultural mecca."

He flipped the camera around, switching the view to the producer and photographer. Struggling in the rain to make sure the gear was working properly and staying as dry as possible, they were oblivious to him. The photographer pulled a large white trash bag from his pocket, wrapping it around the live unit, then wrapped that with an exceedingly long strip of duct tape while the producer held it for him.

"This is my crew," he said, "making sure we bring you the big story of the night. We'd be stupid to be sitting in our rooms, high and dry, instead of being out here in the dangerous elements, making sure you understand the urgency of the situation here in the Big Easy."

He panned the phone around to show the depth of the water that would serve as the background for their live shot. All that was visible in the darkness was the thin ribbons of light from streetlamps reflecting on the thick ripples of deepening water and the countless dimples on its surface from the heavy raindrops.

"This is the floodwater, as it were," he continued and stepped toward the edge of the creeping water. "It's getting deeper. That's apparent as we stand here in the cold rain. We're a few blocks from our hotel, and when we left the warm confines of that fine establishment, the valet told us he'd never seen water get this close to the more highly elevated French Quarter. This is, after all, the lifeblood of the city. Even in Hurricane Katrina, some twenty years ago, the water never got this high in this part of the city."

"We're ready," the producer cut in. "Two minutes until the top of the show."

Lane tapped the screen to flip the camera back to selfie mode. He smiled through the condensation on the lens. "That's my cue, folks," he said cheerfully and in full anchor mode. "We'll see you on television in a few. Don't forget to check the app for the latest from here in New Orleans and across the Southland."

He stopped the livestream and plugged his earpiece into the phone. Then he dialed into the station so he could hear the broadcast in his ear. He took the stick mic from his photographer and took a few steps back into the light the photographer provided with a camera-mounted LED panel.

"That's good," said the photographer. "Can you give me a white?"

"I got it," said the producer. She produced a white card from her jacket pocket and held it out in front of the lens near Lane's face.

The photographer zoomed in, then toggled a switch to set the color balance on the camera. "Thanks," he said. "We're good."

The producer stepped back and checked her phone. She tapped the screen a couple of times then raised her head to Lane. Even through the small opening that revealed the center of her face, it was obvious she was scowling.

"You're a child," she said, adding an expletive descriptor in front of the word *child*. "Absolute child."

"Careful," Lane said and tapped the head of the microphone in his hand. "There's a hot mic. Don't say anything that could get you in trouble."

She balled her hands into fists, gripping the phone as if she meant to crush it. Then she shook her head, a spray of water spinning from her body like a wet dog's. She dialed the control room and brought the phone to her ear, her eyes never leaving Lane's.

"We have thirty seconds until the show," she said flatly. "Then we have about five minutes until they come to you. Can you give them a mic check?"

"Sure thing." He grinned. "Mic check. Chickety check. Chickety check. Two, four, six, eight, ten. Sibilance. Give me a chance. Sibilance. Chickety check."

"That's good," said the producer. "More than enough, Lane. Thanks."

Lane tugged at the bottom of his jacket and adjusted his hood so more of an opening showed on camera. He checked over his shoulder, noticing the water was closer than it had been a minute ago. He motioned to it with the mic. "That water looks like it's rising?"

"That's what happens in a flood," said the producer. "Water rises."

Lane narrowed his eyes and snarled, "I'm not stupid. I'm saying it's rising more rapidly. As in dangerously fast."

The producer huffed and left her post next to the camera. "We're in the show," she said as she approached Lane. "The lead package is rolling."

Lane motioned to the water again when she reached him. "I'm not kidding here," he said, "it's filling like a bathtub. Watch. You can see it inching up the street toward us."

She bit her lip and glanced back at the photographer, holding the phone to her ear. "Hey, could you please shine the light over here for a sec?"

She pointed past Lane toward a white and black street sign twenty yards behind him. The light shifted and revealed the water at about six inches up the sign's pole. Above the water there was a scuff and missing paint.

"Watch that mark for a second," she said. Then her tone changed. "Tank is live. We've got three minutes."

The three of them stood there, the sound of rain slapping against the water the only thing interrupting the silence. A stiff breeze blew across the water, rippling its surface and sending a chill through Lane's body. The shudder, however, came from the mark on the street sign. It was already gone, having slipped beneath the water.

He looked down at his duck shoes. He was standing in water now. The producer was looking at his feet too, then at her own, back at his, and then to the not-so-distant street sign.

"Two minutes," she said.

"Do we have two minutes?" asked the photographer as he adjusted the light back toward Lane. "Should I move back?"

"Give me the live unit," she said. "I'll hold it on my shoulder. You stay where you are. A little water at your feet is no biggie."

He handed her the strap of the bagged live transmission unit. "It's heavy," he said. "The batteries are attached."

The producer took the awkwardly weighted package and, cradling the phone in her neck, slung the package over her shoulder. She stepped back out of the water. "Ninety seconds. Tank is wrapping. Weather is next."

Lane could hear all of this in his ear, as well as the newscast producer as she gave the time cues to his field producer. It was just as well they were being repeated. He was busy configuring the first few seconds of his live shot, thinking about how he'd begin.

"Hey," he said to the photographer, "can you start on me? And when I point over here to the street sign, pan over that way. I'll be moving around. Just kinda go with the flow. I'll find my way back to your shot when I'm ready for it. Other than that, just find what I'm describing and shoot it. Cool?"

The photographer nodded from behind his viewfinder. He was standing with his feet shoulder width apart, his hands on the lens and the grip at the side of the camera.

"You rolling on this too?" Lane asked. "That way we can send it back for the web."

"I always record live shots," the photographer answered. "Habit."

"Cool."

"Thirty seconds," said the newscast producer in his ear. The field producer, who'd taken another step away from the water, echoed the warning.

Lane looked at his feet. He couldn't see his shoes now. They were underwater. But his ankles were dry, as were his socks, so the water hadn't risen above the tops of his low-top duck shoes.

Monica wrapped up the weather, teasing the ten-day forecast later in the newscast, and Courtney Leigh, the news anchor, introduced him. Lane steadied himself, cleared his throat, and eyed the camera. He stared deep in the lens, and when Courtney had finished her introduction, known as a toss, he began.

"The rain here is relentless, Courtney," he said. "It's cold, it's constant, and it's creating havoc here in New Orleans. We're at the edge of the famed French Quarter, and the water is quickly rising."

He looked off camera and guided the photographer toward the

street sign with a subtle move of his head. He pointed at the sign. "See that street sign there?" he asked the audience. "It may be somewhat difficult in the low light. It's one o'clock in the morning here. But if you see that street sign, the water that now creeps up its pole is evidence of how fast the flooding is happening here. When we arrived at this spot a few minutes ago, the water was nearly six inches lower than it is now."

He guided the camera back toward him and moved into the frame. He spoke confidently, slowly, but maintained the urgency he knew his executive producer was craving. He pointed at his feet. "We were standing on dry land as this newscast began. But as you listened to our reporters and learned the weather forecast for the Gulf Coast, this part of the street is now underwater."

The camera lifted back onto his face and he motioned toward a row of two-story buildings to one side of the street. He stepped back off camera and stood close to the photographer. He described aloud what he wanted the audience to see so the photographer could follow.

"These buildings are occupied by restaurants and bars, retail stores, and art galleries. On a typical Saturday night, the lights might still be on," he said, his eyes drifting from one side of the street to the other, "but not tonight. Everything there is dark because of the dire situation unfolding in—"

He stopped cold, leaving dead air. Only the sound of the rain hitting the top of his microphone transmitted the distance from New Orleans to the Southland. His back was to the producer or he might have seen the squeezed look of confusion on her face.

The anchor, whose mic had been left open during Lane's live shot, interjected. She sounded concerned. *"You okay Lane? Can you hear us?"*

Lane didn't respond. He was focused on something barely visible in the darkness on the far side of the street. There wasn't enough light to make it out, but it was about a hundred yards beyond the street sign and the reach of the camera-mounted light.

Then he touched his photographer's shoulder. "Can you zoom in over there?" he asked softly, less confidently than he'd been when presenting the urgent, developing story a moment ago. "I think I see something."

The camera panned and zoomed. The photographer adjusted his focus. Then his head pulled back from the viewfinder.

"What do you see?" asked Lane. He was asking the photographer, but Courtney Leigh answered him.

"It…looks…like…a…body?" she half stated, half questioned.

Lane reached over and clipped the mic onto the clamp atop the camera. Then he unhooked his phone and earpiece and ran into the water.

The photographer refocused on the near distance, following Lane as he sloshed and stumbled into deeper water. The anchor was nearly invisible through the curtain of rain and the splash of water around his awkward, frantic movements in the dark of the night.

Lane couldn't know what the viewers were seeing. He couldn't hear Courtney Leigh narrating his efforts live on television, providing more real urgency than anyone had planned.

Working his way through the water, each step taking him into the deeper flooding, he couldn't be sure why he was doing it. Why was he risking himself?

Was it because he was conscious of the camera rolling? Was it because he knew he'd go viral online? Or was it that, despite the perceived vapidity of a new anchor who liked to sit, read aloud, and collect airline miles, he was genuinely concerned for a person in trouble?

Maybe, if he were honest with himself, it was a little bit of all of that. But right now, as he waded into waist-deep water and approached what he now knew was a body, none of that mattered.

The body was moving toward him, bobbing in the water, carried by the slow current, which contained other flotsam: branches, empty cups, food wrappers, and beer cans.

At first, when he touched the body's cold skin, he didn't know if it was a woman or a man. It was too dark here. Everything was in varying shades of gray.

He dropped down onto one knee, the water hitting him at his chin now, pulled the body toward him, and flipped it over, supporting its buoyed weight on his knee.

Forgetting he was on camera now, streaming live to the world, he brushed the mop of hair away from the figure's face. In the panic of the moment, he wasn't sure of anything more about the person than that they were unconscious and not breathing.

It wasn't until he laid his head on the chest, checking for a pulse, that he sensed the softness of a woman's breasts. There was no pulse.

His own heart now racing, pulsing worriedly, and his breathing accelerated and short, he resolved to try CPR. He'd never done it. He'd never tried mouth-to-mouth either. But he had seen countless sweeps reports on the Southland's News Leader about how to save an injured person. He believed he had no choice but to try.

He tilted the woman's head back, pushing her hair back from her face, and opened her mouth. He fished around in it to make sure there was nothing blocking her airway. So far, so good. Then he pinched her nose, tilted her chin some more, took a breath, and blew into her mouth.

Her lips tasted foul. There was the distinct mixture of floodwater, rum, and vomit. Lane pulled away and gagged. He swallowed hard and tried again. No luck.

He shifted his weight and tried leveraging her body against his knee again, providing some support to her back. Her head tilted back, her hair splaying in the water like tentacles, and she bobbed lifelessly on the surface.

Another round of mouth-to-mouth and chest compressions accomplished nothing. Lane was trembling now. The water was rising. He stood and turned around, forgetting about the camera, the live audience, and called out, "We need help!" His voice broke and an aching knot swelled in his throat. He swallowed hard against it and was reminded of the taste of vomit-spiked floodwater in his mouth. He called out again, his words swallowed by the percussion of the rain on the water, on the roofs of the aging buildings, on the sopping clothing of the woman who floated before him.

He reached down and picked up her body. She was heavier than he imagined a person of her relatively slight size could be. He heaved her onto his shoulder and started trudging toward the camera, unaware or ambivalent to the fact his photographer was still rolling.

He struggled despite the depth of the water mitigating some of her weight, but he pushed forward. He was breathing heavily now. There was a tightness in his chest and a stitch forming in his side. He winced against it, stopping for a moment to stretch his side.

As he drew closer to the camera and his field producer, who had backed away as the flooding encroached, he was startled by a loud roar exploding to his right, accompanied by a blindingly bright flash of lightning.

It wasn't a roar; it was a rumble. And the light wasn't from the sky. Both were from a large city garbage truck rolling through the intersection he was unknowingly crossing.

He stopped short and pivoted toward the truck, the woman's body swinging. It carried too much momentum, combined with his sudden stop, and Lane was knocked off balance. He splashed face first into the knee-deep water, awkwardly twisting his legs. Her limp body flung from his shoulder with a splash and slid forward in the shallows of the black water.

Lane swallowed a mouthful of the rancid water and coughed it out as he worked to regain his balance. Then there were strong hands on both of his arms.

Two men, one on either side, were helping him toward the truck. They were dressed for the weather and wore jackets that announced they were with the city's emergency operations team.

Lane took a couple of weak steps with them and then resisted. He yanked his arms from their grasp and shook his head.

"No," he said breathlessly, his chest heaving. "I don't need help. Thanks. The woman needs help. Where is the woman?"

He pivoted and scanned the surface of the water. Then he swung back to face the two rescuers. No sign of her.

"Where is she?" he said, somewhat dazed. "Where is the woman? She's not breathing."

One of the men put his hand on Lane's shoulder. "It's okay," he said, holding on with a tight grip. "We've got her. There's an ambulance trailing us. Our guys already have her."

Lane glanced past the man in front of him and saw two others hurrying through the water with the woman in their arms. They were carrying her like a wounded soldier; each man had one of her arms draped over his shoulder. Her legs dragged behind, leaving a wake.

"Y'all shouldn't be out here," said the man with his hand on Lane's shoulder. "The mayor just enacted a curfew. She wants everyone—"

"I'm a journalist," said Lane. That last word felt strong coming from his mouth. It was the first time he'd referred to himself using the j-word in years. He'd resolved to call himself a news anchor long ago.

"You're not with the woman?"

Lane shook his head. The ambulance lights strobed off the buildings down the street and reflected on the surface of the water.

"So you—"

"I saw her while I was doing a live shot. I ran over to her. I tried to help her. I swear I did." The knot thickened again and Lane's chest warbled with the threat of tears. He held them back.

"You don't know her, then?" said the man. "Don't have a name? No next of kin? Nothin'?"

"No."

"Well, you did a good thing," said the man. His partner concurred, speaking for the first time by echoing the sentiment.

"You think she'll make it?" asked Lane. "She wasn't breathing. I couldn't find a heartbeat."

The man glanced past him toward the direction of the camera and Lane's field producer. He let go of his shoulder, but he didn't answer the question. He didn't really have to. They all knew the woman's chances were slim. There was no telling how long she'd been facedown in the water, unconscious. The man motioned with his chin in the direction of his gaze.

"You belong to them?" he asked, his New Orleans drawl becoming apparent as he spoke. "That cameraman over there and the lady with him?"

Lane nodded without looking at them. "Yeah. My photographer and field producer."

"He's aiming that thing at us right now," said the man. "Is he putting us on the television?"

Lane bent over, put his hands on his knees, and gagged. Then he nodded. "Probably."

"Yeah." The man shook his head, contradicting his verbal acquiescence. "I don't want to be on television. No, sir, nohow. You be good now, ya hear? And get inside. It isn't safe, even if you're a journalist."

"Thanks," said Lane. "We'll be careful."

The men turned around and high-stepped their way back to the idling garbage truck. The beast of a high-water vehicle cranked as the driver pushed it into gear. It began its slow rumble up the street toward Lane. He stepped out of its path and watched it turn left, down the street where he'd found the woman and where the water was getting deeper more quickly.

It was then Lane saw the large bed of the truck. It was loaded, but not with trash or debris. It was full of people. From the back of the cab to the rear edge of the bed, it was packed with men and women. Some of them held small children in their arms. They stared at Lane as the truck turned and rolled toward the black. A couple of them waved. Lane waved back. But none of them, not a one of the two or three dozen people in the back of that garbage truck, people who clearly had been rescued from the floodwaters, said a word. They were as quiet as if there had been nothing in the truck at all.

Lightning flickered in the distance. Lane was transfixed. This was one truck on one street at the onset of what was going to be two or three days of rain. What more was to come? How many more dozens, hundreds, thousands of people would be facedown in the water or forced to leave everything behind for the crowded, dank confines of a garbage truck on their way to safety?

Lane trudged back to his team. He tried to avoid looking either of them in the eyes. He couldn't do it. Instead he searched the water for his duck shoes.

"That was…" began his producer in a trembling, tentative voice, "incredible. Amazing."

"Freaking A, man," said the photographer. "You were amazing. I didn't think you had that in you. No offense. But…freaking A, man."

The camera was on his shoulder, but the red tally light in the front of the viewfinder was off. He wasn't live and he wasn't recording anything. He was grinning from ear to ear.

Lane couldn't look at either of them. He tried, but there was some sort of magnetic, guilty pull that kept his eyes fixed on the water. Maybe it wasn't guilt. Maybe it was that he didn't want to cry. He knew if he looked at either of them, he would.

After thirty seconds of silence, the rain slapping at them as it had since they'd left the hotel, he finally spoke. "Anybody would have done it."

"Not true," said the field producer. "I didn't do it."

"Me neither," said the photographer.

Lane sighed. "Well, I think we have our story for the rest of the trip, and it's not basketball."

"I agree," said the field producer. "Totally. I'll get on the call in the morning and—"

Lane lifted his head and balled his fists at his sides. He tensed, trying to hold it together as his eyes locked with hers. She stopped cold.

"No," he said, shaking his head. "We start now. The story is now."

CHAPTER 10

April 5, 2026
Santa Monica, California

Danny squirted water from the bottle onto the hot griddle. It sizzled, and steam plumed up toward the vent. He wiped a spatula on his white apron and scraped the charred remnants of ground beef into the catch basin at the side of the griddle.

He relished the humid, acrid odor of the burnt burger pieces. It was a reminder his day was almost over. He dug at a particularly stubborn crumb and sprayed more water. Another blast of steam plumed, some of it reaching his face, and he grimaced like a man too close to a fire.

The crumb scrubbed loose; then Danny guided it into the basin. "I'm the boss," he reminded the crumb under his breath. This was his house.

"You say something?" asked Arthur, the burly fry cook who stood behind him, refilling the wholesale-sized oil bottles. He'd worked at the diner for years. Danny wondered sometimes if they'd built the place around him.

"No," Danny said. "Just mumbling to myself."

"Ha," said Arthur with an amiable chuckle that made his frame shake. "Talking to yourself, huh? I guess that's cool as long as you don't start answering back."

Danny had heard Arthur say the same thing fifty times if he'd heard it once. He smiled at his friend as if it were the first time and nodded.

"True," Danny said. Then he deepened his voice, talking as if he were someone else. "No it's not."

Arthur slapped Danny on the back. "You got jokes. You always got jokes, Danny Correa."

Danny found it remarkable that Arthur thought him comical. Inside his own mind, the one that had only one voice, he was empty of humor. But perception was reality, so he didn't fight it.

Arthur capped the last oil bottle and re-shelved it near the griddle. He stepped close to Danny, lowered his voice, and asked, "What do you think of her?"

His eyes were affixed to the woman settling the cash register, the head waitress and de facto closing manager. Her name was Claudia. She was roughly Arthur's age, Danny figured, somewhere in her mid-fifties. She was single, she was good with customers, and she didn't take crap from anyone.

"I don't," said Danny.

Arthur's shoulders sank and he huffed. "No," he said, dragging out the vowel with frustration. "For me? What do you think of her?"

Danny snapped his head toward Arthur and took a step back to focus on his face. Was he serious? "Are you serious?"

Now Arthur frowned. "Yeah, why? What's wrong with that? I'm a man; she's a—"

"She's a Claudia," said Danny. "I just never thought of her that way."

"What way?"

"Like," Danny fumbled for the right word, "like, a woman?"

"I asked her out," Arthur admitted. "We're going out tonight after work. As soon as we're done and that last jerk of a customer leaves."

Danny didn't have to turn around to know what customer Arthur was referencing. It was Derek. He was sitting in a corner booth, nursing his fourth cup of coffee. Or fifth.

Instead of taking his prescribed breaks, Danny had chosen to work through his shift without a rest. He'd done it not so much because he wanted the lower back ache and shoulder pain that came from a long, uninterrupted stretch at the griddle, but because…Derek.

The unnervingly attractive gazillionaire had waited patiently. He'd occasionally run his sun-kissed hands through his full head of styled hair or checked the heavy two-toned aviator's watch on his wrist. But he hadn't said a word or interrupted Danny in his work.

The time was coming, though, and the meeting and long conversation was at hand. He couldn't avoid it any longer.

"The guy's here for me," he whispered to Arthur. "You and your lady can take off if you want. I got the rest. I can lock up."

Arthur's eyes widened with surprise and then narrowed with suspicion. "Are you…?" He wagged his finger between Danny and Derek.

Danny shook his head. "No, I'm not. He's not. He's with my ex. He's got something to talk about with me. I don't know what it is."

Arthur nodded as if he understood, although there was no way he could. He wiped his hands on his apron and thanked Danny. Then he eased toward Claudia. Danny felt her glare from across the diner, but she apparently acquiesced to whatever Arthur had suggested. Within a few minutes, she'd slapped the keys on the counter in front of him and walked out of the place, arm in arm with Arthur.

When he was sure they were gone, Danny palmed the keys and stepped out from behind the counter. He locked the door from the inside and then spun around to walk the distance of the place to Derek and the last booth.

Derek had his back to him until he slid into the booth across from him. The first thing he noticed were the dark, face-defining circles under his eyes and the pale yellow of his complexion. He had the aged appearance of someone who'd undergone chemotherapy and radiation. He was healthy enough, but there was something there that signaled past illness. There was a translucency to his skin that gave Derek an ethereal appearance. Danny imagined if Derek took another swig of the bitter, room-temperature coffee, he'd be able to see it slide down his throat.

"Thanks for waiting," said Danny, forcing the back cushion to leak air as he leaned against the vinyl covering.

Derek bit at his nail, or what was left of it. Danny noticed the skin around his nail beds was irritated and red. There were traces of dried blood on a couple of them. Derek chewed on the nail, or skin, or whatever he'd torn from his finger. His right knee was bouncing, and it made the coffee cup rattle against the laminate tabletop.

Danny glanced at the cup. "You want more?"

Derek shook his head, stopped bouncing his knee, and raked his fingers through his hair again. He blinked a couple of times and met Danny's gaze.

"Thanks for meeting me," he said, his voice shaky. "I know you didn't want to, that's why you skipped your breaks."

Danny didn't deny it.

"I don't blame you," said Derek, drawing the side of a finger to his teeth, nibbling as he spoke. "That's why I didn't complain about sitting here for seven hours."

Danny planted his elbows on the table and laced his fingers together. He leaned forward, anxious to get this over with and go home to Maggie.

"Here's the thing," said Derek, "I'm not a bad guy."

Danny looked out the window, his own reflection bouncing back at him. It was after midnight. He'd probably missed the last bus.

Derek held his hands palms up. "I get it," he said. "I do. Seriously, though, Danny, I'm not a bad person. I have good intentions. I pay my taxes, I give generously to charity, I volunteer at a food bank…"

Danny dipped his chin and raised his eyebrows. "Do you want some kind of award? Because if you do, I—"

"No." Derek swallowed hard. "That's not it. I'm telling you I have good intentions. That's not to say I don't do selfish things, bad things."

"I can think of at least one," said Danny.

Derek didn't respond directly. "This time, my desire to change the world for the better, to shape it in a way that I think is beneficial to everyone, has backfired."

Derek checked over one shoulder, then the other, as if anyone were in the closed diner, and lowered his voice. His knee was bouncing again, rattling the coffee cup on the table. The spoon fell from the saucer.

"It's backfired in a monumental way," he said, his eyes growing distant. "*Monumental*. And I have no idea how far-reaching it is. It's like I dropped a pebble in a pond and can't stop the concentric circles from growing. Then it starts to rain and there are countless concentric circles. All of them are different sizes, growing and spreading. Now I can't even find the original spot where I dropped the pebble."

The two sat there silently for a moment. Then Danny slapped the table, startling Derek from his reverie.

"I'm getting more coffee," he said. Before he could stand up, Derek put his hands on Danny's to stop him.

His hands were cold, as if he'd dipped them into snow. "Don't leave. Let me finish, please."

Danny sank back down onto the cracked vinyl. He looked at Derek warily. "You haven't said what this has to do with me. And it's late."

"I don't know if it has anything to do with you. That's what I'm trying to find out. You could be one of those little circles. You could be a pebble or a raindrop."

"I'm totally confused."

"I know," said Derek. He was speaking with his hands, which hovered above Danny's on the table. "It's confusing and I'm speaking in metaphors."

"So speak English," Danny said.

"Answer a few questions for me, okay?" asked Derek. "Is it okay if I ask you some questions?"

"About what?"

Derek reached into a bag he had at his side between his hip and the wall that Danny hadn't noticed until now. It was a black leather satchel that Derek unzipped along the top, underneath two extending leather handles. Derek pulled a small black electronic device from the bag and laid it on the table. He pushed a small red button on the front of the device and spun it toward Danny. "Mind if I record this?"

Danny frowned. "Yeah, I do mind. You've told me nothing other than waxed philosophical about pebbles and ponds."

A smile curled at one side of Derek's mouth. "Waxed philosophical," he repeated.

Danny pushed the red button on the device, stopping it. "What?"

"That phrase sounded odd coming from—"

Danny glowered. "A fry cook?"

"You," said Derek. "It sounded odd coming from you. I wasn't about to disparage how to put food on the table. That's not for me to judge."

"Not for you to judge," repeated Danny. "Sounds odd coming from an assho—"

"Okay," said Derek, "I'm sorry. That was rude. Let me ask you the questions."

"No recording."

"Fine." Derek reached into the bag again. He withdrew a yellow notepad and pen. "First question is about your health. Have you had any headaches?"

"What kind of headaches?"

"Bad headaches," said Derek, "like migraines."

"No."

Derek scribbled on the paper in a compact, virtually illegible scrawl. Danny noticed Derek was left-handed.

"What about extreme dehydration? Have you been drinking a lot of water and still not able to quench your thirst?"

Danny shook his head.

"So that's a no?" asked Derek. "I need verbal answers, even though I'm not recording. I need to be sure I'm accurately cataloging what you're telling me."

"No."

"Exhaustion?" said Derek, looking up from his notes. "Have you suffered from exhaustion?"

"Yes. I'm always tired. I could always sleep. That's nothing new. That's probably got nothing to do with your pebble or your pond."

"Describe the exhaustion," said Derek. He was writing. "Is it muscular? Do your eyes burn? Do you feel as if you've been working out at the gym or been beaten up in a fight?"

"Never considered it," said Danny. "Tired is tired."

Derek stopped writing and locked eyes with Danny. His knee bounced. The cup rattled. "Tired is not tired. There is a difference between being tired and being exhausted. And there are different types of exhaustion. Describe yours to me."

Danny sighed. "Okay," he said, trying to focus on the outdoors through the window, trying to see through his reflection, "it feels like I ran a marathon, in the mud, uphill, with the wind in my face."

Derek was scribbling more quickly. "Say that again, exactly as you said it before."

Danny repeated it verbatim then asked, "All of this has to do with the company you invested money into? Interllayar?"

Derek nodded but kept writing. He was mouthing the words as he inked them onto the paper.

"What do they have to do with my fatigue?"

Derek held up a finger until he finished his note. He looked up and took a sip of the cold coffee. He smiled, or more likely winced, at the taste. He smacked his lips and wiped the corner of his mouth with his reddened fingertips. "You said fatigue," he countered. "Is it fatigue rather than exhaustion?"

Danny folded his arms and clenched his jaw before spitting his response. "Yes."

"Danny, help me here."

"I'm not a doctor," said Danny, "and as far as I know, neither are you. The difference is semantics. I think my uphill, muddy marathon description pretty much answers the question either way, doesn't it?"

Derek bit the side of his fingernail and nodded. "I guess. What about déjà vu?"

"Déjà vu?"

Derek chose another fingertip and nibbled. "You keep answering my questions with questions."

"You're not particularly clear with these questions," said Danny. "I'm getting some coffee."

He scooted out from the booth, heading for the last remaining pot. Although it was hot, it was likely stale. He hadn't seen Claudia brew a fresh carafe in four hours, or six. He took a clean mug from the rack above the pot and poured himself a steaming cup. He called back to Derek, "Sure you don't want a refresher?"

"I'm good," said Derek. "Too much caffeine already."

"Suit yourself."

Danny replaced the pot on the hot plate under the drip cup, and the black mud sloshed around in the calcium-stained glass carafe. He drew the mug to his face and blew little ripples onto the surface of the coffee. It made him think of Derek's metaphor. Coffee was even better than a pond, he thought, given the inky blackness of the joe. What Derek was describing, or actually not quite describing, was dark. Whatever was happening was bad. He'd said as much. So coffee, in its light-sucking deliciousness, was a far better example for use in the metaphor than some random, glossy pond.

He reached the booth, set the mug on the table, and slid back into his seat. Then he held the mug with both hands, sliding three fingers of his right hand inside the handle. The steam rose and the cup warmed his hands.

"Yes," said Danny.

"Yes?"

"Yes, I experience déjà vu."

Derek's face stretched with expression. Danny couldn't tell if it was surprise or fright or resignation. It was such an odd look framed by his sunken eyes and sallow complexion. His hair suddenly looked grayer, duller somehow. It was as if Derek had aged remarkably in a short time.

The tremble in his voice was back. His knee bounced.

"How frequently?" asked Derek. "That is, how often do you get that sense that you've experienced something before?"

Danny considered the question and picked up the mug. He blew into it before taking a tentative sip. The liquid was hot, but not enough to burn his tongue, so he drew in a longer sip and then set the mug back on the table, maintaining his hold on it with both hands.

"How frequently?" Derek pressed, urgency in his voice.

"I don't know," said Danny. "I kinda feel like I'm having it right now. Like we've sat here and had this conversation before. It's the taste of the coffee that sparks the sensation."

Derek stared at Danny for a moment, his pen held steady on the paper. He didn't say anything. He didn't react. He didn't move. It was as though he were frozen in time.

Danny glanced at the paper and then at Derek. Back at the paper. Back at Derek. "What? Did I say something wrong?"

Derek sat there another moment before he swallowed again. He looked down at the paper, hunching his shoulders and lowering his head. He scribbled furiously on the paper for what felt like, to Danny, a long time.

His fresh cup of old coffee was nearly empty, the warmth of it having evaporated, by the time Derek asked a follow-up question. This time he didn't look at Danny when he asked it.

"Do you ever feel like you're living someone else's life?"

Danny laughed. That was ludicrous. If anybody at the table was living someone else's life, it was Derek. He'd taken Danny's wife. As a proxy, he'd taken Danny's money. *He* was living *Danny's* life.

"It's not intended to be funny," said Derek, his eyes on the paper. "This is serious."

Danny didn't think it was funny. The laugh was a nervous reaction. It was ironic. It wasn't funny. Of course, he didn't say any of this. He was officially ready to say goodbye to Derek and his delusions, but there was that nagging feeling in the back of his mind that understood that, for weeks if not longer, he'd woken up each morning as if he were in a foreign place.

Sure, it was his bed, his apartment, his shower, his clothing, his dog, his car, his job, his food, his loneliness. All of it was his. He knew this. But it had, in some undefinable way, become foreign.

"Yes," he said reluctantly. "I have felt that way."

Derek exhaled. "Go on." He started writing again.

"I can't describe it other than to say it feels like I'm living my life in the third person, like I'm watching myself from afar. I'm not, I know that. But I get these flashes of it here and there."

"For how long?"

"A month? Two?"

Derek clicked the pen, retracting the ink. He stuffed it and the pad of paper into his briefcase and zipped it shut. He grabbed the handles, sliding out of the booth. He stood at the end of the table for a moment, straightening his clothes.

"I appreciate this, Danny," he said. "You've been helpful. Really helpful."

Danny looked at him incredulously. "That's it? You ask me all of these weird questions, talk in riddles like some techno-sphinx, and then leave? That's incredibly uncool of you."

"I need to read my notes," he said. "I need to put two and two together and figure out if they make four. I'll get back to you when I can tell you more. I promise."

"Do I need to be worried about anything?" asked Danny. "Am I going to die or something?"

It appeared to Danny as if the question of death transformed Derek's face. It melted from weariness to profound sadness. Somehow the lines in his face were deeper, the circles under his eyes darker, his hair grayer.

Derek swallowed. "We're all going to die. That starts the moment we're born."

"Sheesh," said Danny. "You are a jerk."

"Maybe so," said Derek. "But don't fret about it. Let me do the worrying. You've got enough on your plate as it is."

With his free hand Derek reached into his pocket and pulled from it a fold of cash. There was at least a couple of hundred dollars there, if not more. He slapped it onto the table.

"Thanks for your time," he said. Before Danny could protest, Derek was walking toward the locked door. He spun the deadbolt with one hand and shouldered out into the night.

The door clanged shut behind him and he was gone. Danny exhaled, sinking deeper into the vinyl. He spun his cup on the table, mindlessly playing with it for a moment while replaying his bizarre encounter with Derek, when he noticed the black digital recorder sitting on the table.

He glanced at the door and back at the recorder. He cupped his hands around his face and peered through the cold glass window next to him. It was as dark as it had been. He didn't see Derek.

So, already pocketing the cash, he took the recorder with one hand, the two coffee mugs with the other, and went to close up shop. He looked at the clock on the wall. It was late. Too late. Maggie, his faithful mutt, would be wondering if he was ever coming home again to let her out of her crate or fill the bowl with cheap dog food.

CHAPTER 11

April 5, 2026
New Orleans, Louisiana

Bob Monk peeled back the sheer white drapes at the front window of his daughters' rental house. He cupped his hands around his eyes and pressed the edges of his pinkie fingers against the cold glass. He could smell the ginger-ale-tinged whiskey in the vapor from his breath that bloomed and evaporated on the window.

The rain was so intense, so constant in its rhythm on the roof as well as against the glass in front of him that he couldn't hear the drone of the weather report on the television at the other end of the room. His wife and daughters had fallen asleep leaning upon each other on the sofa.

He scanned the front of the property, unable to see much beyond the narrow yard. The street was barely visible through sheets of rain, but he thought he could see water pooling at the curb in the warbling reflection of the streetlight above it. He thought the water was creeping higher up the driveway, although he couldn't be sure. Everything was dark, aside from those reflective, pale yellow, dancing ribbons of light.

"I don't like this," he said to himself. With the barefoot, heavy feet of a man who'd had his share of spirits, he trudged to the front door, unlocked the collection of latches and chains, and swung it inward.

A cool spray of water misted his face as he stepped onto the threshold. It was too dark to see from there, so, without looking down, he stepped down onto the front porch. It wasn't the smooth-hewn pine of the porch that met his foot first. It was ankle-deep water. It was at the door. And it was lapping toward the house.

Instead of stepping back inside, Bob plopped his other foot into the water and shuffled a couple of feet out onto the flooded porch. His eyes adjusted to the lack of light, and then he saw the truth. The water wasn't at the curb. There was no curb. It wasn't creeping up the driveway. There was no driveway. He sloshed toward what he believed to be the edge of the porch, grabbing hold of its wrought-iron step railing, and surveyed the neighborhood as best he could.

Rain was hitting his face, dampening his shirt and pants. His arms were soaked, and the cool droplets were finding paths down the back of his neck. He looked up and noticed he was at the edge of the porch roof.

It was all he recognized. His car was half underwater, as were those of his daughters. The sound of the rain, which normally might offer a soothing salve at the end of a long day, sounding like the barrage of small-arms fire. Attacking. Attacking. Attacking relentlessly as it advanced. Its forces, gathered all around him, were closing in on him.

Suddenly chilled, an involuntary shiver rippled through his body and he took a step back. Like an encroaching tide, the water was riding up his legs. Unless his mind was fooling him, it was an inch or two higher on his ankles than it had been a minute earlier.

Was that possible? Could it be rising so quickly? He glanced over at his car, squinting to better focus through the obfuscating shower. He was certain he could see the surface undulating upward, filling like a basin. He stepped back again, wondering if it was the whiskey. He'd had two drinks more than he should have, that was certain. It was easier to drink when someone else was bartending and handing them to you.

He turned around, careful not to slip, and braced himself against the door frame with one hand. He stepped up onto the threshold, crossed it, and shut the door behind him.

He stood there for a moment in the dark, considering what to do. They had no cars, no boat, and neither he nor his wife could swim. He'd been meaning to learn. He'd always been meaning to learn. Yet he hadn't. His chest felt heavy. His lungs squeezed.

He needed to awaken his women. He couldn't deal with this on his own. One of them might have a suggestion, and both the girls could swim. They were smarter than him. They'd know what to do.

He reached to flip on the light to guide himself back into the living room when he saw it. He stepped back. His jaw slackened and his stomach rolled over on itself.

Water was leaching onto the floor now through the invisible gap between the front door and the threshold. It was moving amorphously, as if searching for him, seeking him. The Mississippi was in the house.

It was like the water knew his secret. It knew he couldn't escape it.

He backed away, his eyes transfixed by the spreading pool. "Kristin, Katie, Kiki!" he shouted, the desperation wet in his voice.

His voice cracked. He cleared his throat and called again.

"Kris-tin! Kay-tee! Kee-Kee!"

He stood frozen, hypnotized by the water.

"Dad?" asked Katie, shielding her eyes from the light. "What is it?"

Kiki followed. Then Kristin. The three of them stood together at the edge of the foyer next to him. They followed his stare. He didn't have to tell them what it was, why he had called them, why he was petrified and anchored to the floor.

The drinks, the two too many, had been meant to ease his mind.

They'd been meant to help him cope reasonably with his worst fear: drowning. That was why his daughter had been generous with the whiskey and less generous with the ginger ale. She knew his fear. She knew he didn't fish, he didn't boat, nor did he do many of the things that native Louisianans did. He didn't see the state as a sportsman's paradise. To Bob Monk, the state of Louisiana was a sea-level minefield.

But it was home. It always had been. And he couldn't leave it despite the danger. Now the danger was swelling around him. No bridges, no levees, nothing to keep him from the water.

Kristin moved to her husband and nuzzled against him. She put one arm around his waist and the other in front of him, her hand touching his belly. Bob put his arm around her and pulled her closer. The four of them stared at the water leaking into the house. None of them said anything until a tendril of it reached Kiki's feet.

"What do we do?" she asked, taking a step back as if the water might burn her. "Can we take the cars?"

"Flooded," said Bob. "Water's too high. It's in the house. There's no street; there's no yard, nothing. We're on a sinking island."

"It's okay," said Kristin softly, in the reassuring voice only a mother of three could offer without sounding condescending or dismissive. "We'll figure this out."

Katie and Kiki tiptoed around the water, and Katie swung open the door. Water poured in over the threshold. It spilled onto the floor, racing for some unseen finish line. The sisters looked at one another and then out the door and into the storm.

Lightning strobed overhead. It was the first flash in minutes and it cast a quick, pallid light across the scene facing them. It wasn't much, but it was enough of a flicker to reveal the gravity of what they faced. There was no walking out of here. Even if they could, they couldn't risk it. Their parents could trip, lose their balance, and float away in what looked from the porch to be a strong current. Large dark objects, as black as the water that carried them, moved and bobbed from one side of the street to the other.

Kiki closed the door, pushing hard against the run of water wanting into the home. She latched it shut and bolted the locks. She pulled the chains. Not that the water cared about locks, latches, or chains, but she did it anyhow.

Katie pulled her cell phone from her back pocket. She stared at the display and grimaced. "No signal."

Regardless, she punched a series of numbers on the screen and held the device to her ear. While she tried to connect, Kristin and Kiki tried their phones. None of them could connect.

Kiki started typing on her device, her thumbs moving up and down in a blur. Then she stared at the screen and cursed.

"Kiki," said her mother, condemning her foul language.

"Seriously, Mom?" She rolled her eyes. "My texts won't go through either. And I *am* a grown woman."

"All right," said Kristin, "all right. It's neither here nor there. We have no way to get ahold of somebody who can rescue us. What do we do?"

"Ideas?" asked Bob. "Should we get into the attic?"

Katie looked up at the ceiling toward a framed access door that, when pulled down by a dangling string, revealed a foldable, recessed wooden ladder. She considered it for a moment then shook her head. "No, we could get trapped up there, and then we'd be in trouble. I don't want to have to figure out how to chop our way through the roof."

"Then the roof?" Bob pressed. "We get on the roof?"

"What about the furniture?" asked Kiki. "What do we do about that?"

"We can raise some of it," he said. "We can take ten minutes and put stuff on top of stuff. Then we get on the roof."

"That's the best bet," said Katie. "It'll suck, but that's what we need to do. I can't think of another way to keep us out of the water, and if we see a boat, we can try to hail it."

"How do we get up there?" asked Kiki.

Lightning flashed again, followed by a boom of thunder rippling in the distance. The water was seeping into the house, now covering their toes.

"Do you have the ladder I got you for Christmas?" asked Bob.

"The one you got us for the lights?" asked Katie.

"That one, yes."

"It's in the garage."

"All right, let's save what we can save."

Together, the family lifted lighter, smaller objects and set them on top of heavier, larger ones. It was a somber task. They all knew, though it wasn't spoken, that none of the belongings would survive the flood if the water got high enough.

The furniture, the books, and the decorative touches that made the sisters proud of their first place would all float or sink. Either way, they'd be trash. Still, they did what they could.

They took piles of clothes, shoes, and handbags and put them into the attic. That would give them a fighting chance at least. Twenty minutes later the water was at their ankles, and Bob suggested they stop, lest they run out of time to make it to the roof.

"I'll go get the ladder," he said, and then ticked off a list of things-to-do on his fingers. "Y'all get bottles of water, snacks, raincoats, portable phone charger, Ziploc bags for the phones, and anything else you can think we'd need. I'll meet you at the front door in five."

Bob made it through the house toward the attached garage. He unlocked the door, slid the chain, turned the deadbolt, and opened the door. Fumbling in the dark along the wall, he found the light switch and flipped it. An overhead fluorescent clinked to life and hummed as the twin bulbs glowed toward their maximum brightness. His eyes adjusted to the cramped garage that served as a storage locker more than anything else. His daughters didn't use the space for their shared Chevy Malibu. Instead, it was a spot for boxes of books and clothes, old trophies, cleaning supplies, and a treadmill they likely hadn't used since they'd moved into the place.

He waded through the ankle-deep water and the junk to the opposite wall of the one-car garage, where he found the ladder he'd bought five months earlier to help his daughters hang LED icicle lights along the roofline.

He wasn't much for the LED lights. He wasn't a fan of the icicles either. He'd told them that. He liked the warmth of the old, hard-to-find, hot-burning Christmas lights. C9s on a straight line along the edges of the roof. That was Bob's choice. It wasn't his house though. He had to let go. His daughters were adults. They were old enough to cuss and pick their own lights.

He pulled the ladder from the wall and swung it carefully around to take it back into the house. The water splashed at his feet as he worked around the stacks of belongings that he imagined would be ruined by the time the sun rose.

Carefully he worked his way into the house and took the ladder to the front door. He placed it on its side, then thought how it would have been easier, though more dangerous perhaps, to have opened the garage door and carried it out that way.

"Girls?" he called. "Y'all ready?"

Kiki appeared first. She was wearing a yellow rain slicker buttoned up to her neck and a backpack that clung to her shoulders and back. Kristin was next. She wore a clear poncho and held a large garbage bag twisted and cinched at the top. Katie was last. She wore a thin windbreaker with the hood already on her head. In one hand she held the strap of a sizable backpack. In the other she had a clear poncho like the one her mother wore.

She held it out to Bob. "Dad, you need something."

Bob smiled and took it from her, sliding it over his head. "Thank you," he said once he had it draped over his body. He surveyed the trio, feigned confidence he thought a patriarch should convey to his family, and exhaled. The water was halfway up his calves now.

"Everyone ready?"

The women nodded, and Katie opened the door, swinging it as far as it would go. She stepped out onto the porch with Kiki, followed by Kristin. Bob was last, bringing the ladder with him at his side. He stepped past the women and out into the pounding rain while Kiki shut the door. The sound was almost deafening, the heavy drops beating on the plastic sheeting atop his head. The sound filled his mind, compressed his thoughts, and made him want to cover his ears.

With the ladder on one side and Katie on the other, Bob carefully descended the steps and left the porch. His first step was tentative. His bare foot hung in the air for what felt like an eternity before he dropped it beneath the surface and found the first step down. Each successive step took them deeper into the cold water. It climbed up his legs to his groin, then his waist. The water was cold. So cold. The beat of the rain on his head was loud. Too loud. His pulse thumped in his chest. It was faster than the rain. It was too fast, the beat too thick.

The only thing that kept him moving as the water reached his chest was his daughter's guiding hand and her soft encouragement.

"You're good, Dad," she said. "You're fine. Almost there. You're doing great."

Bob was dizzy in the water. Each step, the mulch beds oozing between his toes, was more dizzying than the last. But he made it to the spot and, while Katie balanced him, he swung the ladder around to plant it firmly in the bed. He drove it into the muck and stepped on the first rung to dig it more deeply into the inundated ground. He extended it skyward, locked the latch in place, and leaned it squarely against the edge, bending the overhanging composite tile underneath its weight.

Then he motioned for Katie to climb. "Come on," he said above the din of the rain. "You first. Then you help your mother up."

Once she'd climbed the first two steps, Bob stood behind her, holding the aluminum frame in place on the ground and in the muck.

He worried that with the current and the rising water, the ladder could lose its perch and topple, dropping Katie into the water.

She climbed hand over hand until she reached the roof, then pivoted and heaved herself onto the tile, sitting on it with her legs hanging over the top couple of rungs.

Bob squinted through the rain at Katie until she gave him a thumbs-up. Then he stepped from the ladder and, holding it steady, waved Kiki over.

"I thought Mom was next," said Kiki. "Take Mom."

Both parents shook their heads, Bob at the ladder, Kristin on the porch. They wanted their children safe before themselves.

Another wicked strobe of lightning forked in the sky, striking somewhere not that far away. Kiki shuddered and gripped the iron railing, dropping step by step into the black water. Her body seized when it reached her waist. She sucked in a deep breath and exhaled but kept moving methodically. The water, at Bob's chest, was at her neck. It was rising inconceivably fast.

Bob reached out his hand to his daughter, her chin held up as high as she could hold it, and she gripped his wrist with her fingers. He pulled her onto the ladder and stood at its base while she climbed to the roof.

Once she was safely next to Katie, Bob called for his wife. Instead of suggesting she take the same path, he called her toward him on the porch.

A perplexed look on her face, her brow furrowed with confusion and worry, Kristin waded toward the railing to the left of the front door. Beyond the railing, Bob was holding the ladder with one hand and waving her closer with the other. The water was close to the top of his shoulders now.

"You can't make it from the steps," he said, speaking loudly. "It's too deep now. Climb over the rail."

The color drained from Kristin's face. "What?"

"Climb over the railing," said Bob, louder this time. "I can help you get onto the ladder from here. You'll be okay. Just climb and drop. I'm here."

Even through the rain, Bob saw the glistening sheen of tears welling in his wife's eyes. Her chin trembled as she wrung the top of the twisted trash bag she carried in her hands.

"Hand me the bag and climb over," he said. "Now. We don't have much time."

Kristin squared her jaw and nodded; then she bent over the top of the railing and, with one leg at a time, climbed over. She maneuvered onto her feet, maintaining her balance on one foot for a moment until she could grab the railing behind her. She held onto it with one hand and offered her husband the bag.

He took it from her and held it in the same hand that gripped the ladder. Then he looked skyward, his eyes blinking against the bullets of rain. "Girls, hold the ladder from the top. Put pressure on it," he called to them. "Don't let it move."

He took one step and then another toward his wife. His pulse pounding, his sweat mixed with the rain, the whiskey long gone from his body now, he reached her.

She took his hand and slinked down, squatting against the railing. Then, without him expecting it, she jumped.

Bob lost his footing as she flung herself at him. He went beneath the water, sucking some of it into his nostrils. It burned and stung. He shook his head, still under the water in the blackness. Thankfully he found his footing and rocketed himself above the surface, emerging like an orca with a great, raspy breath.

He swiped the water from his face, hearing the cries of his daughters above the slap of the rain, and groped aimlessly for his wife. He found her a foot from him. She was bobbing up and down, struggling to stay above the surface.

She was thrashing and crying, gurgling and kicking, swinging her arms wildly.

Bob tried calming her, reasoning with her, working to get ahold of her. But she was panicking. She was flailing, on the verge of drowning.

Bob backed away, the water to his chin now, and stood on his tiptoes in the muck. He yelled to his daughters to keep hold of the ladder while keeping his eyes on his wife. She was a mess. She would pull him under if he tried to grab her again. He knew it.

So he waited, ignoring his daughters' imploring, desperate cries to help their mother. He waited. The water rose above his chin to his lower lip. Still he waited.

For a brief moment, with her back to him, Kristin calmed herself. Perhaps she was exhausted. Or she came to her senses. Or she gave up. Whatever it was, it provided Bob the opportunity to sneak up behind her, fling his arm around her neck, and drag her to the ladder.

At first she resisted, albeit weakly. She submitted to him and let him work her body onto the bottom of the ladder, placing her hands along the rails and guiding her feet onto the rungs. She was crying, coughing, and shivering.

"It's okay," said Bob, his turn now to do the encouraging, the coaxing. "You're okay. Climb. I'm right behind you."

Both of them now soaked, the plastic ponchos sticking to their bodies, his wife tentatively ascended a single step. Her hands gripped the rails so tightly Bob thought her knuckles might tear through her skin. She started to climb another step but stopped.

"Keep going," said Bob. "You can make it, Kris. C'mon, sweetie. One step at a time. The girls are up there."

He was tilting his head back now to prevent the water from seeping into his mouth. The only thing keeping him grounded was his hold on the ladder.

Their daughters coaxed her upward, and Kristin took another step. Then a third and a fourth. Two more. Three more. Bob was on the ladder now. He was climbing up behind her. He couldn't wait any longer. The water was too high. He climbed. One step, another, another. He closed his eyes, listening to the pounding rain on the plastic stuck snugly to his head. It was loud. So loud. But he kept moving. He urged his wife ahead of him, not looking but still climbing.

Before he knew it, but long after he'd have like to have known it, he was on the roof, flat on his back. His chest heaved. The rain pelted his face, but it no longer bothered him. It was cleansing. It was almost refreshing as he lay there, his family around him.

He opened his eyes and looked in the opaque blackness of the sky, the invisible missiles of rain streaming down from above. He opened his mouth and drank some of it, cleansing his palate and easing his mind.

They were safe. At least for the moment they were out of the water. Then it hit him like a tidal wave.

Where was Keri?

CHAPTER 12

April 5, 2026
New Orleans, Louisiana

The phone rang in Doc Konkoly's room, its red message light flickering in the relative darkness. It startled Konkoly awake and, for several seconds, he lay there staring at the popcorn ceiling trying to remember where he was.

The stiff aroma of commercial detergent on the sheet pulled up to his neck reminded him he was in a hotel room in New Orleans. He had no concept of time, other than that the large rain-speckled window revealed it was still dark outside.

The phone stopped ringing before he rolled onto his side to grab the receiver, and Doc lay there on his back thinking about his night. He remembered drinking at the bar, remembered the loquacious, tip-seeking bartender. And he remembered the news anchor from home.

Then the phone rang again and he remembered the storm. He rolled onto his side, reached across his body, heavy with sleep, and drew the receiver to his ear.

"Hello?" he answered with a groggy voice that he didn't recognize as his own.

"Dr. Konkoly," replied the woman's voice on the other end. She was pleasant sounding despite the urgency with which she said his

name. *"This is Shonda at the front desk. I apologize for calling your room at such an inconvenient hour."*

He cleared his throat. "That's fine."

"We have a somewhat urgent situation developing here on the property," said Shonda. *"Floodwater is threatening our lower levels. I know you are on a higher floor. You aren't in any immediate danger, but—"*

He leaned up on an elbow. "Immediate...danger?"

"You're not in any danger right now, Dr. Konkoly," she said. *"You may notice, however, a loss of power, low water pressure in the bathroom, and—"*

Shonda stopped talking.

"And what?" asked Doc. He was now sitting up in bed, his back resting on the wall-mounted faux-leather headboard.

Shonda didn't respond.

"Hello?" He pulled the phone from his ear and looked at it briefly before holding it again in the crook of his neck. "Hello?"

The line was dead. He reached over to flip on the bedside table lamp, testing it as much as seeking light. It turned on, casting a dim yellow glow in the room. He found his eyeglasses and focused them on the remote, which was beside the phone. He punched the large power button at the top of it and moved his glasses up on his nose.

The flat-panel television opposite the foot of his king-sized bed chimed and powered up. The screen illuminated the hotel's default channel, offering world-class spa treatments and the best jambalaya in the French Quarter. He doubted either claim was true and surfed the channels until he found the same weather report he'd been watching in the bar earlier in the evening.

The screen was split. Half of it displayed the rainbow-infused map of the central Gulf Coast and the relentless bands of severe storms that marched onward; the other half showed live video of flooding streets, of desperate people wading through the water with their children on their shoulders or in their arms, of emergency responders plowing through high water in trucks and boats. It resembled a third-world country, not the kind of thing that would happen in the United

States, let alone the city in which he was currently visiting.

Doc turned up the volume and listened to the reporters describe what he could see with his own eyes. The city was sinking under water. And from the looks of it, even the spots that survived Katrina and the rainstorms of March 2018, August 2017, and May 2015 were sinking below the floodwater.

The city was a fishbowl. And the bowl was overflowing.

He pushed himself from the soft mattress, setting his feet on the floor. He walked the short distance to the television and stood directly in front of it, staring at the endless stream of men, women, and children evacuating their homes. He looked at their faces: bewildered, shocked, sometimes blank with anguish.

Doc reached out and touched the screen, his fingers lingering on the close-up face of a young boy. The child couldn't have been more than three. He held his tiny hands over his ears, his eyes squeezed shut. He was floating in an open red Igloo cooler, bouncing in the wake created by the woman pulling him through the water. She was up to her waist in water and she was crying. Doc couldn't hear her cries, but he could see them in her stretched expression and the tremble of her body as she moved through the chest-deep water.

He couldn't know where in the city this was happening. The location description at the bottom of the screen didn't help him. Yet he couldn't stand in his room and do nothing. That wasn't what people like him did. These survivors would need medical care. They would need a shoulder on which to cry. They would need much more than that.

Out the window, lightning flashed, illuminating the droplets of water that stuck to the glass and curled their way down it in trickles. They looked like converging rivers on the window, seen from high altitude. They swelled and shrank as the trails of water moved and slithered with gravity.

Water always finds the easiest path to its destination, he thought idly.

Doc blinked himself away from the window and found his pants hanging over the back of the desk chair, the belt strung through the loops. He slid into them and pulled on the shirt he'd worn the night before.

It smelled like the bar, a dank mixture of stale cigarette smoke and sour beer. It didn't matter. Where he was headed didn't have a dress code or care if he was washed and starched.

He shuffled to his suitcase, pulling out a folded raincoat. It was really an expensive fishing jacket meant for poor conditions, but it was what he owned. He slid it on, zipping it up, then found a pair of cheap slip-on sneakers he'd worn on the plane ride and put those on over his bare feet. No need to wear socks.

He withdrew some cash, a credit card, and his ID from his wallet, then locked the wallet into the closet safe. He grabbed his room key and phone, stuffed a prepackaged first aid kit into a jacket pocket, then headed for the elevator. The moment he left his room and the door clicked shut behind him, the hallway went dark. The power was out.

Doc cursed, realizing he'd have to find the stairs, as he tapped on the flashlight app on his phone. He used the narrow white beam to search the walls for directions to the stairwell. Then he noticed the glowing overhead signs pointing in the right direction. He picked up speed, half running, half walking, until he reached the heavy metal door that led to the stairwell.

He pushed open the door, it slammed behind him with a thud, and he stood in complete darkness. The echo of the thud cascaded through the well and Doc exhaled. This wouldn't be fun.

He aimed his light down the first set of concrete steps and began the slow, lonely descent. He had sixteen floors until he reached the lobby. At least he wasn't climbing *up* the stairs. That would be far worse.

Each of his heavy steps echoed in the well. He methodically took each one carefully. Even with the dim band of light from his phone flashlight, it was a treacherous descent. He'd been at it for a good five minutes when he heard the metallic *thunk* of a door opening on the floor below where he stood.

He stopped moving for a moment as the door slammed shut again, and he heard two people murmuring to each other. He put his free hand on the cold concrete railing and resumed his foot-by-foot trek down the well.

"Hello?" called a woman as he rounded the flight onto her level. She was standing on the landing with someone else. Doc couldn't make out if the other person was a man or woman.

He accidentally shone the light in the woman's eyes and she squinted, pulling her arm up to shield herself. He swept the light to the other person. It was another woman. Both of them appeared to be the types of guests who were paid to be there by the hour.

"Watch the light," said the first woman, her voice shrill. "You're blinding us here."

"Sorry," said Doc, pivoting back to the first woman. "It's hard to see in here."

"You're a regular Captain Obvious, aren't you?" said the second woman. She was taller, but appeared to be wearing the same sized skirt and top as her smaller colleague.

He frowned at them, though he doubted either of them could see it. There was no point in debating them as to education or profession. He let the snark slide.

"I'm headed downstairs," he said, keeping the light at their stilettoed feet now. "You're welcome to follow me if you like."

Without awaiting an answer, he turned the corner in front of them and took the next flight of stairs. They mumbled something, the unintelligible murmur echoing off the walls, and started the descent.

Once they'd rounded a few more flights, he asked, "What floor were you on?" continuing to take the stairs one plodding step at a time.

"Nine," said one of them.

"Ten," said the other.

The two of them argued it another two flights before they settled on eight. Doc counted in his head, not having caught the last few floor markers with his light. They had to be getting close now.

Another five minutes and they were at the lobby level. That was, they were two steps above the lobby level, which was flooded. Doc's light reflected off the brownish water, a thin rainbow film of grease coating its surface.

"Great," said the taller of the two women. "It's flooded."

Doc turned to her, shined the light on his face, and raised an eyebrow. Then he turned back to the water and scanned the surface from the last dry step to the door.

"Touché," said the tall woman, snickering.

"You and your French," said the shorter one. "You don't speak French. Stop trying to use French words. It's embarrassing."

The two women bickered about romance languages, and Doc came to a decision. Judging by the height of the water on the door, which was below the handle, he figured he could easily wade out into the lobby. The issue would be what was submerged under the water and what danger that might pose as he trudged through it.

It didn't matter, he decided in that moment. He needed to help people. He took a tentative first step into the water, feeling the icy rush of it seep into his shoe, between his toes, and up his leg. His second step was more sure-footed, and then he made the plunge. The water was breathtakingly cold, but it was beneath his hips. Shivering, he made his way to the door, shining the light on the handle. He grabbed it and pulled. At first it didn't give, then he braced himself with one foot against the wall beside the jamb, and it slowly swung open against the water.

The lobby was bathed in the devilish red of the emergency lights. The fiery glow danced on the surface of the murky water, giving it the appearance of being on fire from below.

He hadn't waited for the women, but they were steps behind him. He could hear the splash of their movements.

Not needing the white light of his phone, he turned it off to save the battery and tucked it into a zippered pocket at his chest. It was a water-resistant pocket, and he hoped it was enough to keep his phone alive.

The lobby was surprisingly empty of guests. There were a pair of security guards standing atop the concierge stand. Both of them seemed to be trying to reach somebody on a walkie-talkie. They ignored Doc and his new traveling companions. But the woman sitting on the check-in counter acknowledged them.

"Hello," she said in a familiar voice, and Doc recognized her as Shonda. She was sitting with her knees pulled up to her chest. Her arms held her legs tight, and her hands were clasped in the front. She was soaked and shivering.

Doc nodded at her, started to wade past the desk, and thought better of it. He waded across the lobby toward Shonda. As he approached, it was apparent how young she was. Twenty? Twenty-one? She had to be a college student.

"You okay?" he asked her.

She nodded the way someone trying to fend off an emotional outburst does. She bit her lower lip and squeezed her eyebrows together in a furrow above her dark eyes.

"Where is everybody?" he asked. "Your boss? More than…two security guards? I don't understand."

"I'm the night manager," she said. "We don't have a large staff this late at night. Our maintenance staff is working on emergency power and coping with the water."

"You're it?" he asked. "You're a…college student, no?"

Despite shivering, Shonda appeared to bristle at the suggestion she couldn't do her job. She tightened her grip around her knees and frowned. "Yes," she said. "Xavier. But I'm perfectly capable of—"

Understanding he'd apparently offended her, Doc cut in. "That's not what I meant," he said. "I'm saying you shouldn't be alone. This is too much for anyone by himself. Or herself."

Her frown relaxed. "I can't leave. I'd lose my job. They've got reinforcements coming. Before the lines went dead, the general manager called. He's on his way."

Doc looked to the front entrance to his left. He couldn't see beyond the floor-to-ceiling, two-story frameless glass panels and onto the street, or where the street should have been, but he knew nobody was coming.

"If he can get here," said Doc. "And I'm going to go out on a limb and suggest your GM won't be getting here anytime soon."

"He's Captain Obvious!" shouted the tall date-for-hire standing several feet behind him. "He's good with nuance."

"Really?" whined the shorter of the two. "French again?"

"Ignore them," Doc said to Shonda.

Shonda arched an eyebrow at Doc and glanced at both of the women and then back at him. The faintest hint of a knowing, yet disapproving, smile curled onto one side of her face.

Recognizing this, Doc shook his head. "Found them in the stairwell," he said under his breath. "Not with me."

"He's bourgeoisie," said the taller woman. "Wouldn't be caught with us. He's too good for us."

"Except that he's not," said the shorter one.

"Look," said Doc. "You could come with us. I'm going to try to find some emergency crews…a shelter, and help some people. I could get you to a shelter."

"And lose my job?" asked Shonda. "No thanks."

Doc took another tentative step toward the desk. The cold water moved through his body, sending a chill up his spine. "You won't lose your job," he said. "It's not a safe environment."

"Thanks, but no thanks," said Shonda. She was looking at the entrepreneurial women behind him as she spoke. "I'll be fine."

Doc shrugged with resignation. "Okay. Suit yourself."

He waved a reluctant goodbye to her, trying to formulate some sort of convincing argument for her to come with him. He couldn't, so he sloshed toward the main entrance, the two women crawlers in tow.

The entry doors were large electric sliding doors that were stuck open with about a two-foot gap to squeeze through. Doc sidestepped through the opening and waited for the women, their faces crunched into disapproving sneers and their heels in their hands, sloshing through the water, which was obviously deepening.

The second Doc cleared the opening, he felt the strong undercurrent of the water outside. It was as though he'd stepped from a wading pool into a rapid. He set his gait wider, trying to balance himself against the strong rush of water that threatened to knock him off-balance.

It pushed him sideways for a moment, causing him to have to use his hands as paddles to maintain his foothold on the concrete sidewalk. He told the women, "Hold onto one another. The current is intense."

The first of them, the taller Francophile, waded out only a couple of steps before willing herself back into the lobby. She shook her head vigorously. "I'm not going out there. We're better off in here. That water will kill me."

Doc held out a hand. "You can make it," he said. "I can help you."

The woman's eyes, heavy with shadow and mascara, were wide with fright. She backed away another step, deeper into the lobby. "Not happening."

Her partner in crime, albeit a crime subject only to a five-hundred-dollar fine and up to six months in jail for a first offense, stood with her. She shook her head too. "If she's not going, I'm not going."

"The water is only going to get deeper here," he said, pointing beyond the cover of the hotel's decorative sidewalk overhang. "It's raining. You're no safer here than—"

The taller one saluted with a flick of her wrist. "*Merci,* Captain," she said. "We can take care of ourselves."

Doc shook his head with disappointment. "Suit yourself," he said, and turned to head across the wide street in front of the hotel. He glanced back at the women, their high heels still in their hands. *"Laissez les bon temps rouler."*

The women laughed. "He's got jokes," said the shorter one. "Captain got jokes."

Doc laughed, the tension in his body easing for a moment. He took a deep breath, still bracing his legs at shoulder width to withstand the torrent flowing underneath the surface.

He took one step, then another, and a third toward the street. He shuffled his feet as he neared what he imagined was the edge of the sidewalk. He found it and bent his knee to wade deeper into the water. Trash floated by, spinning in the baby jetties that formed and dissipated in the dark froth.

He took his other foot and stepped from the curb, finding the gutter at the edge of the street, but the current slid him to one side. The undercurrent, stronger than anything he'd ever felt in the trickiest of ocean shorelines, yanked that leg out from under him and pulled him under the surface. He was sucked under, an aquatic tractor beam intent on dragging him to some invisible magnet.

He blew the air from his lungs, bubbles streaming to the surface of the water, and fought to escape the pull. Then his foot was stuck in something, and his body twisted and rolled with the whims of the angry torrent. It dragged him like a rag doll, twisting his body at his ankle, using it as a fulcrum for its whims.

He managed to control himself for an instant and reached down to his foot. His lungs were beginning to burn. He had no air and he was blind in the consuming darkness.

As panic crept into his rational mind, he maintained his wits long enough to understand his foot was caught in a sewer grate, and the force was yanking him downward, trapping him in the swirling vortex. He grabbed at his foot, trying to turn it, to work it free of the grate. It wasn't happening. His throat tightened, the sting of water in his nose distracted him, and the water pushed his body awkwardly away from his foot.

But as that happened, miraculously, his foot was torqued free of the grate. The freedom was invigorating, and Doc pushed himself back the short distance to the surface. He emerged and gasped for air, choking on it, and steadied himself in the street.

Even as he stood as tall as he could, the water was above his chest now. And it was getting worse. He wiped his hands across his face then pushed his hair back. His glasses were gone.

His heart pounding against his chest, his pulse thickly throbbing at his neck, he struggled to regain his composure. He spun in a circle, trying to reestablish his bearings. The hotel was behind him now and to his left. He was closer to the opposite side of the street than he'd first thought and was farther down. It confused him. How had he moved so far from the curb so quickly?

The press of water at his side made it difficult to stand in one place. He danced on his tiptoes, acquiescing to the pull of the current. He was already exhausted and unsure he could make it the rest of the distance across the street.

Doc glanced back at the hotel through the dense curtain of rain and stared at the faint emergency red glow leaking through the large glass frontage. He wondered if he should go back. Maybe Shonda the night manager and the two independent women contractors had the right idea.

It was too far now. He was better off forging ahead into the uncertain waters beyond him. His breathing having returned to normal, at least for the circumstances, he walked diagonally away from the hotel toward the opposite end of the street. The farther he moved, using his hands as oars to fend off the push and pull of the water, the darker his surroundings became.

When Doc found himself clinging to a street sign pole on a corner, he realized he had no direction. He didn't know where he was going or how he could find help. He swung himself halfway around the pole, peering into the darkness of one street and then in the opposite direction.

He'd assumed that emergency personnel would be everywhere, that he'd be able to toss a pebble into the water and a ripple would slap against the side of a high-water truck or rescue boat. He thought for sure he'd find aquatic caravans of desperate families in need of support or guidance. He found none of it.

But as he stood there, again reassessing his hasty decision to leave his dry hotel room, he saw the distant strobe of red and white lights. At first he thought lightning had flashed in the sky. But absent thunder, he kept watching the spot where he'd seen the flicker.

It was there. It belonged to a fire truck or an ambulance. No doubt. He couldn't tell, however, how far down the narrow alley of a street he'd have to travel to reach it. The lights were reflecting off the water and the sides of the buildings. It was faint enough, in the driving rain and light-absorbing dark, that it could easily be a mile from him or a quarter as far.

It didn't matter. It was the only option now. He let go of the pole and waded, half-swimming, toward the lights.

As soon as he'd cleared the corner of the buildings at the intersection, the current eased enough that he didn't have to fight against it. The water was rising still, and he bounced along in it, using the force of his push from the street to propel himself forward. Push with his left foot. Rise. Glide. Sink. Push with his right. Rise. Glide. Sink. He found the movement required less effort now. It conserved his energy. It helped him see above the choppy wake of the surface when he elevated, and it let him more easily evade the floating trash and debris that littered the alleyway.

He couldn't avoid all of it, and at times he caught the strong odor of rotting food and excrement. He bore it as best he could, resisting his burgeoning gag reflex, and bounded forward.

Thankfully he had both shoes. Incredibly he hadn't lost either yet, even when stuck in the sewer grate.

He shivered again. The relentlessly cold shower was biblical. It complicated everything. The flooding was one thing; the absolute darkness was another. The rain was the coup de grace.

Coup de grace, he thought. The taller of the pavement princesses would like the phrasing.

Nonetheless, he persevered. The flickering lights, alternately red and white, were growing brighter. As he drew closer, and the water deeper, he discovered it was coming from a street two blocks up and to the right. He hurried that distance and rounded the corner, emerging into a stronger current.

It wasn't as forceful as the one along the hotel's wide street, but it was strong nonetheless. His calves and thighs thickened with exhaustion as he moved toward the lights. Although he couldn't see their source yet, they were there. Red. White. Red. White. Swirling and flashing against the water and the buildings, bouncing off everything they touched and brighter now because of the absence of all other light.

Then he saw it. At the intersection of the next street, pulled off the main corridor and buffeted next to a corner building, was a large high-water truck. It was black, cloaked in the night and nearly invisible except for the sharp, distinctive angles of its design and its large twin headlights that cast an arcing beam onto the water surrounding it. The water was high enough that it lapped at the truck's grille. Its fog lights were underwater, giving a sense of the depth in a way that Doc hadn't yet seen. Its tires, which had to measure four feet in diameter, were underwater, though the top curves of the wheel wells were visible above the surface.

Around the vehicle, working and struggling, was what Doc had risked his life to find. There were active rescues, families in need, and there were first responders.

Renewed with purpose, he slogged through the water faster, bending into the current and pushing forward against its resistance. He ignored the heaviness in his legs, the ache in his back, and the weight of his waterlogged clothes on his shoulders.

He reached the front of the vehicle, moving past the bright beam of its headlights, and felt the truck's rumbling idle vibrate the water around him. He approached a man who looked like he might be in charge. The man, wearing a bright orange jacket with reflective tape banded across his chest and along his arms. He looked at Doc warily at first. His glare softened when Doc told him why he was there, that he wasn't another person in need of help.

"I'm a physician," he said. "I'm here to do…whatever you need."

The man nodded briskly. He pointed toward the building closest to the truck. On the fourth floor, there were a dozen people crowded onto a narrow balcony meant for three or four at most.

"They're panicking. None of them can swim, I don't think," he said. "We're trying to get them into the truck one at a time. They keep threatening to jump en masse. We can't have that. One group already jumped. We lost a couple in the current. I've got one guy in the truck with evacuees. I've got two guys climbing the stairs inside to get to them and bring them down. We've got a raft that can ferry them the short distance from the steps to the truck, but it's taking a while. They had to clear a lot of debris first. They're working on it."

"Okay," said Doc. "What do you need?"

"I need someone to stand there and calm them. Talk to them. I don't know how many of them speak English. They're migrants. That's an illegal flophouse up there. The roof's leaking on them. But anything you can do to stop them from jumping until my men get up there…"

"No problem," said Doc. "Any injuries yet?"

"Our guy in the truck is sewing up an abrasion on one of the five we've got in the truck now. Not much else, I don't think."

Doc glanced at the back of the truck, to the large open bed in the back of it. He saw the tops of a couple of heads, not much more.

"Do you have a light on the truck?" asked Doc. "That might help."

"We did." The commander frowned. "One of the jumpers hit it, broke it, and went under. That's one of the ones we lost. We're kinda blind here. I gotta get on the radio and call for help if we can get any. Anything you can do to keep those folks up there would be much obliged."

Doc nodded and moved carefully along the side of the truck toward the balcony. He reached a good spot and held his ground there, the water rushing around him. He looked up and, in the flickering red and white light, saw one of the men had climbed onto the outside of the railing. He was preparing to jump.

"Stop!" he shouted. "Too dangerous. *Peligroso.*"

He had no idea if the man spoke Spanish, but he tried it. Then he tried Vietnamese, aware that many of the fishermen who worked the shallow gulf waters were from southeast Asia. Both languages, neither of which he spoke well, had come in handy when he'd volunteered his time at free clinics in various substandard Los Angeles neighborhoods. He'd picked up important words here and there.

"Nguy hiểm," he said, waving his hands. "Dangerous. Stop."

The man held his ground for a moment. Then another man climbed out onto the ledge with him. Now there were two perched and ready to leap.

"No," said Doc, using the most universally understood word he could think to use. "No. Wait. *Esperate por favor. Làm ơn chờ.* Wait. Someone is coming."

The men listened. Both of them, one at a time, climbed back onto the crowded balcony. As the second of the two lifted his second leg over the railing, the balcony shifted. Its mooring loosened at the building's facade.

In an instant, as Doc was exhaling a sigh of relief from having coaxed the would-be jumpers from the ledge, the balcony and the dozen people upon it came crashing down through the red and white strobing darkness. The crack of the landing separating from the building and the constant din of the rain on the rushing water were muted by the shrill screams of the people crashing toward the murk forty feet below where they'd stood a moment earlier.

Doc was nearly frozen, but somehow his aching legs instinctively pushed him to one side and he dove into the icy, putrid water away from the downpour of migrants. Underwater and scrambling to distance himself farther from the instantaneous threat, he felt the percussion of their bodies hitting the water. One after the other it was like an underwater sonic wave.

It enveloped him, disorienting him. Water ran up his nose, sending an electric sting into his sinuses like a bolt of lightning.

Something, or someone, slammed into the back of one leg, the blunt force only minutely dampened by the thing's slap against the surface barely above him. He bellowed out in pain, a cascade of bubbles dancing across his face.

He grabbed at his wounded leg and used the other one to find the asphalt below and propel him up and away, a missile launching skyward.

He resurfaced, grimacing at the solid, throbbing ache in the back of his leg. He shifted his weight, putting his mass on the injured leg. It resisted but held.

Bruised, he thought. It was a deep contusion.

Convinced he wasn't suffering from a fracture or bleeding laceration, he spun back toward the roiling chaos behind him. There was a mind-piercing wail from one thrashing victim, a gurgling call for help from another.

In the waterlogged confusion, Doc couldn't tell which of the dark figures were those who'd fallen and survived and which were rescuers coming to their aid. He waded back toward the rumble nonetheless. More people had fallen than there were those to help them. Chances were whoever he reached first would be wounded, if they were alive.

The first wasn't. The gruesome wounds on the woman's warped body and disfigured face told Doc she'd hit something more than the water. Death was frozen on what was left of her face. Her eyes were fixed open, her mouth agape.

Doc couldn't do anything for her. He pushed past her, wiped the rain from his face, and found the next body. Ahead of him, first responders were trying to calm the wounded and separate them from the mass of bodies clogging the space between the side of the high-water truck and the entrance to the building.

He found his charge floating on his back, crying out through clenched teeth. Bleeding from his mouth and at his neck, the man was holding onto a piece of wrought iron that protruded through the surface of the water perpendicular to his body.

But when Doc evaluated his many injuries, at least the ones he could see in the strobing red and white light, he realized the man wasn't holding the piece of iron. It was stuck there, having impaled the man's thigh.

Doc took the man's hand and squeezed. "Can you understand me?" he said, hoping the man could hear him above the rain and the ambient cacophony of pain. "I'm a doctor. You're going to be okay."

His eyes closed, smiling broadly through his pain, the man nodded. At least Doc thought it was a nod. He held the man's hand, buoying himself in the water and trying to maintain his position at the edge of the chaos without floating too much one way or the other.

He inched as close to the man's ear as he could, keeping his tone measured as he explained the man's predicament.

He imagined the poor soul was in deepening shock, and if Doc couldn't free him from the iron anchor feet below them, he would die. He didn't express that last sentiment to the man, but he didn't lie to him either.

"I cannot move you right now," he said. "Your leg is stuck. I need to free it. When I do, we'll be able to get you to the truck, and they'll be able to take you to a hospital. Do you understand? If so, squeeze my hand."

The man squeezed. It was trembling, like a weightlifter's body out of juice at the end of a heavy set. The man was giving Doc every ounce of life force he had left in him to acknowledge his understanding.

Doc couldn't actually free the man's leg from the iron. It was likely embedded in or adjacent to bone. There was a web of blood vessels, and thick, sinewy muscle. Trying to wrestle or slide the bar free of the leg would not only risk irreparable damage but could lead to blood loss just short of exsanguination. He couldn't risk either. And frankly, he didn't have time to try even if it had been possible.

Instead he'd need to free the bar from the anchoring piece of railing at the bottom of the floodwater. It was his only chance to save the man's life.

"I'm going to swim underneath you and try to free you. Please remain as calm as you can." He let go of the man's cold hand. He heard the sharp rattle in his weak wisps of breath that leaked through his teeth and bleeding nose. Then he dove.

The cold water swirled around him as he dunked himself headfirst the five feet to the street. He opened his eyes as wide as he could, but it did nothing to lighten the darkness. Even the red and white strobe was barely visible beyond the surface. Bodies and debris bumped against him as he groped blindly for the piece of balcony railing somehow stuck at the bottom. The only things that kept him from panicking were his medical training and the silence being underwater provided.

He found a mangled piece of iron railing that bent and twisted like an abandoned smokestack up and up until it reached the underside of the man's thigh, where it disappeared into his puckered, wounded flesh.

When Doc accidentally touched the man's leg, he felt the reactive jerk and recoil. It only proved to further move the iron stake deeper into the leg.

Doc couldn't see it. He felt it as he wrapped his hand around the bar and slid it downward, tracing the bends and crooks until he found one with his fingers that seemed ready to break. He held the bend with one hand while drawing the other to it. He grabbed it and tried pulling, pushing, bending, snapping—none of it worked. He couldn't get the right leverage to finish the job that the four-story crash had started, and the strain of attempting it had robbed him of air.

Using his good leg, he pushed himself back to the surface long enough to suck down another gulp of air. He descended again, fighting against his own buoyancy to dig his way back underwater. He found the same bend in the iron and tried again. This time, though, he placed a hand on either side of the extreme angle then gripped. He held his breath, feeling the pressure build in his ears, exerting his focused energy on the iron. As he relaxed and pushed in a second time, he grunted and forced the air from his lungs. He pushed, maintaining that pressure until he felt the sharp snap of the metal. He blindly reached around the thin pieces of the bar and worked them outward until the final threads of iron holding the two pieces together separated.

Certain he'd done enough to free the man, he propelled himself upward and treaded to the surface. He was breathing hard and his nostrils burned, his eyes blurry from the water and the rain. He took the man's hand again and told him it had worked.

Then he realized the man wasn't returning his grip at all. His hand was lifeless. Doc let go and wiped his eyes clear with the backs of his hands and looked at the man's face.

The smile of pain, that wide grimace that stretched from cheek to cheek, was gone. His clenched jaw was slack. His eyes were closed, but there was no tension there anymore.

Doc called to him again, then tried moving his body closer to him. But the man, who was either dead or unconscious, didn't move. He was still anchored to something.

Doc quickly moved to the man's head and put his fingers at his neck, feeling for a pulse he couldn't find. He floated to the other side of the man's body; then he saw it.

The iron railing hadn't just punctured the man's leg. There was another piece that had speared through his back. The top of it, barely visible at the surface of the water, protruded through his midsection near his navel.

The man was dead. There was no saving him.

Still falling in sheets, the rain made it difficult to distinguish anything in the dim light. But Doc found a woman clinging to the side of the truck. Many of the dozen people who'd fallen were either floating away, sinking, or in the care of the few first responders on scene.

This one woman, however, was alone. She was sitting on the footwell on the side of the truck, holding most of her body out of the water. She was whimpering and holding one arm in the other, her elbow perched in the palm of the opposite hand. Finally, Doc thought, there was someone he could actually help.

His leg was throbbing and his chest burned from his dives beneath the surface. He was cold, his muscles were tightening, and his head was beginning to throb. What had been the faintest of jabs at his temples had spread across the top of his head like a bandanna of pain.

Yet he forged ahead and met the woman at the side of the truck. He ran his hands through his hair and adjusted his soaked jacket at his gut. He tried to smile at the woman, who appeared to recoil defensively as he approached.

Doc held up his hands. "I'm a doctor," he said. "Can you understand me?"

The woman nodded. In broken English she said, "I understand."

"What hurts?" he asked. The noise of crying and wailing had dissipated greatly, but the splash of the rain and the moaning of survivors above them in the truck's bed made communicating a challenge.

She nodded at the crook of her arm, cradling her elbow. Her long black hair was matted to her face, her sharply cut bangs creating an odd frame for her pained expression.

Doc reached out for her arm slowly, locking eyes with her to gain her consent, and gently touched her at her wrist and at her bicep. The woman let go of her elbow. It was swollen, bloodied, and there was a shard of bone sticking out the side of her arm. It appeared to him as if the lower part of her humerus or the medial epicondyle were splintered.

"You have a fracture," he told her. Then he thought of the moniker one of the paid escorts had given him. *Captain Obvious.* "You'll be okay. They can fix you at the hospital."

Her eyebrows furrowed and her expression tightened. "Help me?"

Doc understood her to mean she was asking why he couldn't help her. Now. She was clearly in pain.

"Yes." He reached into the hip pocket of his rain jacket and pulled out the first aid kit he'd brought with him from the hotel. He always traveled with one. It was basic—analgesics, sterilizers, bandages, hot and cold pressure packs—but it was enough to typically suit his needs for intermediate care.

He told the woman to hold her arm with her hand over her breast, demonstrating with his free hand the movement one makes to say the Pledge of Allegiance or sing the national anthem. She mimicked him, wincing with the movement.

Doc opened the kit, holding it against the truck for leverage. He fished through the smaller items, grabbing a package of acetaminophen, to get to a plastic pouch in the bottom. He held the pouch between his teeth while he closed the kit, shoved it back into his wet pocket, then ripped open the pouch.

From inside it he pulled a roll of cotton fabric about two inches wide and six feet long. He wrapped it around her neck, created a sling, and tore the extra length of it with his teeth, knotting it at the nape of her neck. Then he unwound the rest of it and reminded the woman to keep her hand at her chest. Doc wrapped the fabric around her waist, upper arm, and her elbow above the exposed bone. He tore the fabric again and knotted it at the small of her back. He checked her pulse, making sure none of the arteries were trapped. There was a pulse. He sighed with relief and motioned toward the truck. They'd only moved a couple of feet, the woman holding onto the truck to stay above water, when the commander met them.

"C'mon," he said. "We need you in the truck now. We've got to get these people to the hospital. We've done the triage; we're ready to go."

"How many?" asked Doc.

"How many what?" replied the commander, herding the woman toward the rear of the truck, holding her in a way that kept her exposed wound out of the water.

"Dead," said Doc.

"A half dozen," said the commander, heading to the truck's open tailgate and ramp at its rear. "Five or six. Not sure. Too busy."

Doc stopped at the back of the truck, the water lapping at his chest. "You're headed to the hospital?"

"Yeah. We know of one that's open, if we can get there. You coming?"

Doc searched the darkness around him. There was water everywhere. The rain was steady. He was exhausted. He was also certain that he couldn't do anybody any good at a hospital. There were already doctors there.

"I'm coming with you for now," he finally said. "But the second I see a rescue boat or another truck heading into the mess, I'm jumping out."

The commander offered him a hand to climb onto the ramp. "Suit yourself. Everybody's gotta do what he thinks is right."

Doc limped up the ramp, the gravity-reducing buoyancy of water now gone and the full weight of his frame on his injured leg taking hold. He reached the top of the ramp and stepped into the crowded, high-walled truck bed. It looked like a MASH unit. Even in the darkness, the emergency crews were tending to the wounded. There were also the dead. They were kept to one side, not piled upon each other, but laid in such a way as to reduce the amount of space they absorbed in the crowded bed.

The ramp retracted behind him and stowed itself underneath the bed floor. The tailgate closed, clanging shut. The truck's engine roared. Over a loudspeaker mounted to the top of the cab near the broken searchlight, the commander called out, "Hold on, people. We're on the move."

Doc grabbed hold of the side, and a moment later the truck lurched into gear and jerked forward in the water. He took turns eyeing the wounded, who were in good care, and the dead. There were equal parts of both.

He glanced around to locate the woman with the broken elbow. He found her sitting in the corner of the truck bed not far from him. She was still holding her arm despite the sling and the wrap that limited its mobility.

Using the bed wall to steady himself, he worked his way to her side. She smiled at him and thanked him for his help.

"You are very brave," he said.

She shook her head and touched the side of his face with her hand.

CHAPTER 13

April 5, 2026
New Orleans, Louisiana

Dub couldn't walk anymore. The water was too deep now. He was swimming, dog-paddling actually, to keep his head above the surface. He was close to Keri's now, almost certain he'd made the correct series of turns to get back to her street. Now he had to try to identify the neighboring homes he'd seen only a couple of times to guide his path. The problem was twofold: it was dark, and the homes were flooded such that it was hard to know which was which.

He kept spitting as he swam, trying to keep from swallowing the nasty combination of floodwater and incessant rain. His neck and ear pulsed with the after sting of the ant bites. His mouth was bleeding after a floating stick caught him in the face. His body was battered. Still, Dub's resolve was fueled by the urge to find his girlfriend. He couldn't be sure she was still home. He hoped she wasn't home. He wanted her safe and dry somewhere.

Yet as he kicked and pulled himself closer to her home, he sensed in his gut she was there and she was in trouble. He tried not to let his focus stray to the what-ifs and could-bes. He needed to deal in facts.

He pulled and kicked. Pulled and kicked. He was alone in an

endless river bordered on either side by empty, flooded houses. Pull. Kick. Pull. Kick.

Not far from him he heard a splash. It wasn't something falling into the water. It sounded like it was bubbling from underneath it.

Dub stopped swimming. He treaded water, his legs moving as if he were bicycling underwater. He moved his cupped hands under the surface repeatedly, scanning the water around him, searching. The only thing helping him see in the dark was the faint yellow light of a streetlamp that was somehow still lit.

He held his breath, hoping to hear the noise again. Just when he thought he'd imagined it, he heard it again.

Having nothing to lose, he swam toward the noise. As he approached, he realized the house in front of him, feet away, was Keri's. The water was nearly up to the eaves, not much lower than its roof. He looked around him, and then, without thinking any more about it, he dove underwater.

He thought he remembered a window on that side of the house, Keri's parents' bedroom. He dove, kicking and pulling toward where he thought it might be. Maybe he could open it and get inside the house. He could search it in the dark. His impromptu plan instantly changed when in front of him, beneath him, he saw a person struggling, thrashing against something that was keeping the swimmer underwater.

He approached carefully at first, wary of being held underwater by someone panicked, desperate, and on the verge of drowning. He widened his eyes, trying to focus. He could now tell the person was a woman, and her pant leg was caught on the window ledge. She was reaching behind her, her face turned away from Dub.

The current took hold of the woman and slammed her sideways against the house. She kept working to free herself. She struggled, wrestling with her pants at her waist. She unbuttoned her pants, yanked them down, and started kicking them from her body. She couldn't do it. They were too tangled. Dub saw her face.

It was Keri.

Dub fought the current and used every bit of remaining energy to reach her. He slowed next to her, unsure if she knew he was there, and yanked her free of the pants. He grabbed her under her arms. He gripped tightly, pulling her upward as he kicked for both of them. They broke the surface, drifting from the house in the current toward a fence. Keri was gulping air now as she floated in his hands. She spat and coughed.

Dub was behind her now, holding her on his hip as he struggled to keep them both above water. His lungs burned and his arms and legs felt heavy.

Keri blew out water from her flapping lips. "Dub?" she said breathlessly. "Dub? Is that you?"

"Yeah," said Dub, rank water spilling into his mouth when he opened it. "It's me."

He sputtered and gripped her more tightly. Keri was kicking now, helping him propel them. They were underneath the dim yellow streetlight. She laid her head back as if to stare into the light.

In the near distance he spotted their destination: a two-story house that might provide a break from the rising water until they could get help. If help was coming.

He swung her around onto his side when they reached the fence. It was flapping, straining under the force of water against it. Dub brought Keri's hand around to grab the top of the lone fence post sitting firmly above the water.

She grabbed it and Dub worked himself to the other side of the post's decorative top. He treaded water behind her and the section of fence, which served as a sort of dam against the current.

Finally, he was able to look at her. He wanted to smile as much as he wanted to cry. He didn't let either happen. Now wasn't a time for emotion.

"You're hurt," Keri said, her eyes drifting across his face. "Are you okay?"

Dub didn't know where to begin. He had questions for her too. How had she managed to escape the flooded house, only to get stuck at the windowsill? He noticed that the rain had stopped. It was eerily silent without the white noise of heavy drops on rushing water.

"Let's talk about this when we get out of the water," he said. "The house behind me is two stories. As fast as this water is rising, I think we can navigate our way there and we won't have to climb much."

She looked past him toward the house. "You think we can make it?"

They didn't have a choice. He couldn't keep swimming much longer. Of course, he didn't tell her that. He nodded.

"Okay," she said at the moment the wavering fence gave in to the current.

Dub reached for her, grabbing her again with a grip tighter than he intended. She winced.

"I'm sorry," he said. Keri didn't react. He couldn't tell if she'd heard him.

They floated closer to the house and away from the broken fence. Then she kicked. Her feet brushed against his legs under the water before she grabbed at his shirt. He welcomed her into his body as a collection of sharp tree branches scraped their bodies and trapped them in a swirl of water that threatened to pull them under.

"We're okay," Dub said, spitting. "You okay? I'm okay."

"I'm okay," she said, and they somehow floated free of the swirling current and closer to the house.

The rain began again. It was somehow colder now, the drops heavier. They made more noise than before. Or maybe, Dub considered, they were the same but sounded louder because of their momentary absence. His love for Keri was certainly amplified by the moments they spent apart and then reconnected, this one more than any other. Her body, cold as it was against his, fit. It was comforting amidst the chaos, the rush of water, and the darkness that it brought with it.

Something hard banged against Dub's back. He arched it against the jolt of pain.

"Hang on," he said to her, his voice raspy. They spun around in the current, which was pushing them sideways now.

"Hang on," he repeated and tightened his grip. Something else brushed their legs. The sunken threat, whatever it was, passed, and they floated freely. Their bodies spun back and the black water carried them closer to the house.

The rain dimmed everything, giving whatever he could see a smudged appearance. The new moon above provided virtually no light, and the farther they drifted from the streetlamp, the darker their surroundings became.

Keri shuddered against him and coughed again. Then she wriggled from his grasp and her body convulsed. Dub tried adjusting his grasp to keep her against his body, but she slipped free. In a moment she was underwater. Dub reached forward in the water, trying to catch her. Before the panic welled, she resurfaced at his side. She was shaking her head and coughing. Dub reached for her, and Keri took hold of his shirt.

She shrieked, gargling the remnant water in her mouth. Dub wrapped his arm around her again. She shivered, her body trembling now, her breathing heavy. He swore he could feel her pulse against him.

"You okay?" he asked. "Can you make it?"

They were drifting faster now, bobbing up and down in the current that brought them closer to the house. The speed would make reaching the house more difficult. He'd have less time to maneuver.

They were approaching it, but their targeting was off. Dub kicked his legs and used his free arm to spin them, to shift them closer to the house along the edge of the current that seemed as if it had somewhere to be.

They were closer. Closer. And then, at the last moment before they drifted beyond the house, they twirled away from the speed of it and Dub managed to slow them. He backed them to the edge of the composite roof. Both of them slammed against it, and Dub held onto it with his free hand. He pulled Keri onto the roof, inadvertently dragging her bare legs across its rough surface. Then he hoisted himself next to her. They were atop the porch, which was easily six inches or more underwater.

"Wrap your arms around a gutter downspout," he instructed her. "That will keep the current from catching you if you lose your perch."

She blankly hugged the downspout.

Dub moved from that roof to a window ledge and then climbed another three feet above the rising water that already covered the porch's roofing tiles. Once on the second story of the house, he reached down to Keri, spreading his fingers.

"Keri, take my hand."

She didn't respond. She appeared dazed. It was obvious to Dub even in the dark and the downpour that she was almost catatonic.

"C'mon," he implored. "Take my hand. You can't stay there. Keri!"

When he shouted her name and water splashed across her face, she came to life. She let go of the downspout with one hand and reached with the other. Dub couldn't grasp her from that distance. They were inches apart and it might as well have been miles.

She tried again and failed. Finally, at his coaxing, Keri inched herself to her feet, using the downspout to balance herself against the flow of water. She shifted her weight, sliding and almost losing her balance twice as she made her way around to the other side of the downspout where Dub awaited her. When she slipped a third time, Dub extended his reach as far as he could till they connected. Their hands grabbed each other and he lifted her upward. She used something to launch herself the final distance upwards, and they collapsed together on the second-floor roof, her body falling onto his.

They lay there for what felt like so long, the rain hitting their faces, their heaving chests, their tired limbs. Dub closed his eyes, resting his mind for a split second before resuming the arduous task of devising a plan to rescue them both.

Keri shifted her weight and rolled atop him, placing her lips on his. He could taste the salt. He inhaled her familiar, intoxicating scent despite the layers of floodwater and sweat and mud. Her cold hands gently touched the sides of his face, her wrinkled fingertips caressing his cheeks.

"I love you," she said before rolling back onto her side. His heart pounded in his chest, a mixture of adrenaline, fear, and his overwhelming love for Keri.

"We can't stay here long," he said. "The water is still rising. The rain isn't letting up. If somebody doesn't rescue us, we're screwed."

He immediately thought better of what he'd said. Keri's face squeezed with concern.

"I shouldn't have said that," he told her. "We'll be okay. Somebody will get to us before the water does."

Keri exhaled loudly. "It's okay. You meant it. It's okay to say it. I'm not some delicate flower from whom you have to keep the grim reality of things."

"I know," said Dub, "but I shouldn't have said it like that. Especially after what we just went through."

They were facing each other now, the rain dripping down their noses and across their cheeks and foreheads. Dub sensed they were both oblivious to the rain. She locked eyes with him in a way that sent a buzzing sensation through his head and chest.

"What did we just go through?" she asked. "What happened back there? How did you find me?"

"Tell me first what happened in the house," he said. A lump welled in his throat. He tried to swallow against it. "I shouldn't have left you. I don't know what I would have—"

"Don't," she said. "It's not your fault. You were trying to help your…wait…where is Barker? Where is that girl he hooked up with?"

Dub shook his head. "I don't know. I found them. They were at the store. But we got separated."

Keri leaned up on one elbow, her eyes focused on Dub's. He had trouble distinguishing amongst the rain, the remnant floodwater, and what he thought might be tears welling in her eyes. "Are they okay? What do you mean you got separated?"

"I lost the rental car," Dub said. "It got flooded. I started swimming. I found them at the store. There were guys with a boat, and they agreed to take the boat to get you. We tipped over, I fell out, and I lost track of them."

Dub's throat tightened. His mind raced. He went to those dark places, the worst possible outcomes that plague pessimists or realists.

He wasn't either of those. He was too young for those labels, too idealistic. But as a psychology major, as someone who chose to analyze pain and ecstasy and who wanted to swim with demons, he was predisposed to finding the lowest possible depths before working back to the surface.

Keri rolled onto her back and stared at the milky black sky, then closed her eyes, bathing in the rain. A stiff breeze blew across the roof. Dub felt it slice through his wet clothes and saw it pimple Keri's body.

"I wish I had something to warm you," he said softly. "You're shivering."

Without opening her eyes or changing the expression on her face, she moved her hand onto Dub's and squeezed.

Dub closed his eyes too. His pulse hadn't slowed, but his body was heavy. It was like he was wearing lead clothing. He listened to the beat of the rain, the whoosh of the wind, and the rush of a violent current mere feet beneath them.

He thought about the times he'd seen flooding on television as a child. He remembered seeing the torrents of water that ripped through Ellicott City, Maryland; St. Louis, Missouri; and Asheville, North Carolina.

Then his mind went somewhere it hadn't gone in a long time. It drifted to the night Hurricane Harvey flooded his neighborhood and sent his family scrambling into the flooded streets. It was the end of summer. School had started. It stopped when the rains came, when they wouldn't go away, when they dumped more than fifty inches of rain on a city that was equipped for half that much in a three-day stretch.

Dub had long ago suppressed the memories of the night that changed the course of his life. He'd capped the memories in a bottle and shoved it in the back of the bottom shelf out of sight. But it was there again, open and in front of him. A shiver rippled through his body as the images flashed in his mind.

That night was the reason he'd always slept restlessly since. That night was the one that had him escaping the murky, cold bayou water on his father's shoulders. That night was the one that precipitated months of uncertainty, of his parents' constant arguing over money and debt and red tape. That night was, until now, the worst of his life.

After wading through that dank water for more than an hour, futilely trying to find dry land, a pair of men from Louisiana had rescued his family in their small boat. They'd been with what was called the Cajun Navy, a group of volunteers who'd descended upon Houston to help rescue flooded survivors. Those two men were ahead of the curve. They'd positioned themselves near a bayou ahead of that Saturday night and they'd saved his life.

Dub remembered it smelling like raw shrimp and gasoline. He remembered the men wearing large fish hooks clipped to the brims of their worn baseball caps. They spoke with thick rolling accents that sometimes made it difficult for Dub to understand what they were saying as they navigated the streets-turned-canals with a spot beam and a tireless vigor to help strangers.

The memories were there in full color now. They took him from one disaster and dropped him chin deep in another.

As the rain hit his face now, trickling into his nose and draining from the corners of his eyes, he remembered the boaters' faces. He recalled how supportive they'd been, how they'd offered food and towels, and how they'd given him some cheap goggles to keep the water out of his eyes.

He could hear their voices in the dark, calling to his family as their outboard-powered skiff gurgled toward them. They'd called out, promising help, safety, and dry land.

"Dub," they'd called. "Dub, is that you? Dub, we're here. We're coming."

Wait. He opened his eyes. The voices didn't belong to the Cajun Navy some eight and a half years earlier. The voices were more familiar than that. And they were echoing in this world, not a previous one through which he'd already lived.

"Dub! Wave if that's you."

"Do you hear that?" Keri asked.

They wiped the rain from their faces, staring into the dark, toward the streetlamp that gave the dim glow of yellow light.

"I hear it," he said, now certain it wasn't a dream. It wasn't part of his trip down memory canal. It was here. It was now.

Keri's narrowed gaze turned to Dub. "Is that—"

"Barker," said Dub. "It's Barker."

Dub sat up straight on the sloping roof. He cupped his hands at his face and yelled, "Over here! We're over here!"

His voice was absorbed by the rain. He called again, then a third time. The dark shape of a boat moved from the light. It was in the darkness now, a purplish shadow fighting the push of the water.

"We see you!" Barker called back. "We're coming. Stay there."

Dub and Keri stood. Hand in hand they stepped to the edge of the roof, above the overflowing gutter that pulsed water onto the tiles before it dropped back into the gutter and spilled into the rising water below.

The water was only a couple of inches from the gutter now. It was reaching for it. It was touching it and pulling back for a stronger surge forward. It reminded Dub of an incoming tide taking nibbles at the hand-constructed, compacted walls around a sandcastle. With each surge, a bit more of it was underwater.

"Do you see them?" asked Keri. "I think I see them over there."

Dub followed the line of her pointing finger and saw the shape of the boat. In the distance, beneath the pattering rain, the groan and whine of a small engine puttered.

"That's them," he said.

The current was shifting. It was faster now, if that was possible.

How is that possible?

As they had drifted precariously close to missing the roof of the house on which they now stood, he worried the boat and its undersized motor might not be able to navigate its way close enough to get them.

Yet it moved closer, its elongated shape growing. Dub could make out the figures of people on board the boat now. There were four people. Five? They were sitting low against the frame of the boat. One of them was waving his or her arms. It was probably Barker.

"We're coming!" he repeated. "Hang tight."

"Where would we *go?*" Keri murmured. "What does he *think* we're doing?"

The tension in her voice cut through the rain and the cold. She stood there shivering in her underwear and a T-shirt, her arms wrapped tight around her own body.

Dub shifted his weight toward her and put an arm around her shoulder, then moved it to her waist, drawing her more closely to him. Her body was rigid and trembling at the same time.

With his free arm, he waved back at Barker. "We're right here! On the roof. We're not going anywhere."

The boat was within fifty yards now. It was struggling. The bow pitched up and down as the dark figure in the back of the boat tried to fight the current. The boat appeared to be moving diagonally, but it was powering straight ahead.

Dub inched closer to the edge of the roof. His feet were at the gutter. Keri's toes curled around it. Their bodies were ready before their minds were. Dub resisted the instinctive urge to jump to the boat despite its distance from them.

The motor's effort was louder now. The voices on board the boat rose above the rain. Dub could make out four people. Two of the men were Louis and Frank, the owners of the boat. Barker was there, and next to him was Gem. Even from that distance, he saw the exhaustion on their faces, the stress that stretched them long and deepened the creases at their foreheads and around their mouths.

They were close now. Twenty feet. Ten. Five. Dub put his hands on Keri's hips and stepped behind her. She would go first.

Then, short of the roof, the boat spun in the current, its bow facing away now. The motor was spitting and churning water toward the spot where Dub and Keri stood, their bodies itching to jump.

Louis called out, "It's getting away from me. Current's too strong. I can't get closer."

"What should we do?" Keri asked. "I say we jump."

Dub shook his head. "That's suicide. We miss the boat and that's it."

The motor gurgle and sputtered. The pilot yelled out again, "I can't get closer!" The boat was drifting farther away. Six feet. Seven. Eight.

"We gotta jump," Keri said again. "We can't stay here. We're dead if we don't."

The rain fell harder against his head. It pounded like tiny hammers working away at his scalp. The boat was drifting, its motor no match for the current.

"I'm jumping," Keri said. "Let's go."

Before Dub could stop her, she leapt from the edge of the roof and splashed into the water, landing halfway between where Dub stood and the motor, and disappeared into the wash of current.

Without thinking, Dub jumped, landing in the current and dropping just under the surface. His head popped up without fully submerging. The rush of the water filled his ears. The cold stabbed at his chest. The back of the boat was straight ahead. But where was Keri?

"Keri!" he shouted, trying to move forward, to use the current to take him to the boat. "Keri!"

He spun around, facing the house as the water pulled him away from it. He bobbed, and water filled his mouth. He choked, coughed, and spat it out. He was churning his arms and legs, working to fight the water and acquiesce to its power at the same time.

There was the boat. The far-off haze of the streetlamp.

The rain. The boat. The house. The haze. The motor.

And then, Keri.

There she was, at the side of the boat. She'd made it. Somebody was pulling her aboard. She was alive. She was in the boat.

Dub ducked his face into the water and kicked his legs as hard as he could. He swung his arms like a windmill, churning the water as he swam the few feet left between him and the boat. He lifted his head, spotted his target, lowered it again, and swam. He blew air from his nostrils, his arms and legs working. The boat pivoted.

Keri was facing him now. She was leaning over the side of the boat next to Barker. Both of them were leaning over with extended hands. Dub was certain the boat would tip and send all of them into the flood.

Barker grabbed his wrist; Keri took hold of his other hand. He kicked. Dub lifted himself with their help and collapsed onto the floor of the skiff. He heard his heartbeat above the pinging of rain on the aluminum hull.

It took him a couple of minutes to gather the strength to sit up.

By then, Louis had better control of the boat. They were moving with the current, staying away from debris and large structures.

Keri threw herself at him. He fell back, her weight on him. She was crying.

"I'm sorry," she said, kissing his face. "I'm sorry. I just—"

"You just *jumped*," said Dub. "It's okay. We made it."

"You made it all right," said Barker. "And Keri jumping like that was totally badass. It was like when your favorite player takes a three, and you're like, 'No, no, no!' Then it goes in and you're like, 'Yes, yes, yes!'"

Keri moved herself off Dub, but stayed close to him. They were on the center bench now. Barker introduced everyone to Keri.

"Thank you," she said. "You saved us."

"We ain't saved nothing yet," said Louis. "We're riding with the current and trying to find dry land. That's all."

"How did you find us?" asked Dub. "I thought the boat capsized. I thought you were in the water."

Barker shook his head. "No. Almost. When you fell out, you were gone like that." Barker snapped his fingers. "We looked and looked, and we couldn't find you. We thought…"

Barker looked at his feet. His hands were clasped together, one thumb rubbing the other. He ran a hand through his thinning hair. His premature balding was all the more apparent when his hair was wet and slicked against his head.

"How did you find us though?" Dub asked, moving past the uncomfortable, rain-draped silence.

Barker looked up and offered a thin smile, motioning to the woman sitting next to him. "Gem. It was her idea."

Gem demurred. She shrugged. "It made sense. We knew you were coming to find your girlfriend. If you were okay, this is where you'd be. If you weren't, at least we might find her."

"How did you know where my parents live?" Keri asked.

"I remembered the street," said Barker. "Louis and Frank knew where it was. We took a shot in the dark."

Dub thanked them all again. So did Keri. Then Dub said to Louis, "I thought you weren't good with street names."

"I ain't," said Louis, working the stick to control the direction of the jon boat. "But every once in a while, I kinda know a street. Got lucky."

That was an understatement. Dub shook his head and chuckled in disbelief.

"What now?" asked Louis. "Anybody else to save? We ain't got nothing better to do."

Keri didn't hesitate. "My family," she said. "They're all together. My parents can't swim."

"You think you can guide us there?" asked Louis.

Keri nodded.

"Then let's find a way there," he said. "How many of them? Two?"

"Four," said Keri. "My parents and my sisters."

Louis exchanged glances with Frank. "It's gonna get tight, but I think we'll manage. Hold on, everybody. Rescue round two."

"I hope they're okay," Keri said worriedly.

"They will be," Dub said, not sure of it at all.

CHAPTER 14

April 5, 2026
New Orleans, Louisiana

Lane Turner adjusted the damp and mildewed life vest strap at his waist. It was digging into the underside of his ribs. Lane thought about unclipping it and taking it off, but his host aboard the rescue boat had insisted he, his field producer, and photographer wear them. He worked his neck from one side to the other then let go of the vest, focusing on the conversation the pilot was having with his producer.

The rescue boat had picked them up minutes after Lane's attempted rescue of the drowning woman. They'd agreed to keep them aboard until there were too many people who needed rescuing. At that point, they'd have to catch another ride.

It was a risk, given the rapidly deteriorating conditions. The producer had hedged; Lane hadn't. Now they were trolling for survivors north of the French Quarter in an area called Mid City. They'd gotten a call about a family of four needing help.

There were already six aboard a boat that could hold a dozen easily. Lane and his crew, the pilot and his crew. They worked for the city.

The captain, a man named Bellau, was telling the producer about their work as he navigated the boat from street to street. There were colored lights around the exterior of the boat's hull that illuminated its footprint in the water.

"We're part of the city's Search and Rescue Marine Unit," said Bellau in a briny-sounding voice. "New Orleans Police maintains a fleet of thirty-five boats. We're tasked with searching, rescuing, and recovering people lost in any body of water located in Orleans Parish. Sometimes we work with the Coast Guard. Sometimes we're on our own."

A radio crackled, hailing the captain. He held up a finger to the producer and answered the call. The boat listed to one side and then leveled. The large motor on the back spat and chortled, blending the water behind it, propelling the heavy craft forward where the captain told it to go.

"Bellau," he said. "SRMU 29. Go ahead."

The call on the other end was garbled and riddled with static. The rain pounding on the deck made it hard for Lane to hear every word, but he caught the gist of it. Some of the pumps had failed, as had some of the newer, supposedly stronger walls built in the last twenty years, post-Katrina. The call was warning that rougher water might be coming. More pumps were on the verge of quitting under the increased load.

"Understood," Bellau replied. "Update me when you have new information, SRMU 29 Over." He ended the call.

The captain inched the throttle forward. The bow lurched upward. Lane grabbed the side to prevent himself from slipping backward.

"We need to speed it up," said Bellau. "We're running out of time."

"The pumps?" asked Lane. "They failed?"

"Some," said Bellau. "Others will soon."

"I thought they fixed all of that," said the producer. "They rebuilt everything."

"Twenty billion dollars." Bellau had both of his hands on the helm now. "Three hundred and fifty miles of pumps, levees, flood walls, and gates. They circle the city. They're supposed to make us an island, high and dry."

"But they're not," said Lane.

Bellau shook his head. "They're not."

"Why?" asked the producer.

"They were supposed to be built to withstand a one-hundred-year flood, meaning that they would hold back the kind of flood that has a one percent chance of happening. Old Mayor Landrieu wanted ten-thousand-year protection. You know, like they have in the Netherlands. That's what he wanted back then. Didn't get it. Instead, we got stuff that Katrina would have eaten for lunch."

"That's it?" asked Lane. "That sounds ridiculous. Why?"

The captain shrugged. "We still on camera?"

"Yes," the producer answered.

"Then I don't have a comment," he said. "Those decisions were made way above my pay grade. I just do what I'm told. Right now we've got to find some people and help them before we can't."

The producer signaled to the photographer to stop rolling, and all of them took their seats. They bounded against the chop of the water as Bellau motored closer to the address dispatch had given them at the outset of the mission.

Bellau eased the throttle back, and the boat slowed to a near float. The motor rumbled more softly, the water gurgling behind it. The boat floated past what Lane thought at first was a thick tree branch, but when it nearly bumped the hull, he saw it was a body. It was the seventh they'd seen. Seven bodies. If there were seven already they'd seen, he wondered how many more were under the surface. How many more wouldn't reveal themselves until the water receded? His producer had mentioned to him that more than eighteen hundred people had died during Hurricane Katrina. More than one hundred had died during Hurricane Sandy. Harvey killed more than eighty in Texas. There was no telling what kind of havoc this flash flooding might cause. There was virtually no warning, no way to get out. The city's efforts had clearly been too little, too late.

"We're here," he said, pointing at a street sign that was barely above eye level. "Keep your eyes out, fellas."

The two other rescue workers took positions on either edge of the boat near the bow. They shone handheld spotlights out at the houses lining either side of the wide canal.

"We can't see addresses," one of them called back to Captain Bellau. "The water's too high."

The rain had slowed to a sprinkle now, and the sounds of swamp animals croaked and chirped. The air was chilled from the misty rain, but it was thick with humidity. The lights scanned the tops of houses on either side. They were empty.

"They're gonna be on a roof," said Bellau. "That's what the call said. We're on the right block."

Lane motioned for the photographer to start rolling. He shouldered the camera and slid his right hand inside its protective weather gear. The red tally light atop the viewfinder illuminated, and Lane knew the photographer was recording.

He was holding a stick microphone, its wireless transmitter wrapped in a plastic baggie and duct tape. He spoke into it, the top of the mesh almost touching his lips.

"You hear me okay?" he asked.

The photographer nodded. "Good to go. Gimme a level."

Lane lowered the mic a bit, holding it at his chest. "Mic check," he said. "Chickety check. Chickety check. Two, four, six, eight, ten. Sibilance. Give me a chance. Sibilance. Chickety check."

"We're good," said the photographer.

Lane caught the field producer rolling her eyes. "You doing a stand-up for the morning show?"

"For whatever," said Lane. "We could feed this back live and they could post to the web or the app. Doesn't matter to me."

"We don't have a good enough signal right now," said the

producer. "We could send it with a delay. Let the system store it and then forward it. That might work."

"Let's do it," said Lane. "Just follow me. Whatever I talk about, you try to find. Leave the light off and gain up. It'll give it an…ethereal look."

The photographer nodded. The producer protested. Lane assured her it would look good despite the lack of light and the grainy picture quality induced by adding gain, or extra pixels of white, to the lowly lit images. She relented and checked her watch so as to time the hit. Lane counted down from three.

"This is Lane Turner here in New Orleans," he began, looking into the lens. He was speaking in a deeply affected, hushed tone. "I know it's hard to see me, friends. But we're doing that intentionally. We're currently on a search and rescue mission with NOPD. They've given us a spot on their boat as they search for a desperate family of four."

He motioned toward Captain Bellau, and the photographer panned to reveal the captain piloting the boat. Bellau ignored the camera. He had one hand on the wheel and the other on the throttle.

"We understand the family called 9-1-1 and reported to dispatchers they were on the roof of their home. We're on their street now, having come here from the French Quarter. No sign of them just yet."

The camera panned toward one of the two men at the front of the boat, using the light from his spotlight to enhance the picture. The producer held up her hand in the shape of a C, indicating he'd spoken for thirty seconds. In the studio, the time cue was used as a countdown to reflect how much time was left in a segment. In the field, Lane liked to use it to know how long he'd been talking.

"We've learned that the flooding is aggravated by the failure of pumps that, when installed years ago, were intended to stop what's happening now. That clearly didn't work. And the water rises. The calls for help keep coming, if people have access to working phones, but it's tough to get to them."

He paused again and let the camera do the work, showing the men at the bow scanning the water with their lights. The sounds of the reptiles and insects grew louder as the rain softened now to a fine mist. The producer held up her index finger, indicating the hit was a minute in length.

"Maybe the stop in rainfall, however temporary, will help," Lane said. "Stem the tide, so to speak, and give first responders like the men with whom we're traveling the extra time they need to find those in danger. We'll have another update for you soon. Be sure to check back here on our website and on the Southland news app every chance you get. Reporting for now from New Orleans, Louisiana, I'm Lane—"

"Help!" The call was sharp, desperate. It was a child's voice.

The echo off the houses and its carry across the surface of the floodwater made it hard to pinpoint the direction. The camera was rolling, the photographer searching the edges of their lines of sight.

"Help!" the voice repeated. "I'm on my roof. I'm over here."

The lights scanned the darkness, searching the trees, crisscrossing each other across the wide expanse of flowing water. Captain Bellau stopped the engine. He kept his hands on the wheel, moving the rudder to keep the boat away from debris.

The current carried the boat in the same direction and nearly straight down the center of the canal filling the distance between the equally spaced roofs on both sides. Occasionally, the searchlights would bounce off the windows of an exposed second story.

"This is Ken Bellau with New Orleans Police," the captain called out, his salty voice echoing into the blackness beyond the scope of the lights. "We're here to help you. Where are you?"

"On my roof." The voice was so high pitched its owner couldn't have been more than seven or eight years old. "I'm on my roof. I'm by myself."

Bellau keyed the mic on his radio. It squawked and he spoke into it. "This is Bellau. SRMU 29. What's the name on the call slip? We're in Mid City."

The radio crackled and dispatch responded, *"Williams."*

"Thank you." Bellau called out, "What's your name?"

"Kendrick," said the voice, through what sounded like chattering teeth.

Lane couldn't tell where the boy's voice originated. It sounded like it was everywhere and nowhere all at once.

"Kendrick Williams?"

"Yes!" cried the boy. "Kendrick Williams."

"How old are you?"

"Six."

"Where's your daddy? How about your momma?"

There was a long pause. Bellau maneuvered past the canopy of a tree that was half sunken in floodwater. The camera was focused over Bellau's shoulder now, trying to capture what the captain could see. It wasn't much. Beams of light died in the surrounding darkness not more than fifty yards from the boat.

Then Kendrick answered, a whimper that hung in the air with the humidity and the mist. "I don't know."

"There," said one of the men at the bow. "Over there. About ten o'clock. I think I see something through those trees."

"Get your light on it," said Bellau. "Focus on it. Both of you."

Both beams trained on the cluster of trees. Bellau started the engine and moved the boat, pushing the throttle forward gently. The boat eased into gear and jumped against the current as he turned it nearly perpendicular to the rush of water.

"I can't see it," said Bellau, increasing the speed another notch. "I've got to get around those trees."

Once he'd positioned the boat to the side of the cluster, he cut the engine again. The boat drifted backward, trying to find its way into the current; then he swung the wheel around to get a clear shot at what he thought the lights might show him.

At the edge of the beams' reach was a tiny figure against the outline of a roof. It was all shades of gray, varying depths of darkness.

"Wave your hands," he called out.

The figure waved his hands.

"Are the lights in your face, Kendrick? Can you see the lights?"

"Yes. I see them! I see them! Please help me, mister."

"We're coming, Kendrick. I'm going to crank the engine. I won't be able to hear you. Just stay where you are."

Lane motioned to his photographer. The field producer started her watch. The engine rumbled to life, churning the water, moving the boat toward the boy on the roof.

"We've found a survivor," said Lane. "He's six years old, and he's stranded on the roof of his house alone. He told us he doesn't know where his parents are. His name is Kendrick Williams."

The camera moved from Lane toward the house. The spots provided enough light to give the picture a grainy glow. The producer held up a closed fist, the signal for fifteen seconds having elapsed.

"We're getting close," said Lane. "The rain isn't more than a fine mist now. The current here is incredibly strong, however. At times it's as if we're on one of the raging rapids rides at a theme park."

The camera shifted to show the wash of water off the boat's starboard side. The red and white lights underwater gave the wash a bloody appearance in person but more pinkish on digital video. The producer held up her hand cupped in the shape of a C.

"We're getting close to the child now," said Lane. "Captain Ken Bellau and his crew are intent on rescuing him. The call came in more than an hour ago. It's taken us that long to navigate the rough waters to this point."

The camera focused on the roof. The dark shapes drew into focus under the glare of the handheld spotlight. One of the lights was off, as a first responder readied himself to pull Kendrick to safety. He was balanced on the bow, crouching, held in place by a hook and line that kept him attached to the boat should something go wrong.

The line was taut as the officer held out his hands, wiggling his fingers to welcome Kendrick aboard. He was coaxing the child to move from his safe perch inches above the rising water that lapped at his feet on the gently sloping roof.

Kendrick squinted against the bright spotlight that kept him in view. He wore the broad smile of someone too close to an open oven. He was dressed in cotton pajamas that clung to his thin body. He sat cross-legged on the roof, rocking gently. But Kendrick wasn't getting up. He wasn't warming to the rescuer's outstretched arms.

"You're going to have to go get him," said Bellau. The camera moved to put him in frame as he called out to the child, "Kendrick, buddy, I need you to stand up and walk toward the boat."

"I'm scared," said Kendrick, shielding his eyes from the light. "It's hard to see. I don't want to fall in the water like my daddy and momma."

"Turn off the light," instructed Bellau.

The officer holding the light flipped a switch, and they were again bathed in darkness. Lane widened his eyes, trying to adjust. He spoke softly into the microphone, as much out of respect for the work of the first responders as for the heightened sense of urgency it gave his report.

"We're close to Kendrick now," he said. "The poor child—alone, cold, and frightened—is too scared to move from his place atop the roof of his family home. Water is everywhere. It's dark, it's dangerous, and it very well may have taken the lives of his mother and father. I'll be silent now as we watch this unfold together."

The producer gave him a thumbs-up, and then all eyes were on Kendrick. The boy had risen to his feet. His tiny body trembled, his pajamas tracing his soft belly and spindly arms. He took one hesitant step toward the officer, who had one foot out of the boat and the other ankle-deep on the roof.

Kendrick took a second step. And a third. By the fourth, he had his tiny hands outstretched, grabbing for the officer, who swept him up in his arms and then quickly slid back into the boat.

The man kept his arms around Kendrick's shivering body. Kendrick buried his head in the man's chest. Lane couldn't tell if the child was sobbing or trembling. It was likely both.

"Is there anyone else here, Kendrick?" asked Bellau. "Is anyone else with you?"

Lane recalled the captain saying the call slip indicated four survivors on the roof. He glanced back at the empty roof serving as little more than a shrinking island perch for an orphaned boy.

"No," Kendrick said meekly. Lane wouldn't have understood him if not for the adamant shake of his head. "They're gone. They fell in the water."

Bellau had the boat in reverse, backing the boat away from the roof and back toward the main current.

"Who is they?" he asked with his hands on the wheel. "Who fell in?"

"My brother first," said Kendrick, his teeth chattering. "He slipped. My momma dove in to get him. Then my daddy tried to get them both."

Nobody, not even the captain, knew what to say. The camera was still rolling. This private, emotional moment for a child who'd just lost everything he'd ever known was being recorded for transmission to televisions, smartphones, tablets, websites, and apps all over the world. Lane had no doubt it would go viral.

This is what happens in disasters, he thought to himself for the first time in his long career.

This was what really happened. The cameras were rolling when people experienced the worst moments of their lives. They were recording history, sure. But sometimes that history was incredibly personal. A wave of nausea crept into Lane's gut.

He nudged his photographer, who had the camera pointed at the boy, and whispered, "Turn it off."

The producer whipped her head toward him, her eyebrows angled down with confused anger. "What?" she asked under her breath.

"Stop rolling," said Lane, making a "cut" sign by whipping his hand back and forth in front of his neck. "Cut it off."

The photographer hesitated and offered the same, albeit less aggressive, glare as the field producer. He kept rolling.

"Why?" mouthed the producer.

"This is too much," said Lane. "It's too much."

The field producer searched his eyes. Her glare softened and she motioned for the photographer to turn off the camera. It was then, unprompted, that Kendrick started talking again.

"I cried," he said. "I cried a lot. I asked them where they went. I said their names. I yelled. I'm not supposed to yell, but I did. I asked them to come back."

Nobody else in the boat spoke. Nobody interrupted him or consoled him. They let him talk. It was like the spigot was turned and the words came freely now.

"I asked them to come back," he said, his eyes dancing from person to person. "I was by myself. I don't like being by myself. I don't like the dark. I have a nightlight in my room. It's blue. It helps me sleep."

Lane had never had an affinity for children. He wasn't married and had no plans for a family. His life was his work. He was his job; his job was him. But in this moment, in this profound and raw moment, he wanted to get up from his seat and take the child and hold him. He wanted to cry with Kendrick. He wanted to make the child feel safe. He resisted the urge and swallowed the taste of bile that had crept up into his mouth.

"I couldn't sleep on the roof," Kendrick said. "I tried to sleep. I wanted to sleep. I'm sleepy. But I didn't want to be asleep if Momma came back."

Kendrick sighed and laid his head against the officer who'd pulled him into the boat. Nobody spoke for what felt like hours, but was only minutes. The hum and bubble of the motor churning through the water and the distant sounds of sirens were the only accompaniment for the ride amongst floating and sinking debris.

"We're going to take Kendrick to a shelter," said Bellau. "We're out of service until we get him there."

Bellau didn't mention Lane by name. Lane knew it was directed at him and his crew, though.

"Thanks for the access, Captain," he said, faking a smile. "We'll get off at the shelter and leave you to your work. We've got enough here."

"Suit yourself," said Bellau. "It's going to be a long night for all of us either way."

CHAPTER 15

April 5, 2026
Los Angeles, California

"You're going to drown yourself," said Danny. "Ease up there. You're not going to run out."

Maggie was lapping up the water in her bowl as if she'd been for a walk in the Mojave Desert. The sound of her tongue curling scoopfuls into her maw and the spray of it onto the linoleum tile flooring let Danny know he'd been away from home too long.

He was squatting next to her, petting her coat as she drank. "Don't drink too much," he warned. "You'll get bloat."

She stopped drinking and looked up at him with her big dark eyes as if she understood him. She licked her chops and then went back to work on the bowl.

He apologized to her again for being gone for most of the day. He didn't like leaving her. He hadn't spent more than a double shift away from her since the day he'd adopted her for twenty-five bucks from a shelter...

He named her Maggie. It was better than Waggie, which was his first thought, because of how much she wagged her tail when he played with her, rubbed her belly, or took her for long, leashless walks in Santa Monica or Malibu. She was a good dog, a protective dog, who Danny knew in his gut would protect him with her life.

He'd protect her with his too. Somewhere in his gut, he felt like he had.

Maggie switched from the water bowl to the one filled with leftover diner scraps. She gobbled them with her snout buried deep in the mixture of bacon, burger bits, French fries, and kitchen grease.

Danny slapped her on her hind end, said, "Clean your dishes when you're finished," and took the few steps it took to cross his efficiency apartment. He found the television remote where he'd left it and punched on the thrift-store thirteen-inch flat panel he'd scored for twenty-five bucks. It wasn't 4k or 5k or whatever the technology was that made newer sets more expensive and ones like his virtually worthless.

"Another man's trash," he'd said to the gum-chomping clerk when buying the set. She'd ignored him and handed him his change.

He plopped onto his bed, a Murphy bed that he could flip up and hide in the wall behind a pair of French doors, and turned up the volume. He was watching a replay of a live report from news anchor Lane Turner.

Turner left his microphone and waded away from his camera to help a woman. It was riveting television. Minutes later, when it was over, a news anchor for a twenty-four-hour cable network referenced the report as being from a Los Angeles television station.

The anchor then talked over images of the flooding in New Orleans, explaining how all but one of the pumps built to withstand flooding and alleviate the pressure on walls and gates had failed. They had been unable to handle the amount of rain that had fallen on the city within hours. Estimates from the National Weather Service put the twenty-four-hour rainfall totals at more than thirty-five inches. The city was a bowl and it was overflowing.

Following the coverage of the flooding, there was an update on the crash of Pacific East Flight 2929. The weather over southwestern Florida had cleared enough that search crews were able to recover the black box only seventy-five miles from the shoreline. They were hopeful it would provide a definitive cause in the crash that had killed everyone on board.

Danny hit the mute button on the television. Maggie looked up from her dish, apparently puzzled by the silence. She'd scooted the bowl with her muzzle from one side of the small kitchen to the other.

"We need to check something," he said to Maggie. "That last story made me remember I have a souvenir from my long, strange conversation with our sworn enemy Derek."

When he said the name, Maggie cocked her head to one side. She licked her nose and returned to the bowl, seeking out the last of the grease.

Danny pulled the voice recorder from his pocket. He clicked a rewind button until an LCD display showed the recorded track number as 1. He pressed play and a timer began at zero. One second. Two seconds. Three. There was a rustling sound and then Derek's familiar voice.

"This is a question and answer session with jail inmate Clint Anthony, booking number 4492302. The time right now is four thirty in the afternoon, Pacific Standard Time, Saturday, June 21, 2025."

Danny calculated on his fingers; the recording was ten months old. What did a jail inmate have to do with Derek and his company? Better yet, what did any of it have to do with him? He pressed play.

"Mr. Anthony," said Derek, *"thank you for agreeing to do the interview. I only have a few questions. I ask you answer them honestly."*

"Who did you say you were with?" asked another voice Danny presumed was Clint Anthony.

"A private research and technology company," said Derek. *"We sponsored some of the psychological testing you underwent in exchange for a reduced sentence."*

"Okay then," said Anthony. *"Ask your questions."*

"Have you been suffering from any headaches?"

"No more than usual."

"What do you mean?" asked Derek. *"Elaborate."*

"I don't know," said Anthony. *"I've had headaches on and off my whole life. Nothing unusual. I guess maybe I have had a few more since I've been locked up."*

"How frequent are they?"

"A couple a week."

"Are they intense?"

"They can be if I don't get down to the infirmary and get some meds. If I get one in the middle of the night, don't catch it quick enough, then it can get bad."

"What about your sleep patterns? Are you getting enough sleep? Are you suffering from any exhaustion? Muscle fatigue?"

Anthony laughed. *"Seriously? I'm in jail. I don't get good sleep. Nobody gets good sleep."*

"Let me rephrase that," said Derek. *"Are you getting less sleep now than before you did the study with us?"*

There was a rustling on the tape, then the sound of metal scraping against concrete. Derek cleared his throat.

"I don't think so," said Anthony. *"Should I be? Getting less sleep, I mean? What did you do in that study? I don't remember taking any drugs."*

"No, no, no," Derek said, chuckling nervously. *"We didn't administer any pharmaceuticals. But yes, it's possible you'd be suffering from mild insomnia."*

"Yeah," said Anthony, *"that's not happening. I'm fine."*

"Good."

"There is something, though…" Anthony's voice was softer but somehow louder, as if he'd lowered it but moved closer to the microphone. *"I've had really vivid nightmares."*

There was silence for a moment. Derek cleared his throat again. *"Nightmares?"*

"Yeah, like I'm tripping. Like weed and molly and whatever all mixed together. It's that kind of vivid, you know?"

"Tell me about it."

"The dreams are all different. But it's like the end of the world or something. Like the sky is red or black. The Earth is gray and covered in ash. Or it's on fire."

Danny paused the recording and thought about what he'd just heard. He looked over at his dog, who was licking herself on the circular rug at the center of the apartment. Then he touched his neck. He touched his side and felt an ache swell there. It became a jabbing pain, throbbing for a moment before dissipating and leaving his body completely.

His mouth went dry and Danny got up from the bed, crossing the few feet to the kitchen. He pulled a plastic pitcher from the near-empty refrigerator and poured himself a glass of cold water. He guzzled it, trickles of it leaking down his cheeks.

He poured a second glass. Then a third. He was thirsty.

He stood there, leaning against the refrigerator, thinking about the questions Derek had asked him. He wondered what else was on that recorder. Who else had Derek interviewed, and why?

Danny put the glass in the sink then slunk back to his bed. He propped a couple of sagging feather pillows behind his bed, folding them over for support, and pressed play on the recorder.

"You ever read those books about this dude named Marcus Battle?" Clint Anthony asked Derek.

"No."

"Me neither. But I got a cellmate who did. He read all of the books about this guy who lived in Texas after the end of the world. The guy was some ex-military badass who went crazy and killed a bunch of people out of revenge or whatever. Then there's some girl who's like some knife master. She kills people too. A lot of killing. But they're conflicted about it. It's not killing for the sake of it, it's killing to survive. Anyhow, I don't know the whole thing, but I kinda feel like I'm Marcus Battle in these dreams. Like I'm in a wasteland and I'm fighting to survive."

Danny had heard enough. He stopped the playback and wiped the thin veil of sweat blooming on his forehead. He was hot. Suddenly it was hot in his apartment. He pushed himself from the bed again, against the complaint of the worn mattress springs, and found the thermostat. He didn't have a fancy app on his phone to remotely regulate the temperature; he had to do it old school. He ran his finger across the panel, entered a code, and chose sixty-eight degrees Fahrenheit, lowering the target five degrees.

The HVAC system clunked, and a renewed burst of air whooshed through the vent on the wall above his head. He stood there for a moment letting the chill evaporate the sweat before he moved back to the bed.

The television was muted, but images of the flooding filled the screen. Danny tapped the advance button on the digital recorder, randomly choosing track four. It didn't matter, he figured.

The clip began and Derek cleared his throat. *"This is a question and answer session with study participant Gilda Luster. The time right now is nine thirty in the morning, Pacific Standard Time, Friday, October 17, 2025."*

Gilda Luster? Gilda. Gilda. That name rang a bell. He couldn't place it though. Maybe he'd seen it on a ticket at the diner. It was an unusual name, antique even.

"Gilda," said Derek, *"have you been experiencing any episodes of déjà vu?"*

When Gilda spoke, her cadence sounded almost military. It was disciplined and slightly masculine.

"Yes. By that, you mean the sensation I've experienced something before?"

"Yes."

"I have. Two or three times per week."

Danny pictured Gilda with ice blue eyes, eyes that could see through him. He saw her with long hair pulled back tight against her head into a ponytail. She was broad-shouldered and somewhere between athletic and sinewy.

"Tell me about that," said Derek. *"Give me some examples."*

"Well, most recently, I was at the beach. There were crowds there. It was an unusually warm day for October. I remember sweating."

Danny wiped his forehead again with the back of his hand. He picked at his T-shirt. The air was cooler in the apartment but not cool enough.

"The traffic on PCH was bumper to bumper. Cars were honking, their drivers yelling at each other. It wasn't the relaxing day I had planned. I walked down to the surf, letting my feet sink into the sand as the waves washed in and out. The sand was cold. The water was cold. There were storm clouds on the horizon. I think they were storm clouds. They were dark. They seemed pregnant with rain."

"That's a unique description," said Derek. *"Pregnant."*

"I guess."

Danny imagined her narrowing those penetrating eyes and shrugging her muscular shoulders.

"Please proceed," Derek urged.

"The whole scene was somehow familiar. The clouds on the horizon, the crowds on the beach, the stalled traffic on the freeway, the heat. I couldn't place it, but I sensed I'd seen it all before."

There was the sound of scribbling on paper and the clink of liquid spilling over ice cubes in a glass. Danny moved the recorder closer to his ear. Maggie was asleep now on the rug, her back legs kicking as she dreamed. She whimpered, her lips flapping over her teeth.

"Any other examples?" asked Derek. *"Any other times you experienced such a strong sensation?"*

"Yes," said Gilda. *"A couple of months ago I was in the garden."*

"You like to garden?"

"I have to garden. You remember I'm part of a group that is preparing."

"I remember," said Derek. *"You're preppers, people who are stockpiling goods and supplies for the apocalypse."*

"I don't prefer that term, prepper, *but yes. We all know it's only a matter of time before mankind tries to destroy itself. We're planning for that inevitability."*

"You're talking about the OASIS," said Derek. *"A bunker you've built underneath the Getty Mansion."*

"The Getty Villa," she corrected. *"I think the mansion is in your neck of the woods, San Francisco."*

"Yes, you're right. Sorry. But the OASIS is a self-sustaining bunker for your group, right?"

"Not just my group. The plan is to welcome whoever we think might be helpful to our efforts when the time comes. We know not every member will make it to the bunker when it all goes to hell. We'll search for survivors and recruit the ones we need."

"Into the OASIS."

"Yes."

"And what's it stand for?"

"Order of Apocalyptic Survivors In Sync."

"Clever."

"Aren't we getting away from the point?" asked Gilda.

"Sorry again," said Derek. *"But you do you know your involvement is precisely because of the OASIS, right? I think I disclosed that before our first session, before you agreed to take part in the study."*

"I'm aware."

"Tell me about the second déjà vu, the one in the garden."

Danny stopped the playback. He didn't care about another déjà vu. These were the same questions Derek had asked him. There was a pattern there, symptoms of something. Side effects? And the whole idea that there was some underground facility beneath the cliffside Getty Villa sounded ludicrous. It was science fiction.

But wasn't all of it science fiction? The clandestine interrogations, the weblike connections amongst a plane crash and a flood, a jail inmate and a so-called prepper? And somehow he was mixed up in all of it? How could that even be possible?

He'd never agreed to a study. He didn't even like Derek or have a clear handle on what exactly it was the dude did for a living. He'd thought he knew. He didn't. He wondered if his ex really knew.

The thought of his ex sent a sharp pain between his shoulder blades. He took a deep breath and exhaled. He thought about Gilda. Gilda Luster. Gilda. Luster…

He hopped up from the bed. Opposite the foot of it, on a

rectangular writing desk pushed as far into a corner as he could fit it, was his laptop. It was refurbished. It was slow, another thrift-shop find. He'd bought it at Venice Beach from a shopkeeper who went by the name Filter. The guy was an ex-con with a drug habit, but he was good at fixing up junk. He'd wanted seventy-five bucks for the computer. Danny had paid him fifty.

He sat on the cheap plastic swivel chair at the desk and tapped the computer's space bar. The display came to life and Danny entered his passcode. He waited for the operating system to cycle and boot up. It did, eventually. He clicked the icon for his web browser. The bar at the top of the screen slowly appeared with the invitation to enter a keyword into a search engine. He did, then typed Gilda's name and the word OASIS.

His Internet connection was ridiculously slow because he was logged into the open network of someone else in his building. While the old plaster walls of the apartment house didn't do well for wireless signals, the Internet was free this way, so Danny lived with it. He didn't have a choice. He couldn't afford it otherwise. The only reason he had a working television was because basic cable was included in the rent.

The engine stopped spinning and displayed the results. The top of the list was populated with references to cosmetics. The farther down the list of sites he scrolled, however, he found a couple of references to Gilda Luster. There weren't any connections to anything called the OASIS.

One of the references was a people finder website that didn't offer anything of value. The other was a link to an article in a preparedness magazine called *Off The Grid*.

Danny skimmed through it, looking for the mention of Gilda. He gave up, hit CTRL+F, and typed in her name. It highlighted several references, including the caption of a photograph of Gilda working in her garden. It was more a greenhouse with elevated tables and complex hydroponic systems, but that wasn't what caught Danny's eyes. What fixed his attention was Gilda.

She stood behind the tables in a tank top. Her broad shoulders, tanned and muscular, carried a thin, fit physique. Her white blonde hair was pulled back tight against her head into a ponytail. And glaring into the camera, contradicting the broad smile on her face, were intense ice blue eyes that radiated concern, authority, and a hint of paranoia.

Danny wasn't sure how much of his own thoughts and fears he was projecting onto her. It didn't matter. She looked exactly as he'd imagined her. He knew he'd never met her. As he stared at the full-color image on his crappy laptop display, he was confident he'd never seen her in person before. Yet she was familiar. He could almost smell the loamy soil under her fingernails and the dried sweat behind her ear at the nape of her neck where the ponytail began.

He closed the computer and slid out of the chair. He was sweating again. This wasn't science fiction, it was his truth. Somehow, he was embroiled in some weird mind-altering experiment, if that was what it was. He didn't know *what* it was. He only knew he was experiencing side effects similar to two people he'd never met, one of whom he recognized down to the sharp gaze of her eyes.

He'd always disliked Derek for tangible reasons. Now there was something less so. The gazillionaire jerk had done something to him he couldn't quite figure out. And as much as he wanted to confront him and grill him with a litany of questions, he also wanted nothing to do with any of it.

He stepped back to the bed, dazed. He was aware enough to step over the dog before hopping back amongst the dune of sheets piled to one side of the bed. He picked up the recorder and rubbed his thumb along the smooth plastic casing.

His life was tough enough, lonely enough, on-the-edge enough that anything that tipped the scales the wrong way would send him spiraling out of control. It was better to attempt to ignore it, smarter to pretend it was fiction.

Danny stared at the recorder. He considered clicking through the clips and randomly starting another then decided against it. He held the power button until the LCD display went blank. He dropped it onto the bed, amongst the tangle of sheets, and lay back, staring at the ceiling fan.

He focused on the chain flapping, dancing, to the rhythm of the revolving blades. The blades were spinning, a warbling disc above him. He picked one of the blades and tried to isolate it as it moved around and around and around.

He yawned. It was late. Or early. Whatever it was, he'd had enough. He didn't want to think about anything. He wanted to sleep and to dream happy dreams. He drifted off with the image of Maggie in his mind, her feet kicking in short spasms.

He should be so happy.

CHAPTER 16

April 5, 2026
New Orleans, Louisiana

The tightness in Bob Monk's chest worried him, but he couldn't say anything. His arm tingled, and he was clammy. At least he thought he was clammy. It was hard to tell in the damp chill on the roof of his daughters' rented house.

He flexed his fingers in and out, rolling his shoulder in circles.

"You okay?" asked Kristin. "You don't look okay."

"I'm fine," he said. "Just uncomfortable. We've been up here forever."

The four of them were huddled near the roof's peak. There were four or five feet between them and the waterline. The rain had stopped, and the subsequent mist was dissipating. But they were stuck in the chilled air, wet and exhausted. And the water was still rising.

"Mom?" asked Katie.

"Yes?"

"Why were you a waitress?"

Bob knew his children did this when they were frightened. They'd always done it. When his mother had died from Alzheimer's and they were on their way to the burial, the girls were talking about Chevy versus Ford. They'd pressed him on the differences and why one was better than the other. He'd always been a Chevy man. Always. He'd considered at the time, as the ninety-five-dollar-per-hour limousine carried them on gliding wheels toward the aboveground plot, that they were trying to take *his* mind off the day's melancholy.

They weren't one of those New Orleans families who celebrated life with colorful parades or carried the casket on their shoulders triumphantly from block to block. They were grief-stricken. Despite the length of Bob's mother's illness, they'd been floored by the loss of the family matriarch.

He'd decided then, in the darkness of the air-cooled backseats, that they were trying to take their *own* minds off the pain. They'd been too young to really empathize enough and think of him and how he felt. But now, as they huddled together on the roof, he reconsidered the notion. They were intuitive girls. They were kind, if not spoiled and a little jealous of their baby sister having flown the coop. They were trying to take his and his wife's minds off the danger that crept toward them. The girls could swim, after all. Bob and Kristin could not.

Still, asking about Kristin's job as a waitress was a seemingly random question that had come from nowhere. She hadn't been a waitress for more than a year now, and there had never been a discussion about why she'd waited tables for twenty-two years. She'd just done it, pure and simple. Maybe Katie was bored and couldn't think of anything else to ask.

"We needed the money," Kristin said flatly. "Raising a family isn't cheap. Never has been."

"But Dad makes good money," said Kiki. "He supported us."

Kristin wrapped her arm inside her husband's and held him closer to her. They were both shivering. "He does make good money. Your dad works hard, always, and he's a good provider. But everything is expensive. We had three girls and a two-bedroom house. An auto mechanic can only make so much, no matter how many transmissions he rebuilds."

"I should have gone out on my own," said Bob. A wave of nausea crept up from his gut. He winced, trying to keep it from his wife. "Your mom always told me I could make a go of it. But the money was steady. I could fix cars, which I love, and not worry about the business end of things."

"You can be good at whatever you put your mind to doing," Kristin said. "But it's fine. I understood. I didn't mind the work. It paid okay, and the tips were under the table. People were nice. I wish I'd been able to spend more time with you girls though. I do regret that."

"Don't regret it, Mom," said Katie. "I didn't bring it up to drudge up regrets. You shouldn't feel guilty. You were—are—a great mom."

A gust of wind swirled through the trees, rustling the leaves and rippling the water near them. The water was three feet away now. Bob wondered if he was the only one watching it. His neck ached. He stretched it to one side and rubbed his shoulder with his thumb. He took in a deep breath and then exhaled, suppressing the urge to vomit.

"I hate to break up the trip down memory lane," he said. "But the water is getting closer."

Kristin tugged on him, pulling him back toward the peak of the roof. The girls scooted back. They were essentially at the apex now. From that vantage point, even in the dark, they could see the water surrounding them. It was endless, save the tops of houses, trees, and power lines, which hung low over their heads now.

"The rain stopped," said Kiki. "The water should be going down."

"Depends on where it's—" Bob's muscles tightened and he grabbed his arm. He bit the inside of his cheek and tasted the warm, coppery flow of blood filling his mouth.

His wife screamed. His daughters cried out. He couldn't be sure who said what. He couldn't focus on anything but the pain, a tightness in his chest unlike anything he'd ever felt. It wasn't pain so much as a heaviness. Someone was sitting on his chest. The pain, which was acute, was in his shoulder and neck. His jaw throbbed.

He was cold. Shivering now. He was sure he was sweating, even though he couldn't distinguish it from the floodwater and rain on his face and under his arms. His groin pulsed with every unusual-feeling heartbeat.

"I think…" he squeezed out through clenched teeth, "I'm having…a heart attack."

He exhaled again. Each breath was thicker than the one before, more concentrated, more precious. He sucked in the humid air despite the weight on his chest, despite the overwhelming nausea that washed over him like a series of waves, one after the other.

They should have evacuated. The mayor was right. The Evacuspots might have worked. They could have gotten out. They could be high and dry without water at their feet. He could be asleep right now instead of dying. In his mind he cursed the mayor. He cursed the Evacuspots. He cursed the modernist, fourteen-foot sculptures that denoted the gathering points. He cursed butter and cholesterol. He cursed the years of smoking menthols. He cursed himself.

He saw his women trying to communicate with him. He couldn't understand what they were saying, what they were telling him to do, what they wanted from him. How could they want anything from him? He was having a heart attack. How could they ask him to do anything? They couldn't be making demands, could they? He couldn't move, couldn't clench his fist. He couldn't breathe now. He blinked his eyes. Or they blinked for him. Everything was working, or not working, on its own. He wasn't in control. He couldn't feel or do anything other than focus on the pain and the nausea and the dull ache.

But there were hands on the back of his head now. Cold hands on his neck and on his forehead. Even though he was cold, the hands were cold. How many hands were there?

His mind raced. His breathing was quicker now, more shallow.

His eyes blinked again. Slower this time. And again, even slower. It wasn't a blink. He was having trouble keeping them open. He couldn't focus. He couldn't see more than blurry faces looking down on him, blocking the milky black sky above.

Then he couldn't see anything at all.

***

Keri told Louis to turn right onto the next street-turned-borderless-canal. He spun the helm, guiding the jon boat in a looping turn that puttered ninety degrees.

Frank was in the bow of the boat, keeping watch for potentially damaging debris. He was dragging one hand in the water beside the starboard side of the boat next to the bow. But since he didn't know exactly where their destination was, and he was as bad at street names as Louis, he wasn't doing much else.

Keri was his navigator. She knew the way. At least she thought she did.

The city was unfamiliar to her now, like an alien planet whose surface was water and whose long-ago civilizations had drowned in it. There were only the remnant reminders of buildings and lives long ago sunk. The darkness and heavy, moist air added to the grim illusion of being on a foreign moon far from the warmth of a centering star.

This wasn't an alien planet though. It wasn't some foreign moon. It was her hometown, and somewhere in the far end of the city, her parents and sisters were alive and needed help. They had to be alive. There was no other possibility.

They'd traveled for miles now, edging closer to the outskirts of the central city where her sisters' rental home was cemented to the shifty earth. The tops of houses, or their second stories, passed by, and Keri ducked under branches and sagging power or phone lines, challenging herself at every intersection.

Was this the turn? Was it right? Was it left? She couldn't be sure. She told herself she was sure. She wasn't.

The rain hadn't returned, which was good. It made it easier to see in the dark, and somewhat more tolerable to troll the nasty water in search of her family. She did notice the water wasn't receding though. Whenever they were close enough to a house, especially one painted white or yellow, she searched the siding, or brick, or wood, for the hint of a waterline that would tell her the water had reached its crest and was receding. She hadn't seen one yet. Not even a hint.

Although she wasn't a flood control expert or a meteorologist, she knew enough about the way floodwater worked to know it either rose or it sank. It didn't sit stagnant. Not for long, not when the rain stopped.

Then all of her doubt about their path evaporated. She knew where she was at last.

"Turn again," she said, looking past Dub and pointing at the approaching intersection. "I think that's the one."

There was a pole but no street sign. It was familiar enough though, the large aged magnolia on the corner that rose above the white two-story house and protected it with its outstretched branches.

"This is it," she said. "I'm sure."

Her pulse accelerated in her chest. Her breath felt thin as she drew it through her nose. She took Dub's hand and squeezed. This was the street. Four houses in, on the left.

"Go slow," she said to Louis, as if it were her charter. "Real slow. It's hard to see."

The air was warming up again. It was dense with the odor of swamp and rot. Keri didn't smell any of it. Or if she did, she didn't notice. She was too focused on the houses to the skiff's port side. They'd past the first house and the second.

"Do you hear that?" asked Frank. He was staring up to the sky and off to the distance somewhere. Something he'd heard had him straining to focus on it.

"What?" Keri asked, almost standing in the boat, then thinking better of it. "What do you hear?"

"Cut the motor," Dub suggested, "please."

Louis shut off the power, and the boat drifted forward. The only sounds at first were the distinct chirp and croak of insects and reptiles that had been their soundtrack the length of the trip. There was the distant rumble of thunder that felt a thousand miles away. And then she heard it, a woman's voice calling for help. Keri looked to the left, two houses down, but she didn't see anything or anyone. The cry was from farther away.

"I think it's down and on the right," said Dub.

Barker agreed. So did Gem.

Keri resisted the urge to dive into the water and speed to her mother. But why would they be on the right side of the street? Why so far down? *Was* it her mother? Or was it someone else?

She scanned the house tops and the trees. She was second-guessing herself now. How was she wrong? How did she screw up and fail her family?

"That can't be," she said. "They should be here. On the left. At that house. At that—"

She saw the house, fourth on the left. It wasn't her sisters' rental. It was a different style. It was a two-story with a rounded cupola at the top.

Keri slumped, her head felt heavy. Her arms weighed too much and her shoulders ached. She wanted to puke.

But the cry kept coming. The woman ahead and to the right needed help. Her call, louder as they drifted closer in a slow but steady current that pulled them in the right direction, was desperate. Keri could hear it in the woman's voice. There was pain, fear, urgency. She was calling for help, though not for herself.

"My husband!" the woman cried. "He's sick. We need help.

Help!" The voice echoed, carrying across the water. It was distant but not so much so. It was on this street.

"We should help them," Gem said to Keri. "We should help and then go find your family. We have to be close, right?"

Keri nodded blankly. She'd heard Gem but wasn't really listening. She was trying to figure out where she'd gone wrong.

"I'm cranking the motor," said Louis. "We know about where they are, this woman and her husband. If he's sick, we've got to get on it."

Louis set the choke and cranked the motor back to life. Oily smoke drifted across the open body of the skiff. He throttled the boat forward.

They were moving at a good clip now, outracing the current and angling toward the right side of the street. Frank was the lookout. He stood, bent kneed, at the bow. He scoured the rooftops, the elbows of large trees, with squinting eyes that must have cut through the dark. They must have, because he spotted the woman. He saw her husband and two other women on the pitch of a roof four houses from the end of the street on the right.

Keri saw them too and her eyes widened. She leaned over Dub, trying to affirm what she'd second-guessed. This was the right street. It was her mother and father. Her sisters were there too. They'd come there from the opposite end of the street. She'd been turned around.

Her excitement was immediately tempered as they drew close enough to see her father. He was unconscious or worse. He wasn't moving. His head was in her mother's lap. Her feet were in the water. Her sisters flanked her, both of them pale and soaked through. Despite the dark, Keri could tell they'd been crying, might still be crying.

This time she couldn't resist. She stood up in the boat, Dub balancing her by holding her hips. The skiff wobbled and she took Gem's hand with one of hers to steady herself. She set her feet wide and then leapt from the boat, pulling herself free from those trying to hold her.

She landed on her knees and chest on the roof, banging her chin on the rough tile underneath the water. She shook off the sting and crawled the short distance to her parents. She didn't speak. Instead, she threw her arms around her mother, her sisters, and then quickly guided them toward the boat.

By now, Dub and Barker had followed her. They were behind her when she turned to help her sisters. Together they picked up her father, using the buoyancy of the water to move him into the boat at its center. Everyone else made room, shifting to the bow and the stern of the small skiff.

It was crowded and unstable, but as soon as they had her father in the skiff, cold and limp and barely breathing, Frank pushed them free and Louis pushed the throttle all the way forward.

They glided across the water quickly from one street to the next. Keri was focused on her father while the others talked about where to go, how to find a hospital or shelter, what route might be best if they could determine one. Keri's sisters were doing most of the talking since this was their neighborhood.

Keri's mother held her husband's head in her lap as she had on the pitch of the roof. She stroked it repeatedly, running her fingers through his hair. She whimpered but kept her cool, considering.

Dub was at his feet, keeping his knees bent so that he was in a position somewhere between lying down and sitting up. Barker and Gem had moved to the bow of the boat, next to Frank, to give the Monks room.

The skiff was crowded, heavy, and sitting low in the water now. The motor strained when Louis increased the power. He kept riding the throttle, speeding up and slowing down.

They were searching for a needle in a haystack. They had no way of knowing where a shelter might be, let alone one with the kind of medical attention her father needed. Keri was aiming for the closest hospital, or something like it. But in a city with an average elevation of a foot below sea level, dipping as low as seven feet below, there weren't going to be a bunch of options. Monkey Hill was among the higher elevations in the city, and there was a spot called "The Mountain" in City Park.

They were in a part of the city called Touro, north of the Mississippi River and part of the city's garden district. More precisely, they were in the Mississippi now. Her eyes scoured the edges of the street, searching for some sign of anything, anywhere that might help them.

"What's that?" asked Gem. "Up ahead. Are those lights?"

Keri saw them too. A warm, hazy yellow glow hovered above the water some distance ahead. Somebody had power. Louis headed for the light. Like moths they fluttered there, the motor working beyond its capacity to propel them through the water and toward the destination.

As they neared the glow, Keri made out the shape of the building from which the yellow light came. It was a dark, angular shape against the sky. From it, the sound of diesel generators rumbled and burped.

Louis slowed the skiff and steered it toward the building, which Keri recognized. It was the Touro Infirmary. They were on Prytania Street. The old brick building, its burgundy awning teetering above water level, beckoned like an oasis.

She knew it because it was a famous place. It was the first operational hospital in the aftermath of Hurricane Katrina. It was the birthplace of Truman Capote. And it was, most importantly of all, open right now.

There were three other skiffs docked at the awning, tied off to one of the support poles. The second-floor windows at the building's facade glowed with light, one of them shattered. Inside, leaning against the open frame, was a man dressed in blue hospital scrubs. He was waving at them to move the boat closer to the window, yelling something they couldn't understand.

Louis maneuvered the skiff to the window.

"We're open," the man said, "but only for medical emergencies. You got an emergency?"

"My father's having a heart attack or stroke," said Keri. "He's unconscious."

The man waved them to the window and then disappeared inside. He was back with a second person by the time they floated alongside the opening.

The man, tall with dark skin and eyes, was smiling. The man next to him was shorter and heavier. He wasn't smiling. He was all business.

"I'm Drew," said the tall man. "This is Kyle. We're going to help your dad. Get as close to the window as you can."

Dub reached out and grabbed hold of the windowsill, and the men inside the hospital window managed to get Bob through the opening and onto a gurney. Kyle immediately started wheeling him away, hopefully for treatment.

Drew stayed at the window. Sweat beaded on his forehead and in the shallow folds under his eyes. He was still smiling. It was the kind of smile a flight attendant offers when passengers board. It was polite, friendly, but it was mechanical.

"Who's family?" he asked, his eyes dancing across the eight remaining people on the boat. "I can take family."

Keri spoke up. "I'm his daughter. These are my sisters and my mom."

"What about the rest of you?" Drew asked.

"Not family," said Dub.

"He's my boyfriend," said Keri in a way that she hoped might leave an opening for Drew to let him stay too. "He's like family."

Drew eyed Barker and Gem. "And the two of you? Cousins?" he asked with raised eyebrows. "Distant relatives who somehow found each other on one of those genealogy sites?" Before Barker could reply, Drew answered for him with a wink. "Distant cousins it is.

Those sites are amazing, right?"

"We're not related at all," said Louis. "Me and Frank here gotta get going anyhow. More people to save and whatnot."

Drew nodded and waved to the others. "C'mon, climb on in."

Once they were all inside, and Dub had thanked Louis and Frank for their generosity, the boat shoved off. It disappeared into the dark, not even its motor audible over the echoing rumble of roof-mounted hospital generators.

The hospital hallway was stark. Keri smelled Betadine and bleach as the group followed Drew along the wide corridor. It was lined with gurneys and people in various states of consciousness.

"We had to evacuate the first floor," said Drew, as if giving a guided tour. "But we're okay. We've been taking in stragglers as they come, not turning anyone away. It's exhausting but good. It makes me feel like we're doing something in such a helpless situation."

"Are you the only hospital open?" asked Keri.

"I don't know. They tasked me with finding a way to get people into the building if I could. Breaking that window was the only option. We've got another one open on Foucher Street, the other side of the building. I think there's more activity over there."

"Where are you taking us?" asked Kristin, Keri's mother. "Where is my husband?"

"We've got a temporary ER here on the second floor," said Drew. "He's there. We'll take you to a waiting area we've set up. You can wait there. It's crowded, though; you might need to cop a squat on the floor."

"That's fine," said Kristin. "As long as Bob's okay."

Keri noticed her mother's face for the first time in the light. She appeared much older than she had before the flood. She walked with a stoop, her shoulders hunched forward. Her cheeks hung like jowls at her jawline but the skin stretched at the bone. Her skin was pale, sallow, and lacked the color of life. Heavy bags rounded her eyes, her hair was matted against the side of her head, and it was drying in an uncontrolled frizz.

Keri squeezed Dub's hand and let go. Then she took her mother's and pulled it to her chest as they walked slowly along the crowded corridor. Her head was beginning to throb above and behind her eyes.

None of them had yet talked about what they'd experienced that night. None of them had shared how close to death they'd come. None of them were ready for that.

Keri knew her family had struggled to survive. Her parents couldn't swim. She couldn't imagine how they'd gotten onto the roof, how they'd survived.

Her mother smiled at her weakly. It was pained, stretched with concern and preoccupation. At least it was something. It was comforting.

Keri smiled back. She was her mom's baby. She always would be. She was also the prodigal daughter who'd flown halfway across the country to go to college when she as easily could have gotten scholarships at Tulane, Loyola, or LSU. It was appropriate that she hadn't been with them when her sisters' house had flooded.

She'd been on her own, drowning until Dub saved her. Her family had been without her, fighting the rising water themselves. They'd been unaware of her struggles as they battled their own.

She resolved in that moment, in the nauseating stink of a hospital, to do a better job of being a part of her family. She'd call more, text more. She'd come for the holidays and send cards before birthdays came and went. She'd use FaceTime and Snapchat to give her family the sense they were with her and she was with them. She'd tag them and post photo galleries to Facebook. Keri decided these things, as desperate people always do.

"How many people are here?" asked Dub, shaking her from her thoughts. "How many are patients, and how many are…"

"Refugees?" asked Drew. He squared his jaw. "Sorry, probably not the right word."

"It's fine," said Dub.

"I don't really know how many," said Drew. "We've been too focused on managing everything. We're barely keeping our head above, er, keeping up with things."

Nobody else spoke as they wound their way from one crowded hall to the next. Keri rubbed her forehead and winced against the bright light that met them in the "waiting area."

It was a wide intersection of hallways leading in four directions. To one side was a nurse's desk. A half-dozen hospital workers were busy behind that desk, while around it there were thirty or forty people sitting or lying down, leaning on one another for comfort. They were all on the floor.

Keri swallowed against the growing thud at her temples and flagged the attention of the nurse in front of her at the desk. She was a woman in her mid-fifties. Her wiry gray hair hung to her shoulders. Her bangs, which hid her eyebrows, were not flattering. She eyed Keri with pursed lips and a forehead wrinkled with irritation.

"Two things," Keri said to her. "Hoping you can help me."

The woman was unmoved. Keri noticed rings of sweat leaching from under her arms and at her neck.

"One," Keri said, unfazed, "I've got a splitting headache. Could I please get some aspirin? Or even something for a migraine?"

"What's two?" asked the nurse.

"My dad, Bob Monk, just came in here," said Keri, her voice inching toward tremulous. "A guy named Kyle rolled him in. Is he okay?"

The nurse looked down and ran her finger along a piece of paper with illegible scribbles across it. She sighed, as if put upon, and then tapped one of the hieroglyphics. "He's in with a doctor now. I don't have an update."

She looked up after saying this, her features no softer than before.

"Thank you for the information, Keri said. "Do you know when we might get an update?"

The nurse held up the chicken-scratch notepad. "No telling. We've got I don't know how many people here with all kinds of problems. We've got near drownings, lacerations, diabetic shock, a whole bunch of injured who fell from a collapsed balcony. It could be five minutes. It could be an hour or three, I just don't know."

Keri swallowed, trying not to snap at the woman, who she knew was under tremendous stress. She forced herself to smile and thanked the woman again. "I really appreciate what you're doing. I know you likely have a home and family and you're here helping strangers."

The woman's frown, which had appeared set in stone, softened. Keri thought she might even see the slightest upturned curl of a smile at the edges of her dour mouth.

"Thank you," said the nurse. "I appreciate that. I do have a family. They're okay. Our house isn't. But thank you."

The nurse held up a finger, signaling for Keri to stand by for a moment, then stepped away. When she returned, she handed Keri a cup of water and two red caplets. "For your headache. I get them. They can be bad. The blurred vision, the nausea. Take these. They'll help."

Keri popped them into her mouth, downed the cup of water, and thanked the woman again. She worked back through the crowd to find where her group had claimed squatters' rights.

Dub was sitting next to her mother. He was talking to her softly and holding her hand. Her sisters were leaning against one another, their eyes closed and jaws slack. Keri couldn't understand how they could sleep in the adrenaline-fueled confusion of the place. The odors, the noises, and the people all combined to overload her senses.

She found an empty spot next to Gem. "Thanks," she said to her. "You were a big help."

"Of course," said Gem, offering her hand. "I haven't introduced myself. I'm Gemma. Gem for short. I think I've seen you on campus before. Econ 11 maybe?"

Keri leaned against the plaster wall, her spine feeling sharp against it. "Stats 10, I think," she said. "Fall quarter. You're in a sorority, right?"

Gem nodded. "It was a way to meet people. I didn't know a lot of people when I got to campus."

"Me neither," said Keri.

"Barker tells me that your sisters' names are Kiki and Katie," Gem said, smiling slyly. You're Keri. Your mom is Kristin?"

Keri blushed. "Yes."

"Like the Kardashians?"

"Not like the Kardashians," she said. "I mean, I guess the older ones. They have K names. But not the ones on television now. They all have names that sound like nouns."

"True," said Gem. "I didn't mean to offend, but I was thinking it might be tough to keep up with you."

The women shared a brief laugh, a sliver of levity in a night that was drenched with weight. They were interrupted by a man standing over them. He had the look of someone who'd been soaked but had dried again. He was very tall, with a slight gut protruding over the cinched scrubs at his waist. He wore a deep look of concern, and in some way he was familiar. Keri thought she'd seen him before, but not in a hospital. Somewhere else. Somewhere she couldn't place.

"Are you the Monks?" he said to nobody in particular, his eyes dancing across them. "I'm looking for the Monk family."

Keri's mother jumped to her feet, wobbled, and braced herself against the wall. Steadied, she took two careful steps toward the man. Kiki and Katie woke up, apparently aware of the stranger's presence.

"I'm his wife," she said. "These are my daughters."

The man extended his hand and removed the surgical cap from his head. "I'm your husband's doctor," he said. "I'm Steven Konkoly."

"How is he, Doctor?" asked Kristin.

"Let me preface this by telling you I'm not a cardiologist," he said, measuring his words. His deliberate cadence was familiar to Keri.

"You're not?" asked Kristin. "I don't understand. Should he—"

Doc held up his hands to calm her. "He's in good hands. He's going to be fine. Perhaps I should have started with that."

Kristin sighed; her whole body exhaled. "Oh," she said, the air deflating as she spoke, "thank goodness. Thank you."

"We believe he's had a heart attack," said Doc. "He's awake now and resting comfortably. We're not in a position to have the requisite testing done right now. That will have to happen at the first available opportunity."

"What testing?" asked Kristin.

"Again," said Doc, "I'm not a cardiologist. I don't have privileges here, actually. I'm from California. I'm…helping. They're overwhelmed. I offered whatever assistance they require."

"Can we see him?" asked Kristin.

"Soon," said Doc. "He's stable. That's good. But we don't want any excitement at the moment. Can you give it an hour? We'll check his vitals again. Then someone can come back and update you again."

"You're from California?" asked Keri.

"Yes," said Doc. "Los Angeles."

"Oh," said Kristin. "That's where my daughter attends school."

"Do you?" asked Doc, his attention fully on Keri now. "Which one?"

"UCLA," said Keri.

"What's your major?"

"Biology."

"Premed?" he asked.

Keri thought for an instant she saw a look of recognition flash across his face. It was brief, but it was there. "Maybe," she said. "Or research. I don't know yet."

"Good luck," he said. "Maybe we'll cross paths at Reagan someday."

"Maybe," said Keri. She was certain they already had. Not at the medical center, but somewhere.

Doc excused himself and treaded through the crowded hall and beyond a pair of swinging doors. Keri watched the doors slap back and forth until they stopped.

"Hey," Dub said. He'd slipped next to Keri without her having noticed it. "Did that guy look familiar to you?"

Keri swung around to face Dub. She nodded, and she saw as their gazes met that he was as confused as she was. She wasn't going crazy. It wasn't déjà vu, at least not the kind of déjà vu she'd been experiencing more and more frequently. She hadn't told Dub about it. Maybe she should.

"He did," she said softly, leaving it at that for now. "Weird, right?"

Dub nodded, his eyes on the double doors now. "Very. But, hey, your dad's going to be okay. That's a relief. And we're all good here. Everyone is safe."

Keri couldn't help but think it wasn't true. They were dry now, true. They were out of the floodwater, check. But were they really safe? Something she couldn't shake, an oppressive wave that felt as if it were hovering above her, threatening to crash, told her they weren't. They were far from it. Very far from it.

CHAPTER 17

April 5, 2026
New Orleans, Louisiana

Doc Konkoly needed a minute to breathe. Since he'd arrived at the hospital, helping heave one injured patient after another through a broken window and into the second floor, he'd been on his feet.

He'd gone from assisting in one case to leading the charge in the next. He hadn't done emergent care since his residency. It was at once gratifying, terrifying, and emotionally exhausting.

But what had really shaken him was the daughter of the heart attack patient. The Bruin. She'd looked at him as if she knew him, as had the two men sitting on the floor. They also appeared to be college students. All three of them might have burned a hole in his forehead had they stared at him any more intently than they had.

He leaned against a wall and drew his hands to his face. He exhaled, smelling his breath.

You're imagining it, he told himself. *It's the stress.*

Yet he wasn't sure of it. Although he hoped saying it aloud might convince him, it didn't. He reached out to a passing doctor, asking where he could find a restroom. The doctor paused, pointed, and told him where to find one the public couldn't access.

Doc followed the directions and found a men's restroom. He

pushed the door open and stepped into the humid, dimly lit washroom. There was a row of three sinks on one wall, hung against the tile wall beneath a wide rectangular mirror. The mirror reflected the twin urinals and the pair of stalls on the opposite wall. One of the stalls was closed.

Doc moved to one of the sinks and ran his hand under the faucet sensor, activating the rush of water from the tap. He cupped his hands under the warm water, bent over, and splashed it onto his face. It was life-affirming, the idea of heated, clean water. He cupped another handful and splashed his face again, letting the water drip from his chin and down the sides of his neck.

His eyes were closed when the stall door clicked and creaked open. Footsteps echoed, squishing their way to the sink next to him. He blindly reached for a paper towel and patted his face dry.

He looked at the man next to him in the mirror and reflexively nodded hello. The other man did the same while washing his hands; then they both did a double take and looked at each other again. This was no déjà vu. These two men did know each other, at least in passing.

"You're the reporter," said Doc. "The one from LA."

"Lane Turner," said the reporter. "And you're the guy from the bar at the hotel."

"I am. Dr. Steve Konkoly. What are you doing here?"

"Came in with a rescue crew," said Turner. "We've been hopping rides wherever we can get them. About to head back out to the hotel. There are some people needing rescue there now."

"Our hotel?"

"Yeah," Lane said. "My crew's waiting in the boat outside. I had to go to the bathroom while we were here. Too much water everywhere, you know?"

Doc nodded. He reached for another paper towel and wiped the remnant water from his neck.

"You could go with us," said Turner. "I'm sure the two guys on the boat could use the help dragging people out of the water. It's tough work."

Doc started to decline; he could do more good work here. "I don't know," he said. "They probably need me here. I'm about to go get another assignment."

"You can help people out there too," said the reporter, drying his hands. "We could have used you on the last one. One guy was bleeding pretty badly. You could have helped. Who knows what we're going to find this time?"

Doc thought about the people falling from the balcony. He remembered Shonda, the desk clerk at the hotel, waiting for approval to leave her post as the water inundated the lobby.

"Let me tell them I'm leaving," said Doc. "Wait here."

Turner raised an eyebrow. "In the bathroom?"

Doc moved to the door and swung it open. "No, in the hallway, outside the bathroom."

"I was kidding," said Turner.

"I know," said Doc. He needed to find someone of authority. He wanted to be sure that the patients he'd already treated would have good care once he was gone. He also wanted to assure the hospital he wasn't jumping ship, even though he was.

Fifteen minutes later he was in the back of a sixteen-foot ski boat, watching the wake as the reporter and his crew recorded one short report after another, describing what they'd seen during the course of the long night.

Doc only tangentially paid attention to them, or to the three men on the boat who'd taken it upon themselves to search and rescue. It was a private boat. These were do-gooders who wanted to jump into the deep end and help with no compensation or expectation of anything.

All three were from the area, all family men and churchgoers, who were forgoing Easter sunrise services, assuming they'd even be held, to be here.

Easter Sunday. Doc hadn't remembered it was Sunday, let alone Easter. It wasn't much of a holiday, that was certain.

The sky changed from a milky black to a purplish color before the first hints of deep reds and orange smudged their way above the horizon. With the sun coming up and dawn approaching, the night's devastation was at once easier and harder to comprehend.

In the dark of the night, it was difficult to know much more than the presence of water everywhere and in places it should not have been. There was something frightening about not seeing more than that, the reflection of lights on the water, the gray and blue hues of buildings' shadows dipping beneath the rising flood.

In the daylight, though, it was more breathtaking. The water was receding. The debris-painted lines on the sides of now-muted buildings was evidence the worst was over, but worse was yet to come. The tops of trucks poked through the surface of it. Birds drank from it while perched on street signs tilted from their proper place. Bugs danced on it, leaving tiny ripples like those from raindrops. Fish flicked their tails in it, visible life both out of its element but still in it.

Doc saw a couple on a balcony as they passed by. They were in T-shirts and shorts. The clothing looked stained with the drama of the weekend. Their bodies touched, her hip against his thigh. They surveyed the damage with resignation and surprise. She pointed at something in the distance; he squinted. She took his chin in her hand and moved his line of sight. His eyes widened and he nodded. Then he shook his head. She wrapped her arms around him. He put his arm around her and kissed the top of her head.

A lone man paddled past them in a kayak. He plunged one side of the double-bladed paddle into the water, pulled it through, then worked the other side. With each stroke, the point bow of the bright yellow kayak shifted like a compass searching for true north.

The sky was clear and edging toward pink now, the darker watercolors lightening as the sun brushed away the night. The clouds were gone and the air wasn't as thick. The dampness was at the surface now. Thin wisps of vapor rose from the water toward the cooler, drier air.

Doc soaked in all of it, thinking about how this place wouldn't be the same for months. It could be years until these deep, wet scars faded. They might never heal. Not fully. There would always be marks, reminders, stories of the night the city sank.

"It's horrible," said the reporter. He'd maneuvered to the stern of the vessel and inched up near Doc. "I've seen a lot. Never seen anything like this."

Doc sucked in a deep breath of the surprisingly chilled air and nodded in agreement. He turned his attention to Turner and motioned toward the crew. "They go with you everywhere?" he asked. "Same team on every story?"

Doc had no interest in the television news business, but he didn't want to talk about the flood. He needed a beat to think about something else before he dove in again. He sensed they were getting closer to the hotel. They'd already been on the water, maneuvering through canals, for what felt like miles.

Turner checked over his shoulder and shook his head. "Them? No. I'm not typically on the streets. I'm usually in the comfortable confines of a newsroom and studio. I have a desk job, essentially."

"You don't report on the stories you read?" asked Doc. "The stories from the studio?"

Turner pulled his shoulders back and appeared taller all of a sudden. "No," he said. "Not typically. I don't even write what I read. I rewrite it. I tweak what other people write for me, so it sounds like it's something I would say. But most of the stories come from reporters in the field."

Doc lifted his chin toward the field producer and photographer. "What about them?" he asked. "What do they normally do?"

"They're always running around telling stories," said Turner. "They work with all of our reporters. Those two are really good at what they do. They get better assignments than some of the less motivated crews."

"This is a better assignment?"

"It was supposed to be," said Turner. "This was a few easy sidebars to the Final Four. It was free food, nice hotel room, Economy Plus on the plane."

"Didn't end up that way," said Doc. "People died. People don't typically die at the Final Four."

"No," agreed Turner, his expression flattening. "They don't."

He shrank again, Doc noticed. The reporter's shoulders narrowed, as did his glare. He wasn't looking at Doc anymore. He was looking through him, past him. His brow furrowed. The hint of a confident smile was gone.

"We're here," said the man piloting the boat. "We're on the street. Looks like there are emergency workers here already."

Doc shifted his weight and looked beyond the boat's bow. There were a half-dozen boats up ahead, and two or three high-water trucks. There was water halfway up their wheel wells. The water was the color of cafe au lait, and it was receding.

The pilot propelled the boat closer to the collection of boats and trucks. There were people there. Some waded in the chest-deep water, their elbows out like wings working to move them through the depths. Some were in the boats. Some stood, huddled close together, in the backs of the trucks. A shiver ran along Doc's spine.

He wondered if he'd made a mistake by not staying at the hospital. The situation here appeared under control. Even those in the back of the trucks didn't seem frightened or concerned. It was eerily calm here as rescue workers evacuated hotel guests in singles and pairs.

By the time his boat had joined the others, Doc was already hopping out into the water. The familiar creep of it on his legs and through his clothing was uncomfortable. A brief well of nausea crept up from his gut. His body shuddered, but he fought the urge to climb back into the boat pushing ahead.

At one of the smaller boats, a Zodiac with two inflatable pontoons that flanked an oversized outboard motor, he found someone who appeared to be in charge.

"I'm a doctor," he said, the water lapping at his chest. "I'd like to help. Anybody in the hotel in need of medical attention?"

"A few hypothermia cases," she replied. "Some people in shock. A couple of psych patients. Nothing major, though some we can't move yet. Feel free to check. Things keep changing by the minute. There's a lot of water in there."

"Thank you." Doc gingerly spun around in the water and trudged through it, his mouth pressed closed as he splashed along. He mimicked those using their wing-elbows for propulsion.

He felt like a salmon swimming upstream. Not because of the water, though it was pushing at him sideways and keeping him off balance with each step, but because everyone else seemed to be moving in the opposite direction, all coming out of the hotel. There were dozens emptying out of a neighboring hotel too.

"Where are they taking you?" Doc asked one of the people struggling to move past him. The man was wiry, bald, and wore a drenched hoodie that stretched beyond his fingertips.

He looked at Doc with wide eyes. "Out of here," he said. "Somewhere dry."

The man kept moving. Doc stopped the next person who exchanged glances with him, an athletic woman in a sports bra. The water was at her shoulders and she half bounced, half swam toward the boats and trucks.

"They said Baton Rouge," she said. "There are shelters in Baton Rouge."

"I heard Houston," said a third person. "Or Beaumont. I just know it's Texas."

Doc pushed closer to the hotel, deciding it didn't matter where people were going. They were leaving. They were getting out. They were finding somewhere safe to be, somewhere with power and food and clean, potable water.

He reached the double glass doors at the front entrance of the hotel. They were pushed farther open than they had been when he'd left the night before. He waited for a group to move past him, buoyed by one another as they chattered their way through the cold water. At the side of the hotel, a small whirlpool of water was draining into the sewers. That was good.

Doc moved into the lobby, which was much as he remembered it. The water was higher than it had been, but lower than it must have gotten. There was a thick line of silt about seven feet from the floor. The water in the lobby was at least four and a half feet. It could have been higher and was certainly at a level that covered the reception desk.

Despite what the woman in the Zodiac had told him, he didn't see anyone. There wasn't anyone to help, there were only clusters of drenched guests carrying bags over their heads or helping each other dog-paddle through the lobby from the stairwell to the exit.

Coming here was a mistake. He decided he needed to find a way back to the hospital. He'd left a post he should have kept. An image of the college students from California flashed in his mind. He should have stayed and helped that coed's father, the one recovering from a heart attack.

Why had he come back here?

Behind the reception desk there were open doors leading to what he figured were the administrative offices. He waded toward where he remembered the desk being and found the base of it with his feet before hitting it with his knees.

He stood there, his hands underwater, and pressed against the top of the counter, his attention on the open door behind it. He swore he heard a noise coming from the office. It was soft, but it was something. A voice. Definitely a voice.

"Is anybody there?" he called out. "Anybody behind the counter?"

Although there was no response, he swore he could hear

something. He checked over both shoulders. Nobody, at least none of the preoccupied few making their way out of the hotel, was paying attention to him.

He groped his way around the desk, finding the space between the side of it and the wall, and paddled toward the open door. The dim light shining through the glass entrance faded, and he saw the cast of a faint bluish-white glow. He also heard a sweet voice melodically skipping across the lyrics of a song he didn't recognize.

"Hello?" he called again, moving into the darker space of the office. "Anybody here? Anyone need help?"

He inched forward and jumped when something brushed against his leg. His pulse quickened and he considered turning around. Yet something drove him forward, deeper into the office. He was drawn to that faint, ambient glow of what he imagined was an electronic device: a phone, a tablet, or a computer screen. And it had to be portable, since all of the other electronics were off.

The singing was louder now, the voice clear. It was hopeful sounding, something sweet that faintly carried across the waterlogged office space, winding its way around the low-slung cubicle walls that kept him from seeing anything other than a vague shadow swaying. Why couldn't the singer hear him?

Half swimming, half walking, he maneuvered until he arrived within a few feet of the singer and the accompanying light. It was a phone. And it was Shonda, sitting on a chair on top of a desk. She was wearing headphones.

He moved into her field of view and noticed her eyes, visible in the light from her device, were closed. She was singing, her shoulders and head moving rhythmically to whatever beat was drumming in her ears.

She was humming now, and she opened her eyes. Doc smiled at her and she screamed. Startled, she toppled back, and Doc caught her before she spilled into the water or hit her head on the office furniture hidden beneath the surface.

"You scared me!" she shrieked, pulling out one of the earbuds. Her narrowed eyes darted around the room, then fixed on him warily. "What are you doing?" she demanded.

Doc stepped back, raising his hands. "I heard your singing," he said. "I tried calling out to you. You didn't answer."

She waggled the earbud in between her fingers. "I couldn't hear you."

"I'm a doctor," he said. "I'm here to make sure people are okay. I was a guest here. Are you okay? Do you need help?"

"I'm fine," Shonda said. "I'm good."

"What are *you* doing?" he asked. "It's really not safe here, not with all of this water."

"It's my job. I gotta stay here until my relief shows up. Nobody showed up, so I came back here. I've been listening to music, trying to stay dry."

"Nobody is going to show up," said Doc, suppressing a chortle. "You know what happened, right?"

She shrugged. "It flooded."

"You should come with me," he said. "They're evacuating people."

"I can't leave; I've got a paper due. I've got a midterm this week. Plus, I'm at work. I'm not leaving the hotel and the guests."

Doc felt the tension building in his shoulders. "There is no hotel," he snapped. "No guests. No school this week. You won't have a paper due. No midterms. People are dead. The city is underwater."

The reality of it, the scope beyond the flooded lobby and back offices, washed over her face in the bluish-white light. It appeared to hit her, as her tightly drawn expression sagged into disbelief, or finally belief, that staying perched in her elevated throne above the water might not be the best place to stay.

"Come with me," Doc implored.

Shonda glanced behind her into the dark then back at Doc. She rolled the earbud around her fingers.

"How much battery life do you have left on your phone?" asked Doc.

She glanced down at the glow and pursed her lips. "Twenty-one percent."

"Come with me," he repeated.

She nodded, put the earbud back in place, and reached out for help. Doc took her wrists and guided her into the water one leg at a time. She seized at the chill and started breathing quickly. She cursed the water temperature, apologized, and then settled into the discomfort of it. She held her phone above her head.

"Your arm's going to get tired," he said.

"I'm not losing this phone," she replied. "The case floats, but I'm not taking any chances. Everything is on this phone. Everything."

"Fair enough," he said. "Let's go."

Doc wasn't putting salve on a wound or stabilizing a cardiac patient. He wasn't rescuing a drowning man or making a sling for a woman with a compound fracture. He was doing something good though. As he led Shonda through the water, he believed that he was saving her life. If he'd left her there, if he'd never sought out the singing siren, she might have become injured, or severely dehydrated, or died.

He led her through the lobby, and now that they were in the light, he could see the awe drawn onto her young face. She'd retreated before the worst of it. She hadn't seen any of this. It was obvious to Doc as they carefully trod through the water.

"It stinks," she said with a sour look on her face, her mouth turned downward. "This is next-level disgusting."

Doc didn't say anything, focusing on navigating the debris and ensuring Shonda didn't fall or lose her balance in the water. He held one of her wrists gently, tugging her with him as they moved now from the lobby and out into the daylight.

Both squinted as they took their first several steps beyond the open entryway. Shonda drew the back of her hand up to shield her eyes. When she did, her phone slipped from her hand and into the water.

She gasped and started to dive for it, knocking herself into Doc. He held her up, turned, and saw the phone floating in the water toward the whirlpool.

"I can't lose it," she said, her expression having transformed again. Now she was pained. "My life is on that phone."

"I'll get it," Doc said hurriedly. He quickly splashed toward the phone. It was moving too fast now, gaining speed toward the whirling circle of draining water. He hopped off one foot, using the advantage of the water to propel his mass farther than he would have moved on land. He splashed down, holding his chin up to keep his mouth from going underwater, and reached for the phone.

Doc touched it with his outstretched hand, but it dipped into the water and tipped away. He bounced again, leaping as far as he could, and reached again. He gripped it as he dropped into the water on his chest. When he landed, he held up his hand, waving the phone.

Searching for a place to put his foot, he slipped. It caught him by surprise, not finding the surface of the street, and he slid under the surface, swallowing a mouthful of floodwater. He resurfaced for an instant, coughing, but unable to suck in a clean breath of air. Shonda cried out. He heard that, muddied as it was.

He panicked, dropping beneath the surface again. He couldn't breathe. He couldn't find the street. The water swirled around him now. He was disoriented in the brown-hued dark of the water. His vision blurred; his chest burned.

He let go of the phone and tried pulling himself to the surface, but the drain had him now. The water was sucking at his legs, at his body. He fought against it. He kicked, he pulled, reaching for the surface. It was close. It was too far.

He was caught, spinning and sinking. It was a washing machine. It held him in place.

Doc tried to resist the urge to cough again. He couldn't. When he did, when he opened his mouth, more water came in than went out. He was choking now.

He couldn't see, couldn't hear, couldn't breathe. It was happening fast. Too fast. One instant he was chasing a phone with twenty-one percent battery life and the next he was drowning.

His legs gave out first, then his arms. And then his body twitched before it slackened. The drain drew him down, catching him in its jaws. It kept him there until everything went dark. Until Doc's heart beat for the final time and his brain turned off.

His final thought was of the college coed he'd seen in the hospital and the knowing, familiar look she'd given him. They had met before, somewhere. As his life ended, he wondered if they would again. He believed they would. That was his last thought.

The last image in his mind, however, was the faintest hint of sunlight taunting him from beyond the surface of the water. Light before the dark. The morning had come.

CHAPTER 18

April 6, 2026
Los Angeles, California

The first rays of sunlight shone through the lone window in Danny Correa's efficiency apartment. Maggie was on the bed, her body up against Danny's legs. She was licking his bare foot, which was exposed amidst the toga of a sheet that twisted around his body.

"Thanks, girl," he said. "I appreciate that. But no kisses today. I have no idea where my feet have been."

She stopped licking and put one paw on his leg to hold it in place. She looked at him as if she understood him and wagged her tail. Then she went back to the job of cleaning Danny's foot. Danny chuckled to himself. He turned onto his side and checked the clock. It was early. Too early. He'd worked late at the diner Sunday night. It was a holiday, so the double time was a much-needed boon, and Arthur hadn't minded the day off.

He could feel the long hours in his back, even lying there in bed. But he couldn't go back to sleep. He was awake now.

He grabbed the remote for the television, which was on from the night before, and turned up the volume. The morning news was on, and Lane Turner was reporting from outside the Louisiana Superdome in New Orleans. The banner at the bottom of the screen read that the men's championship college basketball game had been postponed indefinitely.

"…*game seems to be of secondary concern for everyone here,*" said Turner. "*Basketball is a sport. It's entertainment. What happened here Saturday night into Sunday morning was much more than that. It was life and death. It still is. Even though the water has receded, for the most part, recovery has yet to begin. People here are trying to process the extraordinary extent of the damage…*"

Danny sat up, propping a pillow behind his head. Maggie looked up at him, no longer in possession of his foot. She hopped down from the bed and crossed the floor to her bowl. She was thirsty, from the sound of her lapping at the room-temperature water.

"*This is among the more deadly floods in American history. From authorities, we know that in addition to the seven hundred and twenty-nine people who've died, sixty-four people are missing. Among them is at least one southern Californian.*"

The screen switched from an image of the reporter in front of the dome, to video of a man wading through water, walking against the tide of people exiting a tall building that looked like a hotel.

"*This is video of that man, Dr. Steven Konkoly,*" said Turner. "*He was here for a medical conference but sprang into action when the flooding started. He saved lives until he lost his own.*"

The video switched from a shot of the doctor walking into the building, to one of him walking out. He was with a woman, who was holding one hand over her head. She tripped, pitched forward, and lost whatever it was she was holding in the raised hand. A phone maybe?

The doctor let go of the woman and dove into the water to retrieve it. It kept bobbing out of his reach. Then he caught it, and he went under. He resurfaced, waving his arms. The video froze.

"*We're not showing you the rest of the video,*" said Turner. "*This is where Dr. Konkoly lost his footing at a drain he couldn't see. Paramedics tell me he was sucked into the drain and trapped there. They did pull his body from the water only a few moments after he slipped under. It was already too late.*"

The frozen video dissolved to a still photograph of the doctor. His name was on the bottom of the screen. It looked like a picture taken from a social media account. It was a snapshot, not a professional photograph. Danny recognized the location of the picture. Chills ran along his spine and his mouth went dry.

The doctor was standing in the Inner Peristyle at the Getty Villa. Behind him was the Temple of Hercules, and beyond that the Atrium. There were Corinthian columns to one side of the snapshot.

Danny could see in his mind beyond the edges of the picture. There was the Outer Peristyle with its long reflecting pool. There was the herb garden. There were the galleries. Flashes of an elevator strobed in his mind. It was like a holiday slideshow, these images.

Then he saw a false wall and a place beyond it. He smelled soil. He felt the wind of a circular pathway play with his balance. He saw camels and a man dressed in traditional Middle Eastern garb. There was a room full of electronics. There was a woman named Gilda.

The reporter was back on camera, talking about other things now, something about the concern for disease spreading among the surviving population. That was always a threat after apocalyptic catastrophes, said the reporter. Danny wasn't listening anymore. He was preoccupied with what had just happened, with the images in his head and the accompanying sense that he had experienced them before or would in the future. His stomach lurched and he swallowed hard.

Danny closed his eyes and shook his head, trying to shake free of the sensation he was somewhere else. He turned off the television and rolled from the bed, tripping on the sheet wrapped at his thigh. At the sink in his bathroom he turned on the cold water and splashed his face, slurping some of it from his hands. The water dampened his dry mouth, satiating the need to drink.

He pressed his hands onto the sides of the porcelain, wall-mounted sink, and locked his elbows. Water dripped from his chin into the sink. He sucked droplets into his mouth and looked up.

"What is going on?" he asked himself aloud. He was sweating now. He felt it under his arms. "What is happening?"

He looked into his own eyes, but what he saw was the reflection of the Getty Villa and all of those things that were not in the snapshot on television. He saw a place he'd never been, not even once.

At least, not in *this* life.

A RELENTLESS DISEASE. NO CURE.
AND NO WAY TO STOP IT.

LOOKING FOR A STAND-ALONE NOVEL
YOU CAN'T PUT DOWN?

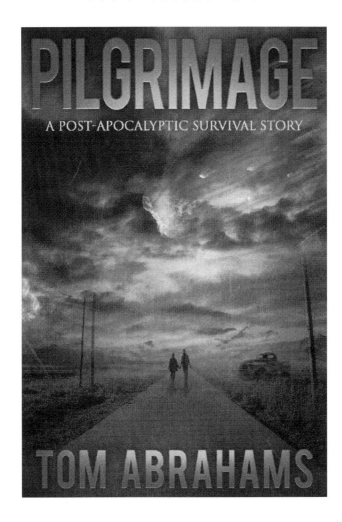

A FAMILY VACATION. AN EXPLOSIVE DISASTER. A
DESPERATE STRUGGLE TO GET HOME.

FOR A FRESH TAKE ON THE APOCALYPSE
ENTER THE DARK WORLD

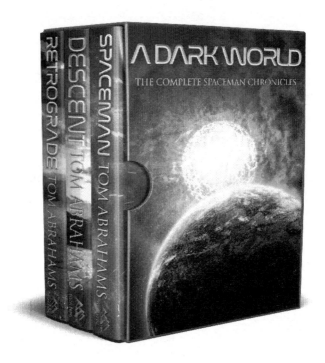

A COMPLETE THREE BOOK SERIES

No communication. Limited power. An unbreakable will to survive.

ACKNOWLEDGEMENTS

Thank you to everyone who's supported The Alt Apocalypse. It's a challenging series to write and I'm so thankful to those of you enjoying the concept of new stories, same characters, different stakes. I'm honored by how you've embraced it.

Thanks also to my team of incredible professionals who help get this book into your hands. Felicia Sullivan, Pauline Nolet, Patricia Wilson, Hristo Kovatliev, and Stef McDaid are all amazing.

Of course, my family always deserves the most gratitude. Courtney, Sam, and Luke give up time with me so I can spend it with these characters, in this imaginary world. I love you three more than any words could convey.

To my parents, mother-in-law, and siblings, thanks to you for all of efforts to support my work and spread the word. I am always grateful.

Made in the USA
Middletown, DE
06 September 2018